AN EXCELLENT WALKER

A PRIDE & PREJUDICE VARIATION

LYNDSAY CONSTABLE

Quills & Quartos
PUBLISHING

Edited by Katie Jackson and Stephanie Eagleson

Cover by GM Book Cover Design

ISBN 978-1-956613-51-3 (ebook) and 978-1-956613-52-0 (paperback)

To my wonderful husband Brad
Because sometimes a good marriage begins with a bad proposal

CHAPTER ONE

K ent held very few surprises for Miss Elizabeth
Bennet.

Thanks to the copious descriptions of the architecture and grounds from her cousin, Mr Collins, the long walks in which she indulged were clearly mapped out in her mind before her very first step onto the hallowed ground. She felt as though she was as familiar with Rosings Park as someone who had been born and bred to it. From which angle she may expect the sun to rise over the manor house, to which direction the wind hailed from when Miss Anne de Bourgh had a headache in her right temple, to how often one may expect a fox to attempt to pilfer the hen house, it was all very familiar to Elizabeth. What could not have been foretold by Mr Collins was the briskness of the air blowing in from the sea or the particular shade of burgundy in the sunrises. Elizabeth imagined those observations were too fine in nature to warrant a note from Mr Collins. The beauty there was compelling. She savoured every moment that she could escape from company and allow her steps to take her to every corner of the great estate.

Charlotte Collins had been Elizabeth's friend for most of her life, and therefore held few new revelations in her conduct. Since her marriage to Mr Collins, the parson of the church of Rosings, it seemed to Elizabeth that her behaviour had not changed a whit. Charlotte was still the ever-constant, practical, steady person she had been since the early days of their acquaintance. It had been an initial curiosity for Elizabeth to witness how Charlotte had acclimated to the treacherous terrain of accommodating several people in possession of intensely self-absorbed natures at once. But, as usual, the ever-pragmatic Charlotte calmly navigated with ease the daily tides and storms of superciliousness.

Elizabeth had expected a dazzling show of obsequiousness from Mr Collins when he was in the presence of Lady Catherine de Bourgh. But, in spite of his effusive descriptions of his patroness, amplified by Elizabeth's own powerful imagination, she was not fully prepared for the degree of unctuousness that she witnessed. It made it difficult for her to keep her tea and cake down. It had started out as highly humorous, and she regretted that her father was unable to witness it for himself. However, like rich foods that are consumed to excess, the sycophancy eventually left Elizabeth feeling heavy and cross. She wondered at Charlotte's ability to withstand it.

The brisk walks on the grounds of Rosings became an absolute necessity rather than an indulgence. The clean air and beauty of Kent served to wash away the grime that accumulated in her mind from too-frequent exposure to the residents of Rosings and its parish house.

After a far pace to the top of Tall Oak Hill, Elizabeth

paused beneath the windblown oak tree. Leaning into the bark of the fine old soul, she closed her eyes and breathed deeply, giving her heart time to slow after the rapid climb up the hill. The wind that was sweeping in from the east tried to rip her bonnet from her head, but she grasped it to keep it in place. Turning to look from whence she came, Elizabeth saw Rosings's chimneys, of which she had intimate knowledge from Mr Collins, peeking out over the treetops. Some tendrils of smoke lay down sideways as the gusty day prevented them from travelling straight up. The scene was spectacular. Elizabeth could not be completely certain, but she thought in the far distance she could just see the bluish haze of the sea. She spied some large birds hovering and thought they must be hawks riding the wind.

This has been a surprise, the beauty of the country here. I was prepared to find fault in everything, but the beauty of nature has won me over.

She had not particularly been looking forward to her trip to Kent to visit Charlotte. However, until the long separation from her family and life back in Hertfordshire, Elizabeth had never realised that the endless stress of dealing with her mother and younger sisters took a toll on her spirits. The visit to Kent had refreshed her in a way that she had not fully anticipated. Even Charlotte had just that morning complimented her on the glow in her cheeks.

"Although I have been the one who most desired for you to travel here, Elizabeth, I believe the air and woods in Kent have done a very decent service for your spirits," Charlotte had commented.

Yes, that has been a very great surprise. Elizabeth frowned. *Though, not the greatest.*

Mr Darcy had suddenly materialised with his cousin,

Colonel Fitzwilliam, the week before. And even though Elizabeth had enjoyed the unexpected variety in the conversation and card playing, it vexed her to have the imperious Mr Darcy always gazing at her with his stormy eyes. Ever since their introduction in Hertfordshire, she had been fully convinced that he was the proudest, most disapproving man in all of England. Elizabeth knew she must be offending him at every turn of her head and casual comment. Not that that in any way caused her a moment of regret. If Mr Darcy was made to be uneasy by some constant fault in her dress or conversation, it was he who should remove himself from Rosings. She did not have the freedom of movement that was enjoyed by men of wealth. Her visit was scheduled at the convenience of others. Still, although she felt no shame in her personage, her heart gave an unexpected lurch every time Mr Darcy entered a room. It was enough to make her self-conscious, though only those who knew her intimately would realise the difference. Thankfully, Colonel Fitzwilliam was a very pleasant man to converse with. His mild, forgiving nature was in sharp contrast to Mr Darcy's.

"Why are all the most pleasing men the ones who are in desperate need of a larger fortune?" Elizabeth murmured to the sympathetic oak tree as images of Colonel Fitzwilliam and George Wickham rose up in her mind's eye.

The oak had no words of encouragement to offer her, only the solid support of one who had seen the history of several centuries pass by his throne upon the hill.

But, if she were to be perfectly honest with herself, Elizabeth did not think that Colonel Fitzwilliam could have seriously engaged her heart even if he was in possession of a lucrative estate. She knew she would most enjoy someone who could challenge her and even occasionally call her to

task when her thinking had taken a wrong turn. Those qualities had made Charlotte such a valuable friend before her
marriage.

Excessive mildness did not appeal to Elizabeth in the
slightest. It was an aspect of her sister, Jane, that she
respected, though it occasionally rankled Elizabeth when
Jane constantly strived to make peace between those who
hardly deserved the consideration. It was always dear Jane
who attempted to heal some breach between their mother
and father or their sisters, seeking reconciliation long after
Elizabeth had given up all hope. Although she admired the
quality in her older sister, Elizabeth thought that in a
husband it would be irksome.

And as for Mr Wickham, an officer in the militia, he had
proved to be induced by cupidity in his recent pursuit of Miss
Mary King. The practical need to marry a wealthy woman
seemed to have easily overcome any preference that he may
have felt for Elizabeth. Upon reflection, she surmised that
even Mr Wickham, though handsome and agreeable, did not
quite fit her notion of the ideal marriage partner. She wished
him well in his matrimonial pursuit for happiness and a
fortune, but it appeared to Elizabeth that he lacked some
deeper quality of serious thought. His observations, though
quick and witty, were simply a means of gaining the attentive
admiration of the entire room.

Elizabeth sighed as she pushed away from the oak to
retrace her steps back to the parsonage. Carefully treading
down the steep hill, she stole a few parting glances at the
racing clouds overhead. By her estimation, she must have
walked more than three miles to Tall Oak Hill. It was a long
distance, even for her, but since the peak was reputed to
possess the most spectacular view at Rosings, she had

determined to make it her destination on a day with fine weather.

On a lark, Elizabeth allowed her feet to escape her in a brisk trot that turned steadily into a gallop when she lifted the hem of her skirts to make a series of leaps down the hill. A stumble at the bottom made her laugh. Her rapid forward course was abruptly halted by a dark green waistcoat of expensive, thick material. The breath flew from her lungs as strong arms caught her sideways fall.

"Mr Darcy!"

"Miss Bennet." His furrowed brow and sturdy grip expressed his uncertainty, as though he observed someone who was not sober enough to walk unaided.

Elizabeth twisted away from his rescuing grasp with a huff of indignation. "Mr Darcy, there was no need for you to halt me as you did. I assure you I was not in danger. You need not have stepped in my path."

He returned his face to its customary mask of stone. "I apologise for presuming that you were in need of assistance. It appeared that you were travelling down the hill at an unsafe speed. I thought you may have been in some distress."

"I was *enjoying* myself. If, according to you, that is a form of distress, then yes, I suppose I was distressed. It was a state of distress that people do sometimes indulge in on a beautiful day when they think they are unobserved by the prying eyes of others."

"Ah, I see. It is just that…it is a very steep hill and the wind is strong."

It took all the fortitude of Elizabeth's spirit not to sigh loudly and roll her eyes at the man standing before her. Was this how Lydia felt when she and Jane corrected her on some point of propriety? No wonder their youngest sister was so frequently exasperated with her older sisters. Elizabeth was on the verge of behaving just as Lydia did when corrected. *Mr Darcy may not react well if I stomp my foot and plug my ears.*

And why was he there? Had she not, just the night before, pointedly announced to the entire dinner party her intention to walk all the way to Tall Oak Hill this morning? Why did he come so far when she had explicitly informed all of her plan? She could almost believe it was an intentional act to aggravate someone whom he considered so low in social standing and deportment.

"You must allow me to escort you back, Miss Bennet."

"Must I?" Elizabeth glowered at him, her arms crossed firmly over her chest and her face warming at the thought that he had witnessed such an unguarded impropriety.

Mr Darcy started, clearly unsettled. "I could allow you to walk ahead of me for several minutes, if you would prefer that. Or..." He appeared not to know where to focus his gaze.

Elizabeth could not help it. She turned her back to him and briefly rolled her eyes heavenward before noticing the dark brown stallion tied to a nearby tree. The handsome animal pawed at the sod, nibbling with his head down before looking up and studying them. Elizabeth smiled back at him. What must he be thinking of the scene before him?

"What is his name?" Elizabeth queried, suddenly curious, with her back still facing the infuriating man.

"My horse?"

"I do not see anything else nearby that would have a formal name, unless Lady Catherine has taken the time to christen every tree in the forest so that she may better scold them into growing in a more upright fashion."

The deep bark of laughter startled her. She turned around, wide-eyed, and looked him in the face. It was so unexpected a sound that she almost thought she must have imagined it. But, no! There stood Mr Darcy, with a wide grin on his face. The effect was so unsettling that Elizabeth smiled back before quickly dropping her gaze down in confusion.

"Aesop. My horse is named Aesop."

Elizabeth looked back at the horse with an appreciative eye. Aesop snorted and looked away, obviously uninterested in the two people before him.

"And do you suppose, if he could speak, that he would have many humorous stories to tell of you, sir?"

"I am more than certain that Aesop could tell a fable or two that would cause my nearest acquaintances to stare. None of us can maintain the strictest propriety at all times, I believe. Such as when we are overtaken by the impulse to plunge down a hill as fast as we can."

Elizabeth turned to see that Mr Darcy's typically censorious eyes had the faintest hint of a twinkle in them. It was like gazing up at the warm promise of a golden shaft of sunshine breaking through a long period of foul weather.

Was he just teasing me? No, it is not possible.

Elizabeth was struck by an overpowering urge—nay, curiosity—to discover some layer of this man that was hidden from the world. How could an individual have a history of such cruelty towards Mr Wickham while also maintaining a close acquaintance with a man of such goodness as his best friend Mr Bingley? Two such divergent images of Mr Darcy could not somehow fit together in the same man, could they?

Knowing that she risked appearing pert, but unable to

vanquish the impulse, Elizabeth said, "And of those fables, is there one that would not offend me? Or am I too bold in my question? My mother does frequently complain that I am often too forward."

"You are not forward at all, in my opinion. A clever mind comes at the price of inquisitiveness, I think. A curious mind needs feeding. If it is starved, it withers and the world loses some of its lustre. If I thought the question was insulting, I would say so." Mr Darcy grabbed a seed head from a tall piece of grass nearby and twirled it between his finger and thumb, evidently gathering his thoughts again after such a frank outburst.

"I think that, well, if Aesop were to tell tales, he would paint an amusing one of me diving into a pond near my home at Pemberley. The heat makes me...unpleasant company at times, and I find the only cure is a swim. The pond is shaded from the sun and the eyes of others, making it a refreshing experience for my body and spirit."

Unbidden, the image of Mr Darcy with his black locks of hair plastered on his forehead came to Elizabeth's mind. Although it was not an entirely unpleasant picture, she had to grin at the silliness of it. He saw the grin and, in the way he tossed the seed head aside with a snap, seemed to regret his sharing of a personal moment.

"It is getting late, Miss Bennet. We should make our way back."

Elizabeth, annoyed that he thought she was laughing at him, knew not how to cure the misstep. In silence, Mr Darcy untied Aesop and led him away from the base of Tall Oak Hill with Elizabeth walking by his side.

CHAPTER TWO

T he walk back started with no conversation, just as all of the unexpected encounters with Mr Darcy in the woods around Rosings always did. It was difficult for Elizabeth to feel fully at ease with his presence so near. The only sound other than the soft crunch of the leaves underfoot and the song of birds overhead was the occasional snort of Aesop behind them.

Finally, with a wave of his hand at the path ahead, Mr Darcy spoke. "So, Miss Bennet, what is your favourite path through the grounds of Rosings thus far? Is there a particular lane of trees or meadow?"

"Ah, there are so many to choose from, in an estate so grand and well managed as this one, I hesitate to make a definitive selection. I would have to say that I do prefer the paths that wind under older trees. I believe the county of Kent has some of the finest old trees that I have ever seen. But, my opinion means little as I have travelled to so few places."

"No, you are correct. From my travels, I can assure you that Kent does possess many more fine old trees than other areas of the country."

"I hope the groves at Pemberley do not receive word of your comment, for they may take offence. As a child, I always imagined that the trees had conversations that we do not possess the ability to hear. Perhaps they gossip with their roots."

With a rare smile, Darcy replied, "Wise counsel. I shall refrain from future comparisons. It would not do at all to have the Pemberley forests cross with me."

Another pause followed. Both took refuge from the uncomfortable silence by gazing around at the very trees that had been the eager topic of conversation just a few moments earlier. The trees entertained the pair by waving their branches around violently in the heavy wind.

"Have you—" Mr Darcy started, then paused to raise his voice against the gusting breeze. "That is, are you planning on seeing the coast during your visit here?"

"I do not believe so. I understand it is not too far from here. How long of a drive is it to Dover?"

"Not far. I believe it would be about a three-hour drive by carriage. Have you visited Dover and its cliffs before?"

"No, indeed," Elizabeth replied with a laugh. "I am afraid my travelling adventures have been limited to Meryton and occasionally London to stay with my aunt and uncle Gardiner. In fact, my sister Jane is staying with the Gardiners at present. Have you had occasion to see her?"

Mr Darcy became suddenly absorbed by the handling of his horse's reins. Elizabeth had a suspicion that what he was about to say was a version of the truth that best fit his present need for an acceptable response. Her eyes narrowed in expectation.

"No, I have not had the pleasure of seeing Miss Bennet. I am glad that she is in London visiting relatives...relatives who reside in?"

"Near Cheapside. My uncle has warehouses there. Their residence is across the road from the warehouses. I believe he could easily afford a more stylish neighbourhood, but he places the time he spends with his wife and children as having higher importance than being seen in the most fashionable neighbourhoods. It is a choice that few would agree with, I am sure, but since the result of his choice is a happy marriage and children who adore him, in my mind at least, he has made the correct decision. He need not spend hours in a carriage taking him to and from his business. Instead, he spends that time in the comfort of a pleasant home among those he loves. What is your opinion of his choice? If chance had made you the man of trade with a family, what would be your decision in the matter?"

Elizabeth asked the question and waited. What could he possibly have to say in response? Mr Darcy had experienced nothing but the very best of society for his entire life. Would such a commonplace predicament be something he could understand?

"It sounds as though your uncle is in possession of a practical mind. I cannot say I disagree with his choice. Though, the case may be argued that some distance from family may very well contribute to the happiness of all."

They had reached an expansive clearing, and Aesop took advantage of their distraction to dip his head into the verdant spring grass. They both paused, allowing the horse his treat.

The gentleman turned to her with a pensive look. "It

would seem to me that someone such as yourself, in possession of a lively mind, may not object to travelling from Longbourn and seeing more of the world. Or possibly being settled away from family."

"As you well know, my liberty to choose how and where I travel and live is very limited. I am content in Hertfordshire. Though, in some ways, you are correct. I would indeed enjoy seeing more of the world, given the opportunity. But such an opportunity is unlikely to ever arise, would you not agree?"

Aesop had come to the limit of his reins, and Mr Darcy was obliged to pull the horse steadily back towards them. The reins again became the sole object of attention as his fingers danced nervously with the leather. Mr Darcy wiped his brow with the back of his hand.

"I must disagree. I think such an opportunity for you to have the freedom to travel with ease is quite likely to occur. In fact, Miss Bennet, it has been for some time now that I have considered you the very lady that I—"

Elizabeth stared, wide-eyed, up over his shoulder.

"Miss Bennet, are you unwell? Should you like to sit upon Aesop for the rest of the walk back to Rosings?"

Elizabeth only shook her head, not daring to blink. The last several words addressed to her had fallen on indifferent ears. As her companion stepped towards her with obvious concern, Aesop flung up his head, the whites of his eyes rolling forward as he reared and jerked his reins from his owner's grasp. The massive horse spun round on his hind legs and raced away, causing Mr Darcy to stumble into Elizabeth, and they both tumbled to the ground.

Muttering flustered apologies, Mr Darcy pushed himself up off of Elizabeth, but she continued to gape in wonder above him.

There, in the sky above the clearing, were floating boats held aloft by giant inflated bags of blue fabric attached by an interwoven net of thick rope.

Elizabeth stared, dumbfounded, as the flying carriages appeared to race rapidly through the sky, driven by the unusually strong winds from the east.

"Good God!" Mr Darcy exclaimed. "Elizabeth, come!" He shot to his feet and extended a hand to her.

Unable to tear her eyes away from such an extraordinary sight, Elizabeth cried, "Mr Darcy! What are those things? Are they machine or beast?"

He grabbed her elbow and hoisted her to her feet. They ran back the way they came, heading to the closest treeline. Mr Darcy did not slacken his pace until they were several hundred feet into the woods.

"Were there soldiers in those flying boats?" Elizabeth demanded, breathless.

"I believe they may have been French soldiers. I distinctly saw coats of blue." He glanced over his shoulder towards the distant clearing. "Those are flying balloons."

"Balloons? Flying soldiers? Be serious, sir. Such things are hardly possible, are they?"

"Miss Bennet, your own eyes do not deceive you. This is one of the plans that Napoleon has contemplated employing in order to invade England. Either by ship, a tunnel under the English Channel, or by air over the Channel. He has been fervent in his attempts. Since our Navy has done such an admirable job of preventing the French Navy from navigating the waters of the Channel, I suppose he has decided to implement plans for an air invasion. It is but twenty miles from the English shore of Kent to the French coastline in the narrowest section."

They both paused, catching their breath.

Elizabeth leant her head back, gazing at the sky overhead to try to catch a glimpse of another flying ship. "What should we do? Attempt to make our way back to Rosings?"

"Yes, though that takes us towards the coast. I am unarmed. Aesop was so frightened by the balloon that I expect he is far from us. I think we have little choice but to attempt to reach Rosings."

"Did you see how many soldiers or balloons there were?"

"I think I saw four soldiers on the ship. Is that correct, by your remembrance?"

"Yes, they appeared to be running about, pulling upon the ropes. Do you think they observed us? I believe I saw them pointing at us!"

"Most likely they were pointing at Aesop, a highly valuable resource to an invading force."

"Invading!"

"There is a chance that these air machines are but a small portion of a much larger force preparing to invade."

"Oh, Mr Darcy! My family! I am so far from them!"

"Your family, north of London in Hertfordshire, with a militia stationed there, has much better prospects than those of us here in Kent. I am sorry to say, but you must forget about your family for the moment and focus on your own welfare."

"And yours."

Mr Darcy visibly startled at this small acknowledgement, and Elizabeth wondered at the flush that rose up his neck as he turned away to glance around them.

"We must attempt to continue in the same direction we were walking before. But I believe we should stay well clear of open spaces where we could easily be seen from above."

"I had not thought of that." She returned her gaze to the small patches of blue sky and clouds that were discernible overhead. "We should hug the treelines of the sheep pastures that are to the south of here. For if we proceed directly to Rosings from this spot, there will be a great deal of open spaces to contend with."

"Yes. I had little idea that you were so familiar with the configuration of Rosings Park," Mr Darcy said with what sounded like admiration. "It is a grand estate to know so well in so little time as you have been here."

"Well, I had extensive explanations and several diagrams to study before I ever left Longbourn. Mr Collins is as attentive a steward of both the spiritual and physical aspects of Rosings as anyone could ever dare to hope for."

Despite the dire situation they were in, Mr Darcy smiled knowingly down at Elizabeth. "Yes, Mr Collins has proved his worth yet again. Here," he said, lowering his voice, "take my elbow if you need. Let us continue in silence, for the sound of voices can travel far through the air. If you need to speak to me, tap my forearm and lean very close."

Elizabeth dropped her gaze at the impropriety of the proposal, but the very nature of their circumstances required breaches of etiquette that would usually not be tolerated. A sudden urge to exchange partners in this misadventure overtook her. Could this not have occurred while she was in the company of Colonel Fitzwilliam or perhaps even Wickham? They were both military men and infinitely more qualified to deal with the present situation; besides, their company would have been more welcome. Yet even she had to admit that, so far, Mr Darcy had acquitted himself well.

They made their way through the uneven terrain of the forest to get to the sheep meadows south of them. The landscape was hilly and wild. Several times, she was grateful for the offer of his elbow as the roots of trees had the aggravating habit of tripping her or grasping at the hem of her dress.

Elizabeth began to feel some fatigue in her legs, slowing her pace. The long walk to Tall Oak Hill, the run from the balloon, and now the unsteady navigation through the woods were beginning to wear on her.

Mr Darcy looked at her with some concern. "Are you beginning to tire, Miss Bennet? There is a stream near here where we could rest and take a drink of water. We may have several hours yet before sunset to make our way back to Rosings. A pause will matter little, I assure you."

"I am very well, thank you. A walk through the woods is no large trial to me. But if *you* are feeling worn, sir, by all means, we should pause."

"Very well. I am feeling fatigued," he replied with a small, wry grin that did not escape her notice. "Let us go down to this bank. We will be out of sight, and we may refresh ourselves momentarily. Allow me to go first, for it is steep and I would like to help you descend."

Mr Darcy jumped down to the bank along a wide stream. He turned and reached both his hands up to her expectantly. Elizabeth's heart raced as she stooped, gripped his hands, and jumped down, landing firmly against Mr Darcy's chest with a quiet gasp. He did not immediately release her hands, and she pulled hers out of his grasp, aware of the warm blush on her cheeks.

"Here," he said, looking around as he did. "This log will do for a rest."

Elizabeth sat, grateful to be off her feet, though frightened of their current situation. She observed Mr Darcy, who stood beside the stream, looking at its waters with a solemn expression. He loosened his cravat and unbuttoned the top of his shirt, then appeared to startle at her attentiveness.

"My apologies, Miss Bennet. I may be more at ease to move freely if necessary if I am not so...so..."

"Choked by the necessity of propriety?"

"Exactly my thoughts."

"Feel free to make any adjustments to your attire that you deem necessary, sir."

His staid demeanour was inscrutable. "Thank you."

"Not at all." Elizabeth smiled reassuringly.

Mr Darcy removed the cravat entirely and stuffed it in his pocket. He began to stoop over the water and then paused, straightening back up. "Again, if you will excuse me, I think I may take a drink from this stream, if you do not mind."

Elizabeth could not help but feel the ridiculousness of his request and formality. This was not the setting of a lady and gentleman's customary stroll. She looked heavenward again and sighed.

"Mr Darcy, if you do not mind my saying, you need not forewarn me of every minor action that you may take before me that would not be in the usual scope of proper etiquette. Our main concern now is getting back safely, not whether we shock each other."

"You are correct, as always."

His statement struck Elizabeth as either incredibly kind or insultingly satirical. But which one remained a complete mystery to her. And since she was beginning to feel hungry, tired, and out of sorts by all that had occurred that morning, she opened her mouth to enquire his exact meaning, but she froze instead.

The impeccably proper, handsome, difficult, wealthy Mr

Darcy was bent on one knee, mud soaking the fabric of his trousers, one hand dipping into the fast-flowing water and bringing his palm to his open mouth as the water trickled through his fingers back into the stream. The other hand was flat on the ground, mud sliding up through his splayed fingers as the cuff of his shirt dirtied itself. He brought his cupped hand to his mouth again and drank deeply with closed eyes, his bobbing Adam's apple evidence of his thirst.

An undeniably new sensation of warmth spread through Elizabeth's face and stomach before settling most definitely in the centre of her chest. Her heart shifted in a most uncomfortable manner as she watched him repeat his movements several times.

Once the gentleman had slaked his thirst sufficiently, he stood and glanced at her. His brow furrowed and his eyes darkened. "Miss Bennet, are you well? Have I offended you?"

"Of course! I mean, I am well. And no, nothing has occurred to offend me. I am not offended in the least. No." She stood suddenly.

"I do not have a cup to offer you, but perhaps you should drink some water as well. We have a way to go before we are back to Rosings."

"Good suggestion. I am thirsty," she said as she approached the water's edge, lifting her skirts in an attempt to save them from the mud. She paused, remembering how the sight of Mr Darcy drinking from the stream had affected her.

"Do you mind terribly... What I mean is, could you turn to face the other direction?"

A sly smile lifted one corner of his mouth. "But what of our suspension of proper etiquette, Miss Bennet?"

Before she could respond, he turned and looked up towards the sky with his hands clasped behind his back.

"Infuriating man," Elizabeth muttered while she stooped as well as she could and took several handfuls of water. Feeling refreshed with something in her empty stomach, she straightened and looked up at the sky. "It will be well past the noon hour by now, I imagine."

Mr Darcy nodded and consulted his watch. "We should move quickly to avoid encountering anyone. It would not be prudent to be out after sunset if we can preferably be within the walls of Rosings. Or on a horse to travel west."

He strode along the steep bank and back again, running a hand through his hair in apparent agitation, stopped, and turned to face Elizabeth.

"Miss Bennet," Mr Darcy said, taking both of her hands in his, "if anything should occur, you must not stop for me. Run as quickly as you can towards Rosings. Or hide yourself well. It is good that you have on your green dress. In addition to being very becoming on you, the fabric serves to blend in well with the countryside."

He looked into her eyes for a long moment before dropping her hands. Elizabeth could not be sure, her thoughts were so muddled from the day, but there seemed to have been something more in his dark eyes than just passing concern for a mere acquaintance. Surely not, though. She must be mistaken. Suddenly the words of her friend Charlotte floated to the front of her mind. Mr Darcy had immediately called upon them at the parsonage after his arrival in Kent. *"I may thank you, Eliza, for this piece of civility. Mr Darcy would never have come so soon to wait upon me."* At the time, she had dismissed this as a mere mistake on Charlotte's part.

Elizabeth nodded in agreement to Mr Darcy's request.

"Wait here until I look about for a moment. Say nothing. Then I will help you up."

Mr Darcy turned to reach up to the tangle of tree roots that lined the bank and pulled himself up with ease. He crouched low for several minutes, looking in all directions. He stood and continued to look about him. Elizabeth wrung her hands, wishing to be up with him and out of the ditch.

Mr Darcy turned and smiled reassuringly down at her. "Come," he said as he knelt and extended his hands to her. The blue sky silhouetted his figure, lean and broad-shouldered. His hair was tousled from all the running and scrambling, and a large patch of mud coated his knee. Suddenly, Elizabeth realised that Mr Darcy was not terrible *all* the time. In fact, despite the danger that they were in, she found herself no longer wishing to replace him with Colonel Fitzwilliam or even Mr Wickham. In fact, there was no one else whom she wished in his stead.

Elizabeth reached her hands up towards his, smiling back at him.

A shot rang out.

CHAPTER THREE

Mr Darcy disappeared from Elizabeth's view. Her urge to scream was immediately smothered by her own hands clasped down over her mouth to silence herself. Terror froze her to the ground. To make a single sound would be to expose her presence to an unknown number of French soldiers.

She remained motionless until the sound of approaching footsteps caused her to throw herself under the tangle of roots that hung over the stream's embankment. As the heavy footsteps drew closer, she heard Mr Darcy moan and a scramble of leaves and twigs breaking. It seemed to her ears that he cried out in pain. Then the sounds of a struggle ensued. Not knowing what was happening to Mr Darcy as he struggled mere feet from her was more than Elizabeth could bear. Her eyes squeezed shut as she tried to wish herself as far from there as possible.

One of the men scuffling above cried out in agony again. The sound sheared through her. Deep in her bones, Elizabeth knew it came from an already injured Mr Darcy. The likelihood of anyone coming to his aid seemed impossible. Fear for him held her captive.

Her eyes darted wildly around and up the other high bank of the stream as she tried to glean whether others were coming or not. Surely Colonel Fitzwilliam or Mr Collins or one of the servants from the house? They were still well over two miles from Rosings by her estimation. Would anyone have heard the gunshot? Perhaps the people there were detained by forces far greater than one French soldier.

With a flash of clarity that tamped down every panicked feeling in her breast, Elizabeth realised that it was she alone who could aid Mr Darcy.

But I am just a girl! was the first response from her mind. *No, I am a woman. A woman who is too free with my opinions and too far-ranging in my walks, according to my mother, to ever be considered a mere girl.*

Elizabeth decided her fate, come what may. She ran along the stream bed, then made a leaping grab at the wall of roots that was within her reach. Her sturdy walking boots made a few sliding plunges downward before she found her grip and began to pull herself up. How she must appear as she wrenched the front of her gown along the muddy bank, coating it liberally with the muck, she cared not.

Once up to level ground, panting with her arms aching from such unusual exertion, Elizabeth ran towards the two struggling figures. They were both on the ground when the French soldier in a blue coat lifted his fist to punch Mr Darcy, and Elizabeth's heart dropped like a stone.

She looked around in desperation. The soldier's musket was out of either man's reach. She ran and picked it up, realising quickly it had already been discharged. She knew enough of the hunting that occurred at Longbourn to be familiar with that much. She glanced about. The reloading cartridges and bullets were still on the French soldier's belt.

Elizabeth stared at the wickedly sharp bayonet at the end of the muzzle and gulped. Could she run a man through with the blade? Even though she was concerned for Mr Darcy, she decided that would be the very last resort.

Flipping the gun over and carefully holding it by the barrel, Elizabeth ran up and crashed the stock down onto the back of the soldier's upper back and head. He paused in throttling and turned to look up at her, dazed. The soldier moaned, slumped, and collapsed to the ground.

Mr Darcy began choking out breaths and coughing. Elizabeth stood over him and, with her boot, pushed the French soldier the rest of the way off of him. She then knelt beside Mr Darcy, supporting him upright with a hand on his back. He, wild-eyed, stared from the prone soldier, to Elizabeth, then back again.

"Miss…Miss… *Elizabeth!* I told you to run! Do you not heed what anyone says to you? Ever?"

Panting from her own recent labours, she withdrew her hand from his back and sat back on the leaves of the forest floor. Angrily, she glared at him. Shoving some wild locks of her dark hair from her eyes, she said, "You are very welcome, sir! Is this how you repay a kindness that saved your life?"

Elizabeth snapped her mouth on further chastisements when her eye caught hold of a shocking sight. The dark green colour of Mr Darcy's coat, just at his right shoulder, had an unmistakable sheen to it. She lifted the fabric from his breast and discovered a bloom of dark red on the white shirt beneath.

"Mr Darcy! You are injured!"

"From his bayonet," he said with a nod at the soldier on the ground.

Elizabeth took a moment to look Mr Darcy over. There was an additional stain of red on the outside of his upper right thigh.

"There, as well. It was a glancing blow, though, not a straight piercing. For that, we are fortunate."

"And the bullet shot that made you fall?" Elizabeth enquired, unable to prevent the panic in her voice.

Mr Darcy simply dropped his chin to his chest. There, among the black curls on the top of his head, was another unmistakable sheen of dark blood. She leant over him and gently parted his curls with her trembling hands.

"It is but a graze as well, I think. The worst of it is your shoulder. We should find a place to clean your wounds as soon as may be so that infection does not set in."

"No, first, we must tie up our friend here so that he may not be able to warn his fellow soldiers. We have no way of knowing if he is part of a larger group or on his own. The very nature of flying suspended from a balloon across the English Channel on such a windy day would probably mean many injuries or deaths upon landing. Regardless, we should keep him from finding others."

Mr Darcy attempted to stand. With a groan, he flopped back to the ground.

"Allow me. Tell me what I should do," Elizabeth commanded in an attempt to overcome her rising alarm.

He gritted his teeth in pain as he removed his cravat from his pocket. "Tie his ankles together with this and his wrists behind his back. Rip some fabric from his shirt if need be. Tie his wrists first. That way, if he awakes, it will be more difficult for him to overcome us."

Elizabeth did as she was instructed.

"Now take off his boots and socks and hide them in the leaves behind that tree. If he does free himself, it will make pursuing us all the more difficult for him."

After several attempts, Elizabeth got the boots off the soldier and concealed them well under some leaves, then turned her full attention to Mr Darcy. His pale face and slowness of his movement told her that they could no longer ignore his injuries. She glanced around the clearing, attempting to discover something that might aid her.

The tan pack of the French soldier lay a short way off, and she ran to retrieve it. Thinking she could grab it and return to Mr Darcy's side, she was stunned when her feet ran one way and her hand on the straps of the pack remained immobile. She tumbled onto her side. The pack was deceptively heavy. Embarrassed, she looked back to confirm that Mr Darcy had not seen her misstep, then scrambled back to her feet.

"Good God! What is in here?" she muttered as she unfastened the straps and rummaged through the bag. It contained several pieces of clothing, tent pegs, shoes, a helmet, some sort of chest plate made of metal, a box of bullets, food, wrappings for an injury, a canteen, a sheathed knife, and many other items. Elizabeth dumped out what she deemed unnecessary. The much lighter pack was flung up on her shoulder as she returned to her patient.

Elizabeth quickly set aside any embarrassment and helped Mr Darcy remove his jacket. Peeling back the right side of his shirt, she cleaned the wound as well as she could and bandaged it up with strips from one of the soldier's shirts to help staunch the bleeding. Having judged the wounds on Mr Darcy's head and leg as less serious—neither was freely bleeding—she determined they could wait for cleaning and binding.

"A decent bandaging job, Miss Bennet. Very tolerable."

Elizabeth started, then pressed her lips together and exhaled forcefully through her nose before blurting out, "Is that your idea of a compliment, Mr Darcy? For something or *someone* to be referred to as *tolerable?*"

"Ouch!"

Elizabeth realised that she had pulled too tightly on the ends of a knot to secure the bandages around his shoulder. "Sorry," she muttered.

"What is wrong with tolerable?" Mr Darcy asked as his eyes squeezed shut in pain. "It is no high praise, to be sure, but it means that something meets the minimum level of acceptability, at least. Is there something wrong with that?"

A flush of anger crept up her neck and warmed her cheeks. She could easily recall what he had said of her at the Meryton assembly when they were first acquainted. Mr Darcy had rebuffed the very kind suggestion of his friend Mr Bingley to engage himself to dance with Elizabeth. The exact response was unreasonably seared into her memory. *"She is tolerable, but not handsome enough to tempt me."* The thought of that stinging humiliation replayed itself over and over in her mind as she stuffed things back into the tan pack.

"I am so *very* pleased, Mr Darcy, that I meet with the absolute minimum level of acceptability in your eyes." Elizabeth staggered back a few steps as she flung the pack onto her shoulder with a little too much force. With one hand on her hip and her chin out in anger, she extended her free hand out to aid him in getting to his feet. "If you would be so kind as to accept my tolerable help, I think we should remove ourselves from this area as soon as possible."

He stared up at her, puzzled. He reached out his hand to take hers, and together, with Elizabeth pulling and then supporting him with her shoulder to his back, they succeeded in getting him to his feet. He stumbled and swayed for just a moment until she draped his good arm over her shoulders.

Elizabeth had the sudden realisation that within the last hour, she had had more physical contact with the bodies of men than she had experienced in her entire life. It was disconcerting, to be sure, but also humorous. A smile reached her face as they took the first few steps forward together.

"Is-is something amusing you?" Mr Darcy asked as he winced with every step of his right leg.

"I was reflecting on the impropriety of the situation, should we be observed by others. It is amusing to me that steps that we must take in order to save our lives would cause no end of comments from those who seek to spread gossip and rumours."

She wanted to add 'like Caroline Bingley' but—not truly understanding to what depth the intimacy between Miss Bingley and Mr Darcy extended—she thought that would be unkind given his present distress. Perhaps he had an intention to marry Miss Bingley or Miss de Bourgh and would find any humorous reference to either lady insulting. But, when Elizabeth reflected on witnessing his conversation and interactions with either of those two ladies, she could recall nothing but strictly civil treatment. In fact, she had thought a few of his comments to Miss Bingley mildly cutting in nature. Then again, how would one know if a man such as Mr Darcy had regard for a lady? He was so solemn, so reserved, so decidedly superior in his manner that a lady would have to guess at his regard rather than witness it through actions or words.

Mr Darcy grunted in discomfort as he walked forward. Their pace was so slow, Elizabeth wondered that they would ever make it back to any sort of shelter that Rosings might offer.

"Yes, I agree, Miss Bennet," he replied, his face covered in a sheen of perspiration. "Ordinary circumstances would find us extremely compromised by the rules of society right now. But those rules are there to be abided by under the best of circumstances. Under the direst circumstances, such as a possible invasion of England by an enemy force, those rules must be succeeded by common sense. I believe..." He paused, eyebrows raised. "I would *hope*, at least, that anyone whose good opinion is worth having would have nothing but praise for you. Their only criticism may be that you did not listen to my explicit instruction to run at the first sight of trouble. I know for a fact that you are an uncommonly good walker and saw with my own eyes this morning that you are a tolerable runner as well."

Elizabeth could not help but exasperatedly exhale.

"Did I say something to offend?"

"That word. Tolerable. It may be considered offensive by some."

"Tolerable? I see no reason that it may offend. I use it frequently when something is satisfactory, but not excelling in nature."

Clearly, Mr Darcy had no memory of his insult to her at the Meryton assembly. The word still caused a surge of indignation in her that could barely be, well, tolerated.

"Mr Darcy, the word implies that something is just barely acceptable. That if that something, or I daresay someone, were just a hair less acceptable, it may cause you to run from the room screaming in fright!"

"That seems a bit excessive. Though I suppose I never considered it like that before. But why should it be so insulting to you? Do you have such strong reactions to other words or just the one?"

"Mr Darcy, you really ought to be saving your breath. We still have a long walk ahead of us."

"You fascinate me, Miss Bennet, and I find that talking takes my mind off of the discomfort I am experiencing. I sincerely apologise if my use of the word 'tolerable' has caused offence. I shall endeavour to remove it from my vocabulary. You have my word."

The moment that silence descended between them, Elizabeth realised the truth of his words. When they spoke, she was hardly aware of the straps of the French soldier's pack digging into her shoulders, or the heavy weight that Mr Darcy applied to her with each step forward. Indeed, if circumstances had been different, it would have been a somewhat pleasant change from the stoic silence that he usually exhibited during their unexpected walks together. Since it eased his suffering, Elizabeth decided that conversation was a small sacrifice that she was willing to make.

"Yes," she agreed, looking up at his face with a polite smile as he looked down at her, "I find our conversation is helping to take my mind off some of my discomfort as well."

The nearness of his dark eyes filled her with a wholly new sensation of disquietude. Unable to name it, she dropped her gaze back to the ground.

"Is the pack too heavy? I should be glad to take a turn at it for a while."

"With what? You have no additional shoulders to spare!

No indeed, we shall rest when needed, and I will be the pack horse until we come within view of Rosings. We know not what lies ahead and may find the contents useful. Besides, to drop it now would leave a hint of our direction to any French soldiers. As you said, that one man may have been part of a larger party."

"Yes, but had he been part of a larger party, I am sure the gunshot would have summoned his fellow soldiers."

Elizabeth had quite forgotten the injury on Mr Darcy's head. The dried trickle of blood from the bullet wound ran down his cheek and under his chin. She glanced down at his thigh and could clearly see that it was still oozing, though not bleeding freely. He winced with each step, and the pallor of his face had worsened.

He must be in a great deal of pain, though unwilling to speak of it.

She glanced around, seeing nothing but the thick, tall trees of Rosings surrounding them.

"I think it would be wise if we were to find a place to rest for a bit and see to your other wounds."

"Perhaps you are right, Miss Bennet. I seem to recall that there is an old hut just ahead. Shepherds used it while tending the sheep at Rosings years ago. As we are getting along in the day, it is possible that we will have to spend the night in some sort of shelter. Or, we should discuss the idea of you continuing on without me to Rosings. You could leave me and—"

"Leave you! No. Out of the question. I will not abandon you, bleeding and unable to walk, while I seek out safety. Do not be absurd. You offered to escort me back to Rosings from Tall Oak Hill, and I shall think it a very severe slight indeed if you do not finish what you started. I will not have it getting around the most fashionable circles of London that Elizabeth

31

Bennet is the kind of girl who takes pleasure in slighting men."

Mr Darcy smiled down at her with a small laugh. "You really are the most—" He shook his head bemusedly.

"Difficult? Contrary? Are those the words you were going to use?"

"No," he replied with his brow furrowed. "Indeed, I was thinking of words that were much more…Well, never mind. I am thankful for your loyalty. Or insistence that I finish this walk with you. However you may put it."

They continued on, their obvious mutual fatigue slowing their pace. When at last they came within sight of a meadow commonly used for sheep, they turned slightly to the left to follow the edges of the treeline, with frequent worried glances at the open space to avoid more shots from French soldiers who may be about, either on the ground or in the air.

CHAPTER FOUR

The sun was beginning to slant downwards as they staggered their way up the crest of a small hill.

"I believe we are on the roof of the old shepherds' hut," Mr Darcy muttered.

"What, we are standing on the roof?"

"Yes, that is what makes it an excellent place to take refuge. You will see. The front is obscured by that tree before us, and the roof was built into the hill. It is quite ancient, I think. My cousin and I used to come here as boys and pretend we were the kings of the realm."

Elizabeth glanced up at his profile, trying to imagine him as a child with the free spirits needed to pretend and play. She thought that maybe she could see a certain curl of his lashes, or a turning up of the corner of his mouth, that perhaps reminded her of a youthful Mr Darcy. It softened his image before her eyes. She could not help but grin mischievously at the picture she saw in her mind.

"What? Why do you smile?"

"Trying to imagine you as a little boy making castles out of shepherds' huts. I am surprised the very finest playhouses were not built for you or that you were permitted to roam so far from the Rosings manor house."

"Miss Bennet, you must know that children much prefer the devices of their own making when they play. They will always hold them in much higher regard than the things that are given to them. Richard and I thought we had discovered something quite special with this little hut."

"Well, if this hut proves to be our salvation for a night, then I would say that you did indeed make an important discovery."

They made their way down the slope with some effort and, as he had indicated, the front was well obscured by a wide tree trunk. The walls were constructed of rough stones stacked upon each other. A thick coating of leaves and moss covered whatever was once the roof of the small structure.

"I can hardly see," Elizabeth stated as they entered the door. Even she had to stoop to clear the compact entrance. Once fully inside, Mr Darcy slid his arm off of her shoulder and slumped against the wall. A stifled cry escaped his lips as he slid to the ground. She shrugged off the pack and knelt beside him.

"You have been hurting much worse than you told me, have you not?"

She needed no answer as the truth of it was clearly seen on his face, even through the darkness. Opening the pack, Elizabeth removed the canteen and brought it to Mr Darcy's lips. He clasped her hand to steady it and drank deeply.

"Does your head hurt?"

"Very much."

She scrounged through the pack to bring out several more

shirts and stockings. One shirt had already been torn to bits to construct the bandaging for his shoulder; the others would be useful for the rest of his wounds.

"Are you hungry, Mr Darcy?"

"Fitzwilliam," he muttered through a grimace.

"Really? Where?" Elizabeth glanced at the door eagerly, thinking that Colonel Fitzwilliam had joined them suddenly.

"No, he is not here. Not a who, it is my name." He laughed gently. "Ouch! Stop making me laugh, it rattles my head terribly and sends an ache from my shoulder all over my body. Since we are in unusual circumstances, we must make concessions. My name is Fitzwilliam Darcy. I do not feel very much like Mr Darcy right now, so can you just call me Fitzwilliam?"

"Fitzwilliam? No, I do not think I can." Elizabeth noticed a slight collapse in his pained countenance, and an inscrutable disappointment that she could not account for darkened his eyes. She knew from her nursing lessons with Longbourn's housekeeper Mrs Hill, and her somewhat recent visit to Netherfield to tend to Jane's violent cold, that the mere act of cheering and encouraging was very beneficial to healing. Willing to do whatever necessary to lift the spirits of her current patient, Elizabeth took a deep breath and ventured, "I have heard Colonel Fitzwilliam call you just Darcy. May I do the same?"

"Must you always have everything your way, Miss Bennet?" Mr Darcy replied with a humoured air.

"That is rich, coming from a man who was born into wealth and used to having his own way with everything. As a woman with four sisters from a family of somewhat limited means, I assure you that I rarely get my way. And when I do, it is because I had to fight for it. Fight very hard, in some instances."

"Darcy is perfectly fine, Miss Bennet." He waved his hand before him as if trying to scatter away a cloud.

"Elizabeth."

"Pardon?"

"You may call me Elizabeth. Till we are through all this and safe back at Rosings."

"Elizabeth. Elizabeth," Darcy repeated in a low, gravelly tone as if he were tasting it. The flavour appeared to please him exceedingly as he leant his head back against the wall with his eyes closed. Apparent relief from pain vanquished the lines of distress from his forehead.

Glad to see him peaceful for a moment, she looked through the remaining contents of the pack. She had left behind many items on the ground near the French soldier, but those she had kept might prove useful. A large flask fell out from a spare set of breeches that she unrolled. It looked very similar to a small flask that she had seen Sir William Lucas sip from on occasion during assemblies or card parties. A merry flush usually came over Sir William's face after his discreet nip, and his naturally jolly mood became even more ebullient.

Elizabeth pulled out the stopper and sniffed. It was some sort of very strong spirit, she was sure. What kind exactly, she could not tell. It might be useful to help dull Darcy's pain. And what else?

She tried to recall the many times as a child that she had found some poor injured animal and run with it, crying, back to the house. Pleading with her mother to help with an injured animal was out of the question as it probably would have resulted in shrieks of horror. Elizabeth had learnt to always run quickly through the kitchen door to find Mrs Hill.

"What have you got there, Miss Elizabeth?" Hill would ask. Snuffling through tears, a young Elizabeth would explain how she stumbled upon the injured animal and beg for Hill's help. The housekeeper always had a warm smile for Elizabeth and a compliment on having such a big heart. *"Just remember, dear, if you have some spirits on hand, any kind will do, from wine to liquor, apply that to the wound after cleaning it with water. And even better, go out near the back flowers and see if there isn't a little bit of mullein coming up. Let's crush the leaves of that plant up and put it in the spirits for a right good poultice for the bunny here."* For the next several days, Hill would help Elizabeth nurse the animal, usually a rabbit but sometimes a small young fox. The furry patient would be kept in a quiet corner of the stillroom. Mama rarely went in there, which was fortunate. Even then, Elizabeth knew how to avoid Mrs Bennet's unreasonable attacks of nerves and rage. Some of the animals she had nursed lived, some did not. The ones that did not heal received a proper burial in the kitchen garden. Hill would stand solemnly by while Elizabeth would do her best to recite scripture and say something in fond remembrance for the animal. The ones that did live were healed and sent back to the wild after a dinner of their favourite food. Those moments of identifying the various weeds that had true medicinal value were still sharp in her mind. The sage bits of wisdom that she had picked up from Hill could be the path to saving Darcy from a severe infection.

Elizabeth glanced at Darcy, who appeared to have slipped into a light doze. Creeping back out the door, she glanced around and listened carefully, with her chest pressed to the tree trunk near the entrance of the hut. Nothing could be detected by her eyes or ears. The birds in the trees were carrying on their lives as usual. If the birds were at ease, that was always an excellent sign that there was no danger nearby.

She cautiously crept down to the edge of the field and saw her quarry. Mullein plants clung to the side of a slope that dropped down in front of her. They were still in their young spring state and not yet grown to their full height with the spike of yellow flowers on top. The fresh young leaves of the plant were just fanning out from the centre and low to the ground.

Lying down on her stomach so that she would not expose herself in the open field beyond, Elizabeth crept a hand forward and grasped the leaves. Their fuzziness reminded her of a recently born lamb. She squeezed hard around the leaves and wrestled with the plant. It flung about for a moment before pulling free from the ground. A spray of dirt hit her in the face. She sputtered and spit the loose soil out of her mouth and wiped it from her nose. With the mullein plant firmly in her fist, Elizabeth pushed from the ground and stood, hearing the terrible sound of fabric tearing as she did so. Groaning, she glanced down to see a large rent in her dress and petticoat.

Her mother's shrill voice echoed in her mind. *"I do not care if there was an invasion, Elizabeth! That is no reason to be traipsing about the countryside, gown torn, hair askew, dirt on your cheeks! What man could possibly want you for a wife?"* Indeed, what man could?

Elizabeth returned to the dark interior of the hut, less frightened than the first time she set foot into the humble shelter. Darcy had slumped to the floor, resting upon his good shoulder with his uninjured arm outstretched and his head resting upon it. She realised that rest was essential, but the proper and thorough cleaning of his wounds took precedence. Hill had always impressed upon Elizabeth the vital need to attend to wounds in the right way.

She removed her pelisse and bonnet so that she could move with greater ease. Kneeling in front of Darcy, Elizabeth placed a hand gently on his outstretched arm.

"Mr... I mean, um, Darcy. Darcy, I need you to wake up for a few minutes. Please." She gently touched the palm of his hand with her fingertips.

His eyes cracked open, then he moved quickly to press himself upright.

Elizabeth rested her hand on his chest and implored, "Please take care, sir—Darcy. You will injure yourself further."

Heeding her advice, he slowly pushed himself up to a seated position with his back leaning against the wall. She handed him the flask of spirits and urged him to drink, which he did, followed by a cough and a wince.

"Good God, that is a strong drink you serve for tea, Elizabeth."

"It is the best I could do on such short notice. It may dull your pain, I think. I need to more carefully attend to your injuries. We were in a hurry before, but I may use more care now. A stab wound straight in like this needs to be thoroughly cleaned."

"Of course." Darcy shrugged out of his jacket and shirt that were just draped over his wounded shoulder.

Elizabeth began to unwind her quickly executed binding, then grimaced once she saw the wound. Although it had only been almost an hour, the injury had an appearance that she did not like. Once again, she used water from the canteen to clean it.

"This will hurt. Perhaps you should take a few more sips from the flask."

"Far be it from me to refuse the request of a lady," he mumbled as he lifted the lip of the flask to his mouth and drank. He exhaled loudly. "I have never had it before, but I believe this is a Chartreuse, a strong liquor that monks in France make using many herbs. The recipe is a well-kept secret, centuries old. It would probably be quite valuable here in England, due to the war."

He sipped and then she took the flask from his hand and poured a small amount over the wound. Darcy groaned in pain.

Elizabeth tore two small squares from her already tattered petticoat and placed them aside, then took the mullein and rolled it between her palms. Once crushed, she lightly doused it with spirits from the flask and sandwiched it between the two cloth squares.

"Perhaps it will be even more effective than wine. It is likely that some of the herbs may be beneficial to the healing of wounds."

Biting her lip with trepidation, she once again poured some of its contents directly on the bayonet wound on Darcy's shoulder. He repressed a groan of pain through clenched teeth. Elizabeth disliked seeing him suffer, but she could well recall how firmly Hill had taught her of the particular dangers of a puncture wound. Quickly, she pressed on the poultice of mullein and Chartreuse. Once his shoulder was bound with the poultice in place, she moved up to his head wound. Through dampening and cleaning, Elizabeth was able to remove most of the dried blood from his hair and view the wound.

"You are very fortunate, Darcy. That bullet could have been the end of you."

"Mmm-hmm."

Elizabeth glanced down. Darcy had his eyes squeezed closed. Whether it was from pain or self-consciousness, she could not tell. The nature of the work had brought her figure very close to his face. Her main concern had been the cleaning of the wound, and her attention had been utterly absorbed by it. She had not realised that she was brushing up against him so closely with her body.

Elizabeth sat back, uncomfortable warmth flooding through her. She could not imagine that, covered in dirt, blood, and grime, and smelling perhaps not the best, she should disturb Darcy's comfort in that way. No, impossible. It was more likely that he was on the brink of thinking her completely intolerable. That very well might be, but she would not have his death on her conscience if she could help it. It would be a disgrace to all that Hill had taught her over the years.

Darcy seized the opportunity of this interlude to take a few more swigs of the flask before Elizabeth grabbed it from his grasp.

"It is a good thing that you did that, for you will not enjoy this," she said with some resentment edging into her voice. She gave a proper splash from the flask to the top of Darcy's head. He cried out for just a second before settling into a moan.

"I think you enjoyed that," he muttered through clenched teeth.

"Well, I can do little to make the pain more tolerable, except by the means of the flask."

"There is that word again, tolerable."

"I know it is one of your favourites, so I used it to humour you and set you at ease. Now, do you think you will be able to clean your leg wound yourself, or shall I?"

They both looked down at the wound and its proximity to an intimate location, then back up at each other. Both looked away quickly. Elizabeth stifled her nervous desire to laugh.

"I can manage perfectly well on my own." Darcy's voice was full of his usual hauteur. "Just hand me a knife from the pack so that I may cut away some fabric."

"As you wish."

Elizabeth retrieved the knife and held things at the ready so that Darcy could manage as well as possible. Several swigs from the flask later, he had done a *tolerable* job with it—she had boldly determined with several discreet peeks that made her heart race—and leant his head back in exhaustion.

"I think you must eat something, sir. You look very worn."

He briefly nodded his agreement, and Elizabeth gathered one of the loaves of bread, the block of cheese, and slices of smoked meat from the pack. Ripping off the end for herself, she handed the rest of the loaf to Darcy. They chewed in silence, both of them evidently having an appetite that was larger than they cared to admit.

Afterwards, Darcy shifted uncomfortably, wincing.

"Is there something that you need? May I be of assistance?"

"I need to... Ahem, I need to go out of doors for just a moment. If you could help me stand, I believe I can manage the rest on my own."

"Is there something out there that you need assistance with?"

"No! I need to attend to...certain needs."

"Oh. Oh! Of course."

Elizabeth moved to help Darcy stand. Once upright, he staggered slightly, and she helped steady him. His good arm was flung about her shoulders as they moved in unison to the door of the hut.

The shadows outside were elongated, and the beginnings of the night air, cool but not cold, stole across the meadow. Together they walked to the far side of the massive tree. He leaned his uninjured shoulder against the trunk. Once she was assured of his relative steadiness, she turned to leave him, but not before glimpsing the gratitude on his countenance as he quietly thanked her.

"Once you wish to return, call for me and I will assist you."

"I assure you, I can manage."

"As you wish. Do not spoil my hard work on your wounds with your stubbornness," she replied coolly as she turned on her heel and ducked back into the hut.

Elizabeth gathered the few extra clothes and a blanket to make a pallet for Darcy on the hay in the corner. She sat down heavily, the exhaustion of the day catching up to her. She was overwhelmed by the urge to place Darcy's dark green jacket over her shoulders and lean back with closed eyes against the compacted mud walls. She recalled all of the concerns that had flitted through her mind just that morning. They seemed rather trivial now. Her mind wandered to various people she loved, scattered throughout the country. Was Jane well in London? Surely she would be well protected there. Her family in Hertfordshire? Again, being farther from the coast and with a militia stationed in the neighbourhood, the likelihood of Longbourn being somewhat safe was strong. The difficult truth emerged that the ones who were likely to be in the most danger were herself, Darcy, and the inhabitants of Rosings Park. She needed to marshal all of her reserves to care for Darcy and herself. They must be a little over two miles from Rosings by now. If Darcy felt well tomorrow, perhaps they could make it back without incident. A creeping unease rose in her when she considered that a search party had not yet come for them, although they were clearly missing and despite everyone knowing precisely where she had intended to go that morning. But they had strayed so far south in an effort to avoid open spaces, they would not be easy to find.

I hope Charlotte is safe. And Colonel Fitzwilliam, Lady Catherine and Miss de Bourgh, and yes, even my cousin, Mr Collins. I hope they are all safe tonight.

CHAPTER FIVE

The sound of a stumble woke Elizabeth from her light doze. Silhouetted in the doorway, Darcy swayed and then began to take an unsteady step inside. Elizabeth jumped up and ran to support him. They made their way to the back of the hut and collapsed together on the pallet.

Darcy lay flat on his back, panting from the exertion. Elizabeth began to cover him with his jacket.

"No, you must keep that for yourself, Elizabeth."

"The evening is warm, sir. Unusually so for this time of year. I shall be well with what I wear."

Darcy closed his eyes, apparently unwilling to argue with her after such a day.

"Would you mind very much retrieving that flask for me, Elizabeth? I should like to enjoy one more sip."

"Have you not had enough?"

"No. Just one more sip."

Elizabeth, hoping that he was not becoming intoxicated,

fetched the bottle. But, if the choice was an intoxicated Darcy experiencing less pain and more comfort, she thought there could be little harm in it.

He took two generous swigs from the flask before she swiped it from his hands.

"There is very little left. We must save some for your wounds, sir. I think you have had enough to ease your pain. You have lost blood today, so I do not think an excess of spirits would be advisable."

The strong drink made Darcy slightly unbalanced in movement and speech. He looked up at Elizabeth through half-closed eyes that seemed slightly out of focus.

She saw he was beginning to ease into a restful state and was glad of it. She moved to rise when she felt his hand rest on her forearm.

"Stay a bit, if you do not mind."

"Of course. Should you like to converse, or rest in silence?"

"Talk to me."

Elizabeth pursed her lips and tried to come up with a neutral topic that would be of interest to them both, without being too stirring in nature.

"Do you know, that is, are you aware of Mr Bingley's intentions in regards to Netherfield? Is he to return? If not, it would benefit the neighbourhood if he gave it up entirely so that another may take up residence there. It benefits no one for it to sit idly as it does now. The neighbourhood, the merchants who supply the house, Mr Bingley's finances would all benefit if he gave it up to a tenant who would be more present, would you not agree?"

Darcy nodded in a slightly lopsided way. Elizabeth

guessed that such a powerful drink was not something he usually consumed.

"I think that perhaps he will give it up," he replied. "His sisters certainly do implore him constantly to do so. It would be better for him financially and put him out of the way of Miss Jane Bennet."

Elizabeth sat up straighter, her eyes open wide. In his current state, Darcy seemed unable to recall that Jane was her sister. Indeed, her most dearly beloved sister.

"Is that so?"

"Yes, it was quite apparent to me that Jane Bennet had very little love for Bingley, though he was in absolute raptures about her. It was more than just one of his passing fancies. This time, he seemed truly smitten. He was in great danger of becoming deeply in love with Jane Bennet. So, I agreed with his sisters that we should try to convince him to give up Netherfield. A loveless marriage for Bingley? I could never forgive myself if I allowed him to stumble into such an irretrievable mistake. No, no, no, silly Bingley. I do have to keep an eye on him sometimes. He is a good fellow and clever in his way, but he is most lacking when it comes to seeing through a ploy like that. Miss Jane Bennet seems even-tempered, but one can tell so little about her intentions and true sentiments that the risk was too great to allow him to continue there. And that family, good God, that family. Except for Elizabeth, of course. Elizabeth is divine."

Elizabeth, deafened by the buzzing in her ears, felt the heat of anger rising. But she remained perfectly still so that she could learn more. So, this was the cause of her sister Jane's misery—the meddling of this man before her. She knew him to be proud and cruel in his treatment of Mr Wickham, but also so officiously meddling as to ruin the prospects of happiness for his best friend? It was almost more than she could bear to resist the urge to flee from that hut and take her chances in the dark forests of Rosings.

"Am I to understand that you thought it your duty as a friend to protect Mr Bingley from a loveless marriage to Jane Bennet? And to do so, you persuaded your friend to leave Netherfield and cease his acquaintance with her?"

Darcy shifted his head to look more at Elizabeth. He blinked several times and then squinted. A look of mild surprise lit up his face.

"Yes, exactly! But make sure that I do not tell Miss Elizabeth Bennet. You see, her very fine eyes would look at me with disapproval in them. And *that* I simply could not bear."

Darcy's eyelids began to droop and soon closed entirely. His breathing became soft and regular, heralding a healing sleep that Elizabeth hoped would last the entire night.

She stood and went to the doorway of the hut, looking out into the night. A sliver of a new moon was rising, giving everything about her a slight glow of silvery light. The fierce wind from the day had settled into a gentle breeze, though the clouds high above still raced by with determined urgency. In the distance, a fox screamed, causing a shiver to run through Elizabeth. But still she stood, unable to withdraw from the unusually warm spring evening to retreat back into the dark of the hut.

Tiredness swept through her body and heart. Her swift burst of rage at Darcy's inebriated confession had already subsided upon reflection. Had not Charlotte warned of Jane showing too little of what she felt? How was Mr Bingley, or indeed anyone, to be sure of the affections of someone who was so cool in her countenance as to be virtually unreadable?

To Elizabeth, her moods were easier to read. But to anyone else, they proved elusive. Jane was not to blame at all. But if Mr Bingley was so uncertain of her regard as not to risk a proposal, it would have only taken a little more interference from his family and friends to cause him to abandon the field altogether.

With a sigh, Elizabeth realised what Jane had lost. One thought of how intensely overwrought their mother was provided a simple explanation of why Jane was so very private with her thoughts and feelings. She was the complete reverse of Mrs Bennet. Their mother was a shrill, overly opinionated trial to the nerves of even the most angelic dispositions. In order to maintain some semblance of contentment as the eldest child of such a woman, Jane had become even more reflective, quiet, and reserved than perhaps had been her natural inclination. And now it may have cost Jane the very happiness she sought with a man suited to her in almost every way.

The futility of it all, the mire of miscommunications and lost opportunities, coupled with the exhaustion of the day and the anxiety of their situation blurred the slice of moon that hovered above the treeline as tears raced down Elizabeth's cheeks. She smeared them away with the back of her grimy hand. What a fright her face and hair must be! A small laugh escaped her when she wondered what Darcy would think of her fine eyes at that moment. Fine eyes? Had he really said that about her? She must have misheard him. Or perhaps the liquid in the flask was just that strong. It must be powerful indeed if it could cause a man who disdained her so fervently to call her eyes fine.

Elizabeth reentered the hut and took up the flask, curious. She pulled out the stopper and sniffed. A small taste passed her lips. A violent fit of coughing doubled her over, her eyes watering again.

Once the coughing had abated, she glanced at the sleeping gentleman. "Well, that explains your admiration of my fine eyes, Mr Darcy."

He was too soundly asleep to respond or awaken at all as Elizabeth curled up beside him on the makeshift bed and fell asleep under her pelisse.

Despite the warmth of the previous day, Elizabeth woke with a chill running through her. Still insensible to the world around her, she pulled her knees up closer to her chest as she snuggled towards the warmth that pressed into her cheek and shoulder. The warmth raised and lowered in a slow, rhythmic manner.

That is odd. As if my pillow is breathing.

An unfamiliar musky scent filled her senses, and her eyes cracked open. Elizabeth looked up and saw the dark eyes of Darcy staring down at her.

Shocked, Elizabeth shot bolt upright, ready to scream loudly before the faintest hints of the previous day began to illuminate her consciousness. Darcy, with his good arm behind his head, had not been forcing her in any way to cling to him in the manner she had been. Embarrassed, Elizabeth realised she was the one who had snuggled so firmly to him.

"Awake at last?"

"You should have roused me earlier, Mr Darcy," Elizabeth snapped as she stood, swayed a bit, and then straightened her spine in a huff of indignation. The soreness in her muscles from the exertions of the previous day were difficult to ignore; that, coupled with sleeping on old straw, made Elizabeth take a moment to regain her sense of balance.

"Of course, but you were sleeping so soundly, I was unable to bring myself to disturb you. Yesterday was quite harrowing, and today may be equally so."

Elizabeth pushed hair out away from shrouding her eyes only to discover that several strands of hay had entwined themselves deeply into her curls. She picked at them, trying to wiggle them free of her naturally curly hair, and then sighed. Discerning a slight upturn to Darcy's mouth as he steadily observed her struggles, she gave up all attempts and simply shoved as much hair behind her ears as possible in an attempt to regain some of her dignity.

"And how do you feel today?" she asked briskly.

"I have a raging headache. My wounds ache. And I am hungry. Aside from that, I suppose I am feeling as well as can be expected."

"The headache may be from whatever this is." She picked up the flask and held it at arm's length.

"Chartreuse," he said with a wince and rub of his forehead.

"It gave you quite the loose tongue last night."

"What?" Darcy, clearly alarmed, leaned up on his elbow.

"Yes, it did," Elizabeth replied flippantly while she prepared another loaf of bread and some of the cheese for him.

Silence settled as she brought the simple repast to Darcy. He frowned, looking down at the food.

"Did I say anything that was, um... What exactly did I say?"

Elizabeth drank deeply from the water canteen before passing it to him. She strived for an expression of nonchalance as she said, "Well, we discussed the future of Nether-field. How it may be necessary for Mr Bingley to give it up in the best interests of the neighbourhood—"

Darcy visibly relaxed as he took a bite from his bread, chewing enthusiastically.

"—and then you explained how you endeavoured to sepa-rate Mr Bingley from my sister, breaking her heart in the process, by the way, and then told me not to mention any of it to Elizabeth Bennet or her fine eyes."

Darcy froze, keeping his eyes fixed on a point before him, clearly not daring to look up and meet Elizabeth's earnest gaze. Turning pale at the effort, he sat all the way up, then hung his head low. In a barely audible, pained whisper, he asked, "Did it truly break your sister's heart?"

Elizabeth had been prepared for many things—outright denials, lecturing on the differences of wealth and standing, anger at her accusation, even an excuse for the mild halluci-nations caused by large swigs of Chartreuse. This, however, caught her completely off guard. There was more than phys-ical pain showing on Darcy's face.

"Yes. It caused Jane deep grief. She truly loved Mr Bingley. She has battled low spirits since his leaving Netherfield. Her sorrow is such that, if I am to be totally honest, she may never fully recover from it."

"Oh. I see," he murmured as he rubbed his hand harshly over his eyes. The quiet that followed was unbroken for several moments while Darcy kept his eyes shaded, his elbow resting on his knee. Elizabeth remained motionless as the weight of the words circled the stale air.

She soon stood and went to the door, glimpsed outside to see if anything was stirring, and then risked a brief exit to attend to her personal needs.

When Elizabeth returned, she saw that Darcy had eaten a good bit more and was attempting to stand. She rushed over and easily dipped underneath his left arm to support him the rest of the way to his feet. He swayed uneasily for a moment before getting his feet under him.

"What hurts the worst?" she asked, full of genuine concern.

"My head, my shoulder, my leg, and no small amount of my pride." Darcy looked down at her. She looked up, astonished at this bluntly honest response. His face was so close to hers that she looked away quickly, her heart beating in her ears.

"Elizabeth, you must believe me when I say that I acted out of an incorrect judgment of your sister's feelings towards my friend. I admit, I was foolishly encouraged in this assessment by Bingley's sisters, but I accept full responsibility for giving him poor advice and concealing her presence in London from him."

"Excuse me? You are saying you also lied—"

"Concealed, not lied," a flustered Darcy added.

"This is the same in nature! You lied about Jane being in London for all these months? Did you also advise that Caroline Bingley claim both of Jane's letters went amiss?"

"No, I never told her anything of the sort. That is all Miss Bingley's doing."

"But you concealed Jane's presence from Mr Bingley? You lied to him about that?"

"I did *conceal* that fact from him. I never lied about it."

"Mr Darcy, you can attempt to make a silk purse from a sow's ear all you wish, but it will never be a silk purse! Call it what you wish to salve your conscience, but you did indeed lie about my sister's presence in London."

He grimaced, shaking his head. "Perhaps you have a point, but I must beg to differ from you. I can honestly say that I was truly unaware of the depth of your sister's feelings for Bingley. Now that you have enlightened me, I will attempt to remedy my misstep as soon as we are able to return to civilisation. That is, if England is not now in the hands of Napoleon."

Despite the flurry of resentment Elizabeth felt at the additional revelation of Darcy's concealment—and the agitation encouraged by his close proximity—she pressed her eyes shut and took a cooling breath. "Yes, I agree that we should focus all of our resources on getting back to Rosings. This conversation can wait until another time. I would very much appreciate any effort you can put forth to repair the damage done by yourself and Mr Bingley's sisters to the two most deserving, good-hearted people of my acquaintance."

Elizabeth continued to help Darcy to the door, knowing that he had needs to attend to in private as well. She eagerly dropped his arm and left him standing in the doorway with one hand resting on the wall. Her attention turned to packing their few belongings for the walk back to Rosings. With a fierceness of purpose, Elizabeth began to roll up the blanket from the pallet as if it had personally insulted her. She swung round to Darcy again, dissatisfaction bubbling up in her.

"Just so you are aware," she continued as Darcy turned to look back at her, while she crouched on the ground next to the half rolled-up blanket, "I find it quite ironic that you should be so mistaken about my sister's honest affections towards Mr Bingley. *Some* have said that you have such a reserved pride in your bearing that no one can possibly know what you are thinking. Forgive me for being so bold, but should *your* affections ever be captured by a woman, I am quite sure she would have little idea of it, you are so reticent in your feelings. The very quality that made you misjudge Jane may be considered to be just as strong in your nature as well. That should make Jane an object of your compassion, not your derision."

Elizabeth turned back to the poor blanket with renewed strength and rolled it quickly to within an inch of its life. She glanced back over her shoulder and saw that he was still gripping the frame of the doorway, his face thoughtful. Darcy scowled, perhaps not trusting himself to respond to what she had just said. He began limping out of the door, then paused and turned his head back towards her.

"Elizabeth, while I am out, perhaps you could put on the breeches that were in the soldier's pack."

"Pardon? You cannot be serious. Why on earth should I put on a man's breeches?"

Turning his face back to the outside, Darcy looked up at the tree tops and continued, "Your dress. It is damaged. It is very...distracting." He walked out the door in short, unsteady steps, reaching for the trunk of the tree before the hut.

Elizabeth looked down. She had not realised that the slit from the day before, during her trip to wrestle the mullein plant, had extended from her hem all the way up to the middle of her thigh. It went clean through her petticoat as well, which had been the source of several fabric squares for the poultice and for cleaning wounds. She had deemed it the most likely piece of clothing to be clean and best suited for such a service. While crouched over, almost her entire leg must have been exposed. Elizabeth rolled her eyes and huffed in frustration. As if being a nurse and pack mule was not enough for her to manage while evading enemy forces, she now had to consider the impropriety of her dress offending Mr Darcy. No doubt he would add this to the extremely long list of embarrassments committed by herself and her family. Oh well, once they were through this, they need never see one another again, would they?

With a grumble, she shook out the breeches from the Frenchman's pack and held them up to her waist. The soldier had been slight in frame, but regardless, Elizabeth would be positively swimming in them with her slim figure. She took off her walking boots and slipped the breeches on, cinching the waist tight. To accommodate the extra volume, Elizabeth cut her dress so that she had more freedom of movement. The breeches ballooned out from the slit in her gown in the most ridiculous manner.

When Darcy reentered, he glanced at her with a barely repressed smile while he clutched the frame of the door. Elizabeth put her hands on her hips, daring him to say anything.

"So, shall I grace the very finest houses in London, do you think?"

"Actually, you look surprisingly—"

"Ridiculous?"

"—charming."

"Oh. Well. That is kind of you to say." Her self-consciousness provoked her to cross her arms over her chest. Her recollection of Darcy mentioning her fine eyes last night erupted in a deluge of conflicting emotions engulfing her as she looked up at his glittering dark eyes. He had so quickly explained his actions towards Jane and Mr Bingley, but had said nothing to counter the statement he had made as to the quality of her eyes.

Either he must not have heard me, or he was too embarrassed by such a ludicrous statement made under the influence of alcohol that he wishes it would be forgotten completely. That is quite all right with me. The less said the better.

Still, something in his gaze had left Elizabeth with the impression that propriety was perhaps not his main concern when he requested that she wear a French soldier's breeches. She turned away quickly so that she did not have to look into those coal-black eyes anymore. Either the strain of this misadventure or her lack of a good night's sleep made the effect of his scrutiny unsettling.

CHAPTER SIX

When Elizabeth turned her full attention to the packing of their meagre things, her thoughts of Darcy and propriety faded. Worries of whether her family and friends were safe filled her heart and mind. How did their home of Longbourn fare? What would she do if she was unable to safely travel through the countryside? How long would she have to impose on the kindness of friends and acquaintances before she could reunite with loved ones? And of course, the ever-present concern for her family's future if something happened to her father hung over all others like the sword of Damocles ready to deliver a fatal blow.

It had been long understood by herself and her sisters that, upon the death of their father, the estate of Longbourn would be left to their cousin. Mr Collins had asked Elizabeth to be his bride first before he honoured her friend Charlotte Lucas with the exact same proposal less than two days later. It was well that a man of Mr Collins's passionate temperament was able to secure a happy return so soon after his refusal from Elizabeth. It belied a character that was either extraordinarily practical or tragically foolish. For the sake of her unwavering respect for her friend Charlotte, Elizabeth chose not to examine too closely which of these two it might be. Occasionally, she felt something like regret that she could not have secured her family's future without also sacrificing her happiness and sanity. For being married to a man such as Mr Collins would have been a terrible sentence for her, she was sure.

With a sigh, Elizabeth securely tightened the straps of the pack and made to rise so they could resume their interrupted trip to Rosings. Just as she stood and swung the straps onto her shoulders, she heard a terrible crashing thump to the floor. Upon turning to the doorway of the hut, she witnessed Darcy's crumpled form lying motionless at the entrance.

Elizabeth dropped the pack and rushed to his side.

"Darcy! Mr Darcy! Fitzwilliam!" she cried as she shook him gently, trying to rouse him. The only effect was a groaning response. Elizabeth pressed her palm to his forehead and sensed the unmistakable warmth of a fever. She had been so meticulous in her care of his wounds, but now a fever had begun regardless. With a frustrated sigh, she realised the error of her ways. Darcy had attended to the wound on his thigh, not Elizabeth. Although the injury had appeared superficial in nature, if he had not cleaned it thoroughly, that may have allowed infection to enter. And now their foolish concession to propriety might cost Darcy his life.

Elizabeth bit her lip in anger at herself. She was the one with experience caring for an injury, not Darcy. Even though she had only cared for animals, Hill had always made perfectly clear that what they were doing could be equally applied to people. She should have absolutely forced her way into being allowed to tend that thigh wound as well. A future of being haunted with malicious gossip about her behaviour with a wounded man was preferable over a future with the guilt of an unnecessary death on her conscience.

With a grunt of effort, she rolled Darcy onto his back. She brought the canteen to his lips. He swallowed a small amount, which Elizabeth took as a hopeful sign. A dampened cloth pressed to his forehead helped to revive him to a mild state of sensibility.

"Darcy! You must rouse yourself so that I can take you back to the bed! Are you listening?"

Elizabeth rushed to reassemble the pallet for him from the night before. After a good fluffing of the hay and replacing the unwound blanket, she returned to his side. It took several shakes and some stern words to get Darcy to rise unsteadily to his feet. Elizabeth snuck herself snugly under his left arm again to help him the short distance to the bed. He collapsed onto his back with a moan.

Elizabeth once again wet his lips and forehead. She shook the canteen and dismay gripped her. There were only a few splashes of water left.

"We shall need water soon."

"Water?" His tremulous voice divulged the fog of fever.

"Yes, I would not like to return to the stream. I have no doubt our friend the soldier was able to wiggle himself free by now. Although he would be barefoot, I have no desire to relive that encounter."

"Barefoot?" Darcy replied with a toss of his head. "No, no, no. That will never do. He must not come into Rosings barefoot. Lady Catherine would never tolerate that sort of indiscreet behaviour. My aunt will be furious."

He laughed aloud, longer and louder than anything Elizabeth had ever heard from him before.

"But, it would be terribly funny!" he added through his laughter.

Elizabeth could not resist joining him and giggled at the image of a barefoot man with the shrieks of an indignant Lady Catherine raining down upon him.

"Water..." Darcy murmured as soon as his laugh died down. Elizabeth gave him the last sip.

She began to take stock of all of his wounds after he had settled down with the water and a cool cloth to his forehead. The worst, the shoulder stab, looked rather well as Elizabeth removed the bandages and poultice. She examined it closely. There was no foul odour that wafted up from it, even though she sniffed very near the wound. His head injury looked and smelled equally well. Now, the one that was the least in severity and greatest in concern, his thigh wound. Carefully, she peeled back the layers of the dressing and saw the angry, bright red flesh around the slash. She scowled, furious with herself. With some of the last remaining splashes of Chartreuse, she cleaned it well. Looking about, Elizabeth found the remaining leaves of the mullein plant and made a generous poultice from them, the last drops of Chartreuse, and a few additional squares from her vanishing petticoat.

With a weary sigh, Elizabeth sat back and admired her handiwork. It was then that she realised that her recent revolt against the strictures of propriety would be put to the true test. Darcy had done a slipshod job of binding his thigh over his trousers. For Elizabeth to properly bind the wound, she would need to remove his breeches. Elizabeth rubbed her fingertips on her forehead and squeezed her eyes shut, hoping for an idea that was less questionable to present itself. Hill, with her rosy cheeks and her beefy forearms crossed over her ample chest, seemed to materialise in front of her. *'I know it's squeamish work, Miss Elizabeth, but do you want your patient to live or not?'*

Elizabeth gazed at Darcy, lying there helpless with his chest rising and lowering too rapidly, his shirt open, a thin sheen of sweat on his pallid face. She removed the poultice and temporarily placed it aside, then took his forest green jacket, beginning to look a little worse for wear, and covered his waist to his upper thighs with it. She tucked it under him as well as she could manage in an attempt to keep it strictly in place. After exerting more force than she had imagined would be necessary, a panting Elizabeth wrestled off Darcy's riding boots and stockings. With a deep breath of fortification, Elizabeth reached under the green jacket and, by touch alone, attempted something she had certainly never tried before. She began the process of removing a man's breeches. After several more minutes of averting her eyes when his riding jacket shifted and careful tugs, Elizabeth stepped back with Darcy's recalcitrant trousers hanging from her hand, feeling oddly triumphant.

"There! Hill would be proud," she said with a smile of satisfaction. Then, looking down at the men's breeches still swaying from her hand, she added, "I think."

Elizabeth set herself to the vital task of dressing Darcy's leg wound. The flesh around the cut was warm to the touch, but she hoped that she had caught it in time to help him fight off the infection. She again placed the poultice on the cut and bound it up. Each pass of the cloth under Darcy's leg caused him to groan in pain. Elizabeth very carefully tied the bandage, making sure that each knot was constructed with care and with as little jostling as possible. It amazed her that one smaller wound of less severity than the others could have been the source of such trouble. She sent up a silent prayer that she had done enough to stop the wound from deeply festering.

Now, her main concern was the fever from which Darcy suffered. She picked up the water canteen lying nearby to take a drink herself and press Darcy into taking more. The labour of shifting Darcy and removing his clothing had tired her. Elizabeth had a newfound respect for the servants who bound and wreathed them in clothing every day. It was not such a simple task as it appeared.

The canteen felt too light and Elizabeth knew that it was empty. Worry clouded her vision as she looked about the abandoned hut. There was not even any Chartreuse left. It was clear they needed water, but from where?

To risk going farther away from Rosings, back to the stream where Darcy had fought the French soldier, seemed inherently unwise. She could make the trip quickly, but the risks were too great. She could make the trip in the opposite direction to Rosings, but what would she find there when she arrived? More trouble than she currently faced? Somehow, her spirit revolted at the very idea of leaving Darcy. It was not something that her heart would even allow to be considered. Perhaps it was the wisest course to leave him alone and feverish, but the mere thought produced a tightness in Elizabeth's chest that surprised her.

Elizabeth sighed, the very immediate concern of her thirst pressing her to make a difficult decision. She looked around the hut. Would not a shepherd build this structure near a water source for himself and his animals? Her thoughts turned to a boisterous pair of small boys calling this the castle of their kingdom. If they spent many hours here, surely there was a spot to refresh themselves nearby.

With a dry throat, Elizabeth turned to the dozing Darcy. She placed her hand on his unwounded shoulder with a gentle nudge.

"Darcy, may I ask you something? Oh, do wake for just a moment. Please." She gave him a very slight shake as he turned his head towards her with a moan. "Is there water nearby? There must be water near this hut, but I do not want to wander about in the open looking for it. Can you rouse for just a moment?"

He moaned again and cracked his eyes open. Looking about him in puzzlement, he said, "Is the kingdom under attack? Where is my best knight, Sir Fitz?"

Elizabeth dropped her head, trying to repress a smile. An idea dawned on her. *I should speak to him in the place his mind is at. If he believes that he is in the kingdom from his childhood, I should address him as such.*

"Your highness—" She repressed a giggle with a cough. "—times are dire. We are in need of supplies. Most importantly, water. The king surely knows where water can be found."

Darcy peered at her with an eager sincerity. "My queen? What is it you require?"

"Water. We need water."

"Ah, just through the gate, to the left. There is a mighty spring hidden in the mountain-shaped rocks. We hid it so enemy forces will not attempt to poison the well during a siege of our castle."

This sounded very promising indeed. She made to stand, but Darcy's hand shot out and restrained her. He held her wrist firmly in a surprisingly strong grip. With an ardent look in his dark eyes, he said, "Have I told you today, my queen, how very much I am in love with you? Your beauty stuns my senses into stillness."

Elizabeth, her thirst increasing with every passing moment, had little patience for the fairy-tale fever that had its hold on Darcy.

"Yes, my dear, you are very kind in your words to me, always. Well, some of the time, anyway."

She gently peeled his hand from her forearm and made her way to the door with the canteen in her hand. After a brief pause to ensure that no French soldiers were near to their hiding spot, Elizabeth quietly made her way along to the left of the entrance to the hut. There, just a little farther up the hill, was a mound of rocks a little less than half her height.

Elizabeth placed her hand on the top rock; it felt unusually cool to the touch. The faint smell of moisture in the air around the funny little mound told her that perhaps this was the very spot that Darcy had described. She took a last careful glance around and then began removing the rocks, one by one. As she progressed, the rocks increased in dampness until she reached a layer covered in water. Removing several wet stones, a small pool of crystal clear water emerged. Elizabeth had never before been so grateful at the sight of water and bent over to drink deeply. After her thirst had slackened, she filled the canteen, placed it to one side, and bent over again for several more swallows.

She lifted her head with a smile and wiped her mouth with the back of her hand. Looking up into the sky through the branches of the trees, she watched the lazy clouds waft by. White and billowy, their wide girth and stately march were the direct opposite of their hurried form the day before. The absence of the bizarre balloon boats with their baskets of soldiers was a relief. If the French had attempted a trip across the English Channel today, it would have been terribly slow going for them. A dark cloud on the horizon made her frown. It was due east from the shepherds' hut. A storm?

Elizabeth gasped as she sprang up and moved as close to the edge of the meadow as she dared. It was not a storm cloud—it was smoke, coming from the direction of Rosings Park's manor house. It billowed even more fiercely than before. Each second caused the monstrosity to belch and roll out folds progressively more expansive.

To cause such a quick blaze as that, to produce that enormous amount of smoke, perhaps Rosings itself is on fire! What could be happening? This not knowing is infuriating!

Elizabeth ran back to retrieve the canteen and returned to the hut. Darcy was unmoved from his previous position. She felt his forehead, first with the back of her palm, and then with her lips by leaning over him. Hill had always told her the very best way to be certain of a fever was to measure it with lips, not hands. *"The same way that a hot soup won't burn your finger, but may scald your lips and tongue most awful. So, when nursing a person, use your lips when you can to observe the state of a fever."* Elizabeth had employed this very technique to nurse Jane back to health at Netherfield. As she leant over Darcy with her eyes closed in concentration, the heat from his forehead felt no better, but no worse, for which she was grateful. He was still far too warm for comfort, though.

Elizabeth pulled away from him to see his eyes open and gazing up into her face.

"Darcy, your fever is no better. Nor has it worsened. But...but I am fearful for you." Her voice had trailed off to a barely audible whisper. This proud, difficult man who had scorned her every move as barely acceptable had been her whole world for the last day. The thought of him disappearing from her life forever wrenched her heart with a shock of discomfort and confusion. Her eyes began to water.

Darcy brought a hand up to her cheek and cradled her face. The palm of his hand was warmer than it ought to be. His eyes and breath were more expansive than usual as well. Elizabeth hoped against hope that they were soon found by friends or his fever broke.

"Fear not, my queen. I am here to defend you," Darcy said, his voice lower and huskier than usual.

Elizabeth could not resist a smile at his feverish declaration. Never in her life—even through her most long-ranging walks through mud, sudden snow showers, or the occasional angry bull who would chase her out of his meadow—had she been so grimy and dishevelled. She laughed trying to even compose in her mind what the reactions of the Bingley sisters, Mr Collins, or Lady Catherine would be if they were to witness her in her present state. Never mind that she had perhaps saved the life of their beloved Mr Darcy. Never mind that they had been chased by flying machines and shot at by French soldiers. There would be no reason that could excuse her filthy condition, let alone having spent the night with a man in the wilds of Rosings Park.

"I am afraid I am far too lowly and improper to make you a good queen, sir. Some of your, um, subjects would have a litany of objections. Your mistake is due to your fever. I am no one's queen, and after last night, I may never be the consort of anyone."

Darcy looked up at her again as she brought the water flask to his lips and put a damp cloth on his head.

"I find that impossible to believe." He sounded confident, even in his delirium. "You are extraordinarily lovely. Your mind has a quickness to it, an ability to find humour in the most unlikely places, and your eyes…your eyes…"

Elizabeth, suddenly aware of how close their bodies were, sat up further, pulling away from him. His eyelids floated shut as he appeared to enter a light doze.

The fevered ramblings of Darcy had distracted her temporarily from the thought that there was a wicked column of smoke snaking into the sky from the vicinity of Rosings. That probably meant the French soldiers had ignited something in that area. Again, Elizabeth thought of her dear friend Charlotte Collins and hoped that she would be well. *But it would be the next logical step for the French to extend their way this way, to the west, would it not? That may bring them just past this spot.*

Elizabeth's worried eyes looked to the entrance of the hut, the only thing that could give their position away. Standing quickly, she went to gaze out of the doorway. She clasped her hands together tightly and blew out a breath. She could just see the black cloud billowing in the sky to the east and left of their hut.

Elizabeth smiled wryly, feeling her tension subside. She had thought of it as 'their hut'. With her inclination to see the amusing side of things, how did this dark shepherds' hut compare with the wonders of Pemberley?

"And of this kingdom, I am mistress!" she muttered as she looked at the meadow below and the pile of rocks that surrounded the recently uncovered spring. She shook her head at the amusing thought and carefully made her way out. Above their hut, farther up the hillside, a tree had recently fallen. Perhaps as recently as in the terrible wind of yesterday morning.

Elizabeth tramped up the hill with the hem of her skirt hitched above her breeches. A loose branch about the width of her wrist was separated from the main trunk of the fallen tree. She paused, taking a moment to look about her, listening for any sounds that were not native to the forest. After several moments, Elizabeth decided that she was unobserved and probably safe. She reached down and grasped the branch and began to drag it towards the shepherds' hut. It was much heavier than she anticipated, and the branch proceeded to seek out any little crevice or rock to tangle itself up with. The leaves of the limb were still green and full. Several times, she had to yank with her entire weight to encourage it along the path she had intended.

"How is it...ugh...that you appear so...ugh...light and airy upon the breeze? And yet you are actually...ugh...very heavy!" she said to the recalcitrant debris.

After much huffing and puffing, Elizabeth had managed to wedge the branch between the entrance of the hut and the tree before it. She took a few steps back to admire her handiwork. A bead of sweat ran through the dirt on her cheek as she nodded approvingly. Scratches from the branch and twigs ran up her forearms. Leaves and bits of bark from the branch were settling into her curls, tangled in among the hay.

"Not bad. It will help to disguise us at least. The entrance of the hut has all but disappeared. Time will tell if Darcy is able to move tomorrow or not." Was she developing the strange habit of talking to herself? She glanced around and saw a single red squirrel in a nearby tree. He sat on his hind legs, chewing away at a nut as he examined her handiwork with a bold, critical eye.

"It is not as bad as all that, is it?" she asked. The squirrel did not reply, just gazed at her with indifference while his jaw worked furiously. Suddenly, the little man dropped his nut, braced himself on all fours, and tilted his head to one side. Motionless, he watched and listened. Elizabeth turned to look where his focus was, past her in the direction of the now lessening smoke column. She saw nothing. But when she turned to question the little man in the tree, he was gone. Elizabeth did not like that at all.

He senses what is invisible to me. I would be wise to heed his warning.

She squirmed her way through the branches of her makeshift door. Once more, she heard a terrible ripping of fabric. One particularly sharp branch scraped a cut along her forehead and upper chest.

The hut was even dimmer than before now that some of the sunlight that had previously filtered in was blocked. Elizabeth squatted at the entrance, peering out through the leaves and branches and around the tree trunk as best she could. After several minutes, her legs began to ache from their cramped position. She grumpily wondered if the little man in the tree had not been having a bit of fun at her expense.

Then she heard a sound that, although she could not make it out at all, did not belong in the forest. Another sound that made Elizabeth tilt her head in the manner of Mr Squirrel to aid in her hearing. She quietly parted some of the branches to clear her view. Far to the left, a flash of blue, unnatural in the forest in any season, struck her eye. A crashing of branches and thuds against sod told her that horses were just breaking through the outer edge of the meadow. Two fine horses, one she recognised as belonging to

Colonel Fitzwilliam and one from the Rosings stables, galloped full tilt across the meadow. They had no bridle or saddle on them. It was as if someone had opened their stall doors and slapped their haunches to whip them into a frenzy.

The horses paused, snorting, and restlessly stopped in the centre of the meadow. They lowered their heads for a quick snack before they snapped back to full alertness, gazing at the direction from which they had just come. Even from afar, she could see the animals flatten their ears, the whites of their eyes showing, ready to flee in an instant.

Then Elizabeth heard the French voices. Two men in blue jackets of the French infantry stole into the open space. They moved slowly towards the horses. One held a rope dangling from his hand.

Although Elizabeth's French was excellent, she strained, trying to decipher the speech of the men from a distance. They were too far to understand, but the meaning of their movements and posture was clear. They wanted those horses. But the horses had other ideas entirely, as they sometimes do. No doubt the severity of the fire had alarmed them thoroughly, and now the chase they were subject to by men who no doubt looked and smelled unfamiliar to them had them in the highest state of skittishness. As the men slunk forward in their approach, attempting to sound soothing and nonchalant to the animals, the head tossings, stomps, and snorts of the beasts only increased.

The French soldiers were as close as they were going to get to the little hut on the hill. Elizabeth prayed that the horses would be coy enough to lure them farther away. She held her breath, every sense in her body on high alert at the smallest sign that the soldiers detected them.

"Elizabeth!" A low moan from Darcy sounded behind her.

CHAPTER SEVEN

Elizabeth almost jumped straight up. In her alarm at the scene unfolding before her, she had forgotten to attend to Darcy.

"Elizabeth!" he demanded slightly louder. She glanced back at him and then returned her focus to the scene outside. The soldiers seemed not to have noticed anything amiss and continued their stalking of the horses. She cautiously stood and made her way to the back of the hut. Sitting close on the ground beside Darcy, Elizabeth leant upon his chest and rested her hands just below his throat.

"Darcy," she whispered, her face just inches from his, "I must beg you to speak softly. Our lives will be in great danger if you raise your voice any higher."

"But I want to proclaim myself to you and before the world!" he said in a still louder voice.

In consternation, Elizabeth glanced at the hut door. If she risked leaving his side, he might raise his voice even higher. She bit her lip at the anxiety pressing in from all sides. Her palm tested Darcy's forehead. It seemed as if it were less warm than previously, but she could not be certain.

"You must listen to what I have to say. You must," Darcy said, wrapping his good arm around her waist to pull her in tight to him.

Her first instinct was to pull away from his embrace, but she thought that if she was to do so, it would rouse him to an even more agitated state. Sighing, she decided she must play a game with him once again.

"Darcy, my head aches terribly," she whispered to him. "If you have any kindness for me, I beg you to only speak softly, in very hushed tones. I shall hear you quite well as I am so close."

His fevered black eyes appeared to glitter. "You are indeed so close to me, Elizabeth. I am not at all opposed to it. Indeed. I am not."

All Elizabeth could think was that her ruse had worked. He had replied to her in soft whispers. His lips had formed each word with gentle care, and she found herself, despite their current predicament, impelled to gaze at those lips. Those lips that always seemed pressed together in stern disapproval. Now, they seemed wonderfully warm and close.

"Miss Bennet, you must allow me to tell you how ardently I admire and love you."

"What?"

"Since almost the very first moment I saw you, my love has grown at such a pace that I was dizzy. It has wreaked havoc with my heart."

"No, I do not think—"

"I do not care that you have no fortune. I do not care about the situation of your family. The impropriety of your sisters and parents can be avoided. I do not even care how I

73

shall be ridiculed and mocked by those in London's high society. Your position in society is so much lower than mine, I never regarded you seriously as a future wife. I have fought so long and hard to repress all regard for you, but it has been such a struggle, and I now admit defeat. You must relieve my suffering and consent to be my wife. We will marry as soon as possible."

Those lips that had been so inviting just seconds before were begging for a brisk slap from the palm of Elizabeth's hand.

Only Mr Darcy could somehow concoct a marriage proposal that flatters and insults equally!

But no matter what bizarre fantasy that his fevered brain may be indulging in, Elizabeth could not forget the very real danger lying just beyond her flimsy screen of branches that covered the door. Instead of pressing away from him, she leant fully into his embrace, feeling the length of his form along the side of her body.

"You do me a great honour, sir, but I must...I must consult my father before giving you an answer."

"Let us go to him now! At this very moment."

Darcy lunged as if to rise. Elizabeth pressed more of her weight on his chest to keep him still. She had the sudden remembrance that beneath the makeshift jumble of jackets and shirts, Darcy was practically nude. The thought of a swift slipping and rearranging of the garments made her warm. She pressed herself even more firmly against his chest.

"No! Please, sir, you forgot my aching head."

"Yes, of course, forgive me. My head aches terribly as well."

"So, do you not agree that it would be wise for us to rest here for just a few more moments? Am I not pleasing company?" she said with the most ridiculous batting of her eyelashes. Elizabeth's hours of observing the coquettish tools used by her youngest sister Lydia had not been totally wasted. As much as she disapproved of Lydia's techniques that kept most of the officers at her beck and call, Elizabeth had to concede that such arts seemed to work. She felt the full weight of her foolishness, but was prepared to do all she could to keep Darcy there and quiet.

With a gasp, Elizabeth realised that perhaps those tools worked too well. Darcy had tightened his grip on her even more, and she pressed so close to him that the pounding of his heart could be felt on her chest. The heat from where their skin contacted felt molten. Any effort Elizabeth made to slide from Darcy's grasp only increased her awareness of how close he was and how little she really wanted to be released by him.

"But you, what is your answer, Elizabeth?" he asked with deep urgency in his voice.

"I must first consult my father, as I told you, sir," she whispered back to him, her lips so close to his.

"But, you!" he said, his voice gaining in volume. "What is your answer? If there was no father to consult? If we were free of all worries of propriety and family?"

"Darcy! Please! Fitzwilliam, do be quiet," Elizabeth hissed at him, trying to break through his growing agitation.

"I must know, I suffer from not knowing, please! What is your answer?"

Elizabeth looked in his eyes, so close to hers. Was there real anxiety there? Was he speaking truth? Or was this the result of pain and fever? Surely, he could have no real design on her. She had been as clear in her disregard for Darcy as good manners would allow. He had been equally as clear in his opinion of Elizabeth being too inconsequential and unappealing to tempt him in any romantic way. He would not gain wealth or title from her or her family. *Is Darcy capable of wanting to marry just for the sake of love? Is he truly speaking of love to me?* She shook her head at the improbability.

But then Elizabeth felt a sudden, deep urge to know for herself if he was in earnest.

"I am not afraid who knows, Elizabeth. I will gladly accept the scorn. Perhaps even the scorn of your family as well! I no longer care. I shall go now and shout it from the rooftops. Then you will be convinced. Then you will be compelled, for pity's sake, to give me an answer."

He again made to rise, and again she pressed him down with all her strength. Then, not knowing what to do to calm him and feeling an impulse rise in her that was persuading her to act, Elizabeth pressed her lips gently to Darcy's. The sweet sound of silence filled the hut.

Darcy sank back, clutching her to his chest, as they repeated their kiss again and again. His pressure upon her lips grew with each passing second, real passion behind every brush of their lips. Elizabeth knew she should pull away from his embrace, but the desire to stay was so much stronger that she rested in his arms and pressed herself against him even more.

Finally, after an amount of time that Elizabeth could give no account for, Darcy relaxed back so fully that she pulled her lips from his. Her breath was quick as her racing heart slowly settled.

"I have my answer. At last. I surely have my answer, dearest Elizabeth," he murmured as he sank back, slipping into a restful slumber. Before she thought better of it, Elizabeth pressed up and rested her lips on his forehead. It was not as warm. He was in much less danger now. In smiling relief, Elizabeth's lips puckered, leaving the smallest of kisses on his insensible forehead before she pulled back and sat up.

A wave of exhaustion washed over her. With a shake of her head, she recalled the Elizabeth Bennet of a little over a day ago. Her greatest concern was how to evade the company of Mr Collins and Lady Catherine de Bourgh as much as possible. Or when her next letter from Jane was to arrive. Or whether or not Mr Darcy would pop up unexpectedly on one of her long walks. Such a fundamental change had occurred in such a harrowingly short time that it astounded her that she could even be considered the same girl.

She gazed down at the man she had kissed. His breathing was calm and regular. A healthier shade upon his handsome face gave every hope that a full recovery could be expected. A few unruly locks of his hair had tumbled low on his forehead, and she reached up to brush them back with a lovingly proprietary air.

Elizabeth snatched her hand away, dismayed and frightened by the warm, expansive feeling in her heart. What was she doing? This was Mr Darcy. The very fiend who had bungled the happy courtship of her sister Jane and Mr Bingley. Though, now that she had a deeper understanding of his motives, Darcy was less of the villain than she had thought. Now she saw him more in the light of an officious meddler who believed he was acting for his friend's benefit. Still, the damage he had wrought might be permanent. There might be no repair of the wreckage from his interference for her sister's future or her sister's heart.

And Wickham! What of poor, deserving Wickham! How could he possibly defend himself against the charge of ruining the future of a man whose career could have been so much happier and secure.

Funny, I have not thought of Wickham at all for the past day. He used to travel the roads of my thoughts frequently.

Another realisation intruded upon her while she quietly chewed on a piece of hardened cheese. What would have happened to her had Darcy not discovered her during her walk yesterday? With a glance at the dozing man, Elizabeth realised that she might very well be indebted to him for her life and honour. The thought made the cheese stick in her throat.

Feeling the need to move her body so she could achieve some relief from her racing thoughts, an energised Elizabeth slowly crept towards the door of the hut. The meadow below them was empty; there was no sign of horses or coats of French blue. She sighed heavily, relieved beyond all knowledge.

Tomorrow, if Darcy feels well, we shall attempt our way back to Rosings or the parsonage. I long for word of Charlotte.

The next morning, Elizabeth perceived a shuffle beneath her as she roused from a deep slumber. Her hip ached, and she was chilled.

Why am I so uncomfortable? The main source of warmth against her cheek and shoulder squirmed terribly again. *Let me sleep…*

With a start, Elizabeth sat bolt upright, fully recalling her circumstances of dirt floors and a barely dressed man lying next to her. Warily, she looked down at the wide awake and fully conscious Darcy. His handsome, alarmed face was dappled by the rising sun as it pierced the tangled doorway of the shepherds' shelter. The only expression Elizabeth could imagine on her face was one of sheer horror. Her hair was almost certainly completely down and tangled with mud, straw, and twigs. Her dress was far beyond repairable. Her face was surely a smear of dirt, tears, sweat, and scratches.

Darcy cleared his throat. "Miss Bennet, have you seen my —" He pulled his eyes from his stern gaze at Elizabeth and redirected them upwards to the ceiling. "—my breeches? I would be much obliged if you could direct me to them. They seem to have been misplaced."

Elizabeth shot up without a word and grabbed them from on top of the soldier's pack. She had discovered a small sewing kit in the pack the day before and had done her best to repair his breeches. It was slapdash work, but functional.

"I would have washed them, you see, there is still blood, but it seemed unwise to risk it." She handed the trousers to him. "The French soldiers were outside yesterday, and I dared not attempt it."

Darcy grimaced in pain as he sat up and took the breeches from her, shifting to keep the jumble of jackets and shirts in place over his body.

"You see, your breeches," she continued, nervous and flustered, "I had to remove them to tend to your leg wound. It was becoming infected and prompted your fever yesterday, I believe." A blush steadily climbed her neck and face, possibly with the blood that had, in its sudden absence, left her hands feeling oddly numb.

Darcy's stoic silence and blank face stayed on the task of examining his breeches and then slowly slipping on the rest of his shirt which had only covered half of his upper body.

She was overpowered by an unreasonable impulse to

defend her actions. "It was difficult to remove them, and I could not easily put them back on, you see, especially since you were delirious from the fever."

"Would you mind, very much, Miss Bennet, stepping outside while I dress?"

"But you may need—"

"I will manage by myself! You have done quite enough!"

She spun away, indignation swiftly overcoming her embarrassment. By the time she reached the doorway, Elizabeth was in the middle of one of her 'clouds of fury' as her sister Jane used to call them. She stepped to the door, barely pausing to make sure that it was safe to go out, then squeezed herself past the tree limb, scratching her face and arms further. Once outside, she grabbed the branch and wrenched at it with all the strength that a proper fit of anger could muster. With loud mutterings about proud, ungrateful gentlemen, though in words not quite as proper, she wrestled the limb from the door so that Darcy might exit with greater ease.

When she turned around, a few splinters now implanted in her hands, the infuriating gentleman was at the door of the hut, wide-eyed and still. He stared at her with undisguised astonishment. His breeches were on, his shirt still unbuttoned hung loosely open, and his feet were bare.

"The branch hid the door of the hut from the French soldiers!" Elizabeth declared with a wild swing of her arm towards the meadow.

"Ah, I see. And they were in the meadow?" Darcy replied, dropping his gaze.

"Yes."

Darcy nodded, looking around briefly. "You discovered the spring?"

"You told me where it was."

"I told you? I have no memory of that." His brow furrowed.

"Among the other things you said, you told me that you and your cousin Fitzwilliam had covered the spring to protect it from poisoning by enemy forces during a siege. You called him Sir Fitz. The both of you spent quite a bit of time defending this little kingdom, it seems."

Darcy, staring at the wet pile of rocks nearby, smiled broadly. "I had forgotten about that." His smile slipped to a frown of concern as he returned his gaze to her. "Did I say anything else, during my fever?"

Elizabeth tore her eyes from his piercing stare to look at the ground. Memories of his animated declarations, fond pet names for her, and the silencing of his talk with her kisses caused all her words to flee.

After an awkward pause, Elizabeth muttered unconvincingly, "You said things, of course, but I can hardly remember them."

Darcy stared at her as though examining a tradesman who was charging an exorbitant fee.

Finally he broke the silence. "Would you mind stepping back inside while I attend to some needs of my own, Miss Bennet?"

"Of course, *Mr* Darcy."

"Thank you."

"Not at all, your highness."

Elizabeth huffed past him, her head held high, into the hut.

CHAPTER EIGHT

The morning passed in long stretches of quiet as they readied themselves to continue their journey. Elizabeth's foul mood dissipated, focusing instead on the impending and possibly perilous walk back to Rosings.

"This is the last loaf," Darcy said as he passed the larger portion of bread to Elizabeth. They sat on a log near the rock spring as they ate, enjoying the warmth gained from the dappled sunlight under the canopy of tree foliage.

"I do not think I have ever eaten or drunk anything from France before," Elizabeth said pensively. "Imagine, this bread travelled to us from the Continent. Through the air! Can any of your acquaintances claim to have had flying loaves of bread from France? Even among the most elegant circles of London?"

"No, I do not believe they can," he said with a small smile.

"Well, it shall provide you with an amusing anecdote for

the London elite, will it not? I doubt I shall ever have French bread again. Which is a shame because, as stale as it is, it is delicious. Better than anything I have ever had in my life."

"You are right, Miss Bennet. It is the most delicious bread that I have had as well. And I must say the Chartreuse liquor quite grew on me as well. Although it was the most powerful liquor I have ever had."

Darcy's use of her formal name pierced her with a small pang of sorrow. He was no longer saying 'Elizabeth' when addressing her. She found it difficult to grasp after all they had experienced together.

But then, he does not recall most of it. I am the only one of us who remembers my kisses on his lips, him calling me his queen, his loud demands to see my father to ask for my hand in marriage.

"I think you enjoyed the Chartreuse a little too much. Between that and the fever, I expect you remember little of the past two days."

Darcy did not respond, his brow furrowed as if he searched for any thread of memory he could grasp. The silence extended, and Elizabeth regretted mentioning it as it seemed to distress him.

He turned to look directly at her. "Miss Bennet, allow me to say that although I do not remember everything I said—"

Elizabeth placed her hand on Darcy's knee and brought her finger to her mouth to silence him. His eyes widened, glancing down at her hand, but he obeyed. Movement on the edge of the meadow below them had caught her eye. She inclined her head ever so slightly in that direction to convey her purpose. Both of them became perfectly still, watching and listening. Finally, when their suspense was at its height, a familiar haughty brown head emerged into the meadow and dipped down to have a snack of grass.

"Aesop! Oh, Darcy, what a piece of luck! Finally, something to give us hope." Elizabeth took Darcy's hand in hers and squeezed it with a joyous smile. His face brightened, and he smiled back at her.

Elizabeth ran down to the meadow, not wishing to lose the opportunity to catch a hold of Aesop's reins. She entered the open space, risking all to have a chance to help Darcy with more ease. Although she was no horsewoman, she strode up confidently to Aesop and took his reins. Far from recoiling from her advance, the noble animal seemed glad to see her and nuzzled her on her neck and head. She laughed at the bright green colour that stained his lips, revealing that he had had a drunken bout of his own on all the fresh grass of spring.

Exuberant, Elizabeth led Aesop back to where Darcy was limping very slowly down the hill, using a makeshift walking stick to aid him. The horse snorted at Darcy and tossed his head, defying his master to be cross with him.

"Foolish old man! If you had not taken fright at the first sight of those balloons…" Darcy muttered as he scratched the horse affectionately on the neck.

Elizabeth, still smiling, rubbed Aesop on the other side of his neck. The horse took on the air of a great monarch who was not at all surprised by the adulation he received from his peasants.

"Though we can hardly blame him, I think," Elizabeth said. "There are few people who would not start at such a sight as flying soldiers. So in a horse, it is entirely forgivable. Is it not, Aesop?"

The animal nodded vigorously. Darcy took the reins and slowly led him towards a tree stump at the edge of the meadow. Elizabeth ran back up to the shepherds' hut and retrieved their pack. At the entrance of the hovel, she paused. It was not possible for her to leave their little, dark, cramped hut without a feeling of gratitude.

For it is likely you saved our lives. Thank you.

"Of all this, I was once mistress. Perhaps even the queen," she said aloud for the benefit of Mr Squirrel who had appeared in order to make his farewells. "And thank you to you as well, sir. For if you had not warned me of the approach of the French—"

"Are you speaking with someone, Miss Bennet?" Darcy looked concerned as he gazed up the hill towards her.

"I am thanking...a friend."

"And who was this friend?" Darcy asked as Elizabeth met him at the stump.

"Mr Squirrel, there in the tree. It was due to his alarm that I knew of approaching French soldiers."

Darcy glanced at the animal, still supervising their departure, and then back at her.

"Miss Bennet, perhaps as we travel back, you can tell me exactly what happened during the day of which I have no memory."

Elizabeth looked away and blushed at the very notion of telling Darcy *all* that was said and done.

"I shall do my best, although a lady must have her secrets, do you not think? We are alive and, for the moment, safe. Let us be content with that."

A worried look crossed Darcy's face. His mouth opened as if to press the matter, but there must have been an especially moving appeal in Elizabeth's eyes that convinced him to shut it with no further word on the subject.

It took several minutes of coaxing Aesop with soothing words from Elizabeth to make the feisty beast pause long enough for Darcy to attempt to mount. Elizabeth held the reins as Darcy eventually mounted, slowly and aided by the tree stump, with his face showing the pain the effort caused. They hesitated for a moment while he regained his composure. A slight sheen of sweat covered his wan face, and his mouth was in a grimace of pressed lips.

She scrutinised him worriedly. "You are quite pale from the effort."

"I am well enough," he said with a grunt as he shifted his injured leg with his good arm.

"It is too bad we have no more of the liquor, it would help to ease your pain."

"I think you have witnessed the effects of me drinking that liquor quite enough. Although you are too gracious to tell me of it."

Elizabeth looked away, feeling the truth of his words deeply. "I am sure that anyone could tell of words that were spoken in moments of duress that we wish not to be repeated. It is of very little consequence, sir," she replied flippantly, in hopes of dismissing the subject entirely. She imagined that Darcy, a man so accustomed to being in control of his world and behaviour, was quite anxious to know what had happened. But she knew not how to soften it for him, being herself so hesitant to reveal their interactions.

Darcy's face darkened from sensations of clearly more than just physical pain. Solemnly, he looked down at her with his good hand extended and said, "Come, Miss Bennet. Let us be on our way."

"Surely there is not room upon Aesop's back for both of us at once. I can easily walk. It is no hardship." Darcy's stony gaze stayed locked on her, his hand still extended. "Besides," she continued in an effort to stem his insistence, "after almost two days in the hut, my limbs could do with the exertion."

"Miss Bennet, if we are taken unawares by the French, I can hardly defend you and get us out of harm's way with you walking before me! It is better that we stay together."

"But will he be able to carry us both?" She wished to avoid being so close to him, although she knew the good sense of his words.

"This horse is the most spoiled, well-maintained animal this side of London. And you are no bigger than a young sapling. He will carry us just fine," Darcy replied, his hand still outstretched.

Biting her lip, Elizabeth scrambled up the stump and leant over behind Darcy. Aesop, curious about all the commotion around an activity as simple as getting on his back, perked his ears up and snorted.

"What are you doing? You should sit before me so that I can keep you safe," Darcy exclaimed. "You cannot ride behind me."

"I very well can and shall," Elizabeth stated, wishing to avoid his close embrace. Memories of pressing close to his chest, the motion of his heart through the thin fabric of her gown, feeling that she imposed herself on him with her kisses far longer than was necessary, impressed on her the exceedingly great need to keep things a little more formal. "I shall manage very well back here. That way the pack can stay on my back. Besides, I am equipped to ride as the young farm boys do, see?"

Elizabeth hitched her skirt high, exposing her still trousered legs, and leant into the space behind Darcy. He grabbed her arm and helped her cross the breach between the stump and Aesop. She flailed momentarily, her legs swimming in the air as she pushed her stomach across the back of the large horse. She clumsily swung her leg over the animal. Aesop snorted and danced, causing her to squeak in fright as she attempted to settle herself. She grasped her arms around Darcy's chest and hugged his back tightly.

With a grunt, Darcy said, "Would you mind loosening your grip slightly, Miss Bennet?"

"Of course." She had not realised that she was gripping him with so much ferocity. Her arms loosened but stayed in place as the sensation of riding without a saddle on the back of a massive horse quickened her pulse. She glimpsed Darcy's profile in time to see how he happily smiled when he tentatively placed his hand on top of hers that rested on his chest.

"Ready, Miss Bennet?"

"Of course!"

With a click of his tongue, Darcy encouraged Aesop into a light canter out of the meadow. Elizabeth's grip tightened again and Darcy glanced back at her, yet the smile had not left his face.

CHAPTER NINE

T hey kept to the woods as much as possible while trying to find fairly level ground for the horse to navigate. The additional burden of Elizabeth on the horse's back did little to dampen Aesop's enthusiasm for the adventure. He bounded up each slope with quick determination. Each time the animal lunged up an incline, Elizabeth squeezed her eyes shut and hugged Darcy tight.

After some blunt questions from Darcy, Elizabeth, in a hushed voice, recounted as much of the past day to him as she thought proper. Beginning when he had fallen to the ground as the fever overtook him, up to the moment of their awakening that morning. She made certain to mention the column of smoke she had witnessed from what she thought was the direction of Rosings. In case it was nothing to cause alarm, she did not dwell upon it for long. It may have been little more than a field fire that got out of control or a barn that burned. Darcy was tired and in pain, so adding to his worries would have served little good.

He became more solemn as the narrative continued, which she took as some form of his judging her decisions to be poor ones. She had certainly left out retelling of his passionate delusions towards her. Elizabeth could not even begin to think of telling him of her indecently creative method for keeping him silent while the soldiers were in the meadow below the hut.

A time of silence ensued after she had stopped talking. She was beginning to feel some resentment rise in her from his lack of response. She knew him well enough now to know that he was most comfortable when he had some time to gather and organise his thoughts. Darcy was incredibly intelligent, but not swift in the workings of his mind. She had grown up with several varying examples of extremes in this trait, thinking of her mother and her sister Lydia as being swift in the workings of their minds, but not burdened by the need to deeply plumb a subject with insight.

I know others may have done a much better job of it, but, given my resources, I think that I deserve an acknowledgement of some sort. One small 'Thank you' would suffice.

Darcy finally cleared his throat. "And you pretended to be a subject of my kingdom in order to gain directions to the spring by the hut?"

Elizabeth was relieved that he could not see her face to notice what she was sure were some telltale signs that she was telling only half-truths. Darcy's gaze did have the most annoying habit of making her feel warm and uncertain. She could not imagine a time when she would *ever* be able to tell him of his claiming she was his beautiful queen with whom he was madly in love.

To dispel the image, she pressed her forehead into his back. But this was perhaps not the wisest course of action as

Darcy's strong, musky scent filled her senses. The memory of his laboured breathing and dilated eyes as he paid her compliments only increased.

"Exactly! I pretended to be a subject, and that tricked you into giving away the location of your hidden spring. Perhaps you thought I was your court jester. I have been known to make people laugh."

"Mmm. I very much doubt that I believed you were the court jester," Darcy mumbled.

She kept her head resting gently on his back as they continued their journey. The past two nights had been chilly and uncomfortable. Elizabeth's attention had been bent towards Darcy's well-being. As a result, her body was as tired as her mind. The warmth of his body and the motion of Aesop under her soothed her into a light doze.

"Good God!"

Elizabeth started awake, her hands clutching around Darcy even more firmly at the sound of his exclamation.

"What? Darcy, what is it?"

He remained speechless, so Elizabeth peeked over his shoulder. She gasped, unprepared for what she saw.

There was Rosings. It was a shell of the once stately country home it had been. Small columns of smoke still snaked upwards, and Elizabeth could feel the heat coming off of the rubble despite no flames being visible. All the windows of the stone husk had been melted or shattered out. The interior of it had burnt to the ground. It was a bizarre sight, since the very formal, symmetrical shrubberies around it were relatively untouched. In the centre sat the wretched, twisted hulk of the remains of one of the finest homes in England.

Aesop continued his wary advance as his passengers were too stunned to stop him. They reached the foot of what had once been the imposing stairs up to the front door. Ironically, the front door stood unblemished, ready to receive morning callers as if absolutely nothing had changed.

A liveried servant, with soot covering his hands and face, approached.

"Mr Darcy? Is that you, sir?"

"Manson?"

"Yes, sir."

"What happened? Did the French do this?!"

"The French soldiers were here yesterday, sir. They attempted to make off with horses before we set them free. Then they made for the house. But Lady Catherine locked all the doors. She ordered us all out the back and sealed herself and Miss de Bourgh inside. When the soldiers started crashing the windows, she must have lit the fire."

"*What?*"

"Yes, sir. I saw her myself as she stood at one of the top windows. She was shouting about 'no French pollution on my watch' or something to that effect. By then, the soldiers were off after the galloping horses, and the fire was too big for us to save them. I'm sorry, sir. We begged her to come to the front door and unlock it, but Lady Catherine would have none of it and shouted down about how we all should be ashamed of ourselves, or something like that." The man bowed his head. "They are gone, sir. Perished in the flames."

"Lady Catherine, Miss de Bourgh, and anyone else?" Darcy asked with a weary voice.

"Only Mr Collins, who climbed through a shattered

window to attempt a rescue. We can't seem to find him either."

Darcy covered his eyes with his hand and let out a low moan. Elizabeth felt him swaying slightly. Manson stepped closer, reaching up to Darcy as if he might need catching. Elizabeth tightened her hold on him.

"Are you all right, sir?"

"I, yes, I..."

"Mr Darcy was badly wounded, and he needs some rest. Is the parsonage still in good repair?" Manson blinked upon seeing Elizabeth a little more closely and stared in wonder at her attire and condition.

I can hardly blame him. What a fright I must be.

"As far as I know, ma'am. That's where you may find Colonel Fitzwilliam. I've been staying on here, sleeping in the empty stables. Trying to keep away any thieves that may be sneaking about."

Darcy inhaled sharply. "If you need me for anything, I will be at the parsonage. We shall make sure some food and bedding are sent over."

"Yes, sir. Thank you, sir."

"And Manson, I am in your debt. Your dedication will be remembered in the future."

With that, Darcy turned a reluctant Aesop towards the parish house. The confused horse took one last look in the direction of the stables, no doubt thinking he had more than earned his feed and hay for the evening.

Elizabeth felt Darcy's strong frame yield slightly as they travelled the short distance to the parsonage. Indeed, before she was even aware of it, a tear for her cousin Mr Collins slid down her cheek. Whatever may have been his shortcomings, and they were too numerous to list, he had spent his last moments in a valiant effort to save Lady Catherine from herself. She hoped that Lady Catherine's daughter Anne had not been forced against her will to stay within the ancient home as it flamed around her. The thought ran a bitter chill up Elizabeth's spine.

When Aesop finally stopped before the parsonage, Elizabeth and Darcy simply paused, unmoving and not speaking. The tidy house looked very much as it had more than two days before when Elizabeth had departed it for her very long walk to Tall Oak Hill. To imagine that so much had occurred in that short time, much of it beyond anything she could have ever conceived, was so startling that the home seemed almost unreal to her.

Unbidden came the thought, *This is the last time I shall touch Darcy*. She started. *Why should I care?* She could not say.

With that question unanswered, Elizabeth slowly released her hold upon Darcy's waist and pulled her chest from contact with his back. With an awkward swing, she threw one leg over and slid down off of Aesop's back. The horse sidestepped away from her, and her feet hit the ground with a hard thud. Her muscles, so unaccustomed to riding a horse, caused her quivering legs to buckle, and she fell back onto her bottom. With a defeated shrug, Elizabeth dropped the French soldier's heavy pack from her shoulders.

"Elizabeth!" Darcy exclaimed.

She heard rapidly approaching footsteps and looked up from the ground to see Charlotte rushing towards her from the front door. Behind Charlotte, Colonel Fitzwilliam ran out of the house and took Aesop by the reins. Darcy winced as he tried to swing his injured leg to dismount, his eyes locked with Elizabeth's, as though determined to come to her aid.

"Colonel Fitzwilliam! Mr Darcy is badly injured and needs assistance."

Colonel Fitzwilliam nodded, speechless, as he helped his cousin down from the horse. Charlotte crouched next to Elizabeth, her hand on her shoulder, her brow furrowed.

"You see, he never asks for help, he is such a proud, difficult fellow..." Elizabeth said softly, as if to herself. She looked up and saw the loving worry in Charlotte's eyes.

That was enough for Elizabeth to completely lose her composure. She leant into Charlotte's open arms and burst into tears. Every strain of worry, duress, physical exertion, and even uncertainty of her complex feelings for Darcy over the last two days flooded out onto her calm friend's steady shoulder.

Through her bleary vision, she sensed Darcy's concerned attention on her. Colonel Fitzwilliam, who was supporting Darcy after his unsteady descent from Aesop, regarded Elizabeth with undisguised wonder.

By this time, a servant from the house and one from the stable had arrived and were tending to Aesop and picking up the Frenchman's pack from the ground. Darcy turned his head towards his cousin and muttered, "It has been a trying two days. I believe Miss Bennet is feeling the effects of it." Then the two gentlemen made their painstaking way into the Rosings parsonage.

The two ladies sat silently in the middle of the gravel drive.

"Elizabeth, let us move to the house. You are in need of some time to recover from your travels," Charlotte said aloud, then whispered into Elizabeth's ear about the curious looks of the servants.

Charlotte coaxed Elizabeth to rise and walk into the

house. Elizabeth sniffed and strived to regain her composure, but it was a difficult task. Her weight on Charlotte's arm bolstered her equanimity, feeling comforted by her steady friend's presence.

Once Elizabeth was settled into her room, she gazed about in some wonder for several moments. A bath was ordered to be prepared for her and a tray of food was sent for.

Charlotte sat across from Elizabeth and took both her hands in an unusual display of affection. "My dear friend, we were all so concerned for you and Mr Darcy. No trace could be found of you! Colonel Fitzwilliam and the servants did search for you. And several of those terrible flying carriages were on the ground very near the area you had gone out walking. The soldiers were told to—"

"Soldiers! Are there English militia in the area?"

"Yes, there are now. Just this morning, they arrived very early."

"Oh, Charlotte, what is the state of England? Do you think that our families in Hertfordshire are well?"

"I believe they are well. It seems, from the scraps of news we were able to gather, that a mighty fleet of French ships was set to cross the Channel with the balloons, but a sudden change in the weather and the power of the English Navy caused almost the entire column of invading ships to be destroyed or captured. It was a perfect day otherwise. Thank goodness for the winds that were too strong for them."

"But the French soldiers we saw! We had to run from them!"

"It seems that the majority of the balloons that actually survived the journey across the Channel landed here in Kent, several apparently in our area. I expect that most of the invading forces have been captured or killed by now. Indeed, it may be that you and Mr Darcy were among the few who saw action from the French invasion. I suppose that you and he will be quite the heroes."

Elizabeth slumped in her seat, forgetting all appearance of propriety before another. "I feel too worn and hungry to be anything like a hero."

At that moment, a servant entered bearing a tray laden with all of Elizabeth's favourites. She knew Charlotte was to thank for that small kindness, but she could hardly stop to acknowledge it. Her belly was so terribly tight after several days of meagre portions of tough bread, cheese, and meats. She had deliberately eaten as little as possible to save most of it for Darcy and the uncertain future that they faced.

Elizabeth ate with a hearty appetite for several minutes until, with a bite of cooked apples halfway to her mouth, she froze and gaped at her friend in horror. "Oh, Charlotte! Mr Collins! I am so sorry, it completely fled my mind until this very moment!"

She dropped her spoon and reached out with her hands. Charlotte had lowered her head at the mention of her recently deceased husband. Her face was shielded from Elizabeth's view, but she did hear a sniff from her friend. When Charlotte looked up, there was a moistness to her eyes that told of true grieving, though perhaps not the throes of anguish that some may have felt upon the recent loss of a beloved marriage partner. Elizabeth thought she understood. Her friend was indeed grieved, but not heartbroken.

"I begged Mr Collins to stay with me, when we first saw the smoke rising above the trees, but he insisted that his place was by the side of Lady Catherine."

Elizabeth bit back her sharpish response that had almost

escaped. Mr Collins's place was by his wife and to protect her and the female servants of his house from enemy forces. Instead, he imagined himself some sort of foolish knight errant on a quest to save Lady Catherine from a fire that was created by her own hand. The shame and fury Elizabeth felt for her deceased cousin caused her only a little guilt upon reflection.

Even I refused to leave Darcy's side out of a sense of duty and honour. God knows Darcy must hate the very sight of me after so many indiscreet moments together. Not to mention my complete loss of all control upon seeing Charlotte.

These thoughts, layered with sadness for the loss of Mr Collins, distracted Elizabeth from the plates of hot food before her. She suspected that Charlotte would rapidly recover from her loss, since there could have been little more than warm regard on her side for a husband of such mean understanding, limited information, few personal charms, and undignified behaviour. With a shock, Elizabeth realised that Longbourn was no longer entailed to Mr Collins.

What will become of Longbourn, my home, and my sisters and I with Mr Collins dead? Who shall inherit? And what of Charlotte? The main reason she married Mr Collins was to secure her future here at the parsonage and then later as mistress of Longbourn!

Elizabeth, blushing from so many mercenary thoughts at such a time, peeked up at Charlotte. But Charlotte's face had returned to that mild look of calm detachment that so frequently could be seen upon her countenance. Surely, knowing Charlotte's prudent nature, these thoughts had already occurred to her. Elizabeth could detect no bitterness at the recent undoing of all of Charlotte's best-laid plans for a secure future. But there was a hint of something in her friend's face, perhaps worry, that kept her from thinking

Charlotte was completely free of all concern regarding her future.

"He did make a valiant effort to save the lives of two women, Charlotte. It is comforting to know that he will be remembered in such heroic, selfless light."

"Yes."

Elizabeth cleared her throat and, sensing that Charlotte no longer wished to speak about her recently departed husband, picked up her spoon to resume eating the stewed apples. She chewed slowly now, savouring the flavour of the dish that satisfied her on so many levels. Just outside the window, the skies were blue and beautiful with no hint of strong wind, columns of smoke, or flying soldiers. And for that, Elizabeth was exceedingly grateful.

CHAPTER TEN

Elizabeth awoke to the sweetest sensations known to man. A soft bed under her, a full stomach, a clean body, and early spring birdsong of a beautiful morning. She sighed deeply with a smile, knowing it was late in the morning but not caring a whit. She considered lying there all day. Through the birdsong, she heard voices outside.

The full power of her curiosity returned to her, Elizabeth eagerly rolled herself out of bed, then stifled a yelp. The soreness in her muscles was acute, the intense activities of the past several days making themselves known through recollection and pain.

Elizabeth pulled back the curtains just a crack to see Charlotte, Colonel Fitzwilliam, and a man whom she presumed to be the physician, if his black leather bag was any indication, standing in the drive as a horse was brought up by the stableboy. The physician mounted and departed. Colonel Fitzwilliam and Charlotte remained standing there. Just before the colonel's horse was brought into the drive, he lightly grasped Charlotte's hand and smiled down at her. Instead of withdrawing it immediately, Charlotte left her hand in his and smiled back up at him. Some words passed between them that brought a new sort of light to Charlotte's face that Elizabeth had never witnessed before.

Elizabeth, feeling the flush of someone who had inadvertently witnessed a private moment, pulled back into the room.

Charlotte and Colonel Fitzwilliam!

The longer she pondered it, the less extraordinary it seemed and, after a very few moments, Elizabeth was well acclimated to the idea. Perhaps Charlotte had found someone to inspire true affection in her heart. Elizabeth wondered if the two had a long understanding or if it were something that was newly formed as a result of their current adversity.

Love does bloom under hardships and trials.

Elizabeth shook her head, discomforted by that thought and not wishing to examine further her own recent experience.

There was a knock at the door, and Charlotte entered with a tray. "I thought you may be up. The curtains of your window were swaying."

"Ah, yes. Thank you, Charlotte. You need not have done this. I can eat downstairs very well."

"Not at all. I was not certain you would wish to leave your room today. I am glad to see you so well recovered, Eliza. Indeed, you look very well."

Elizabeth sat to eat and invited Charlotte to sit with her.

"Was the physician here for Darcy? I mean, Mr Darcy?"

"Yes, he was." Charlotte began to pour the tea. "And I must say you have a very impressed admirer."

Elizabeth froze. "Who?"

"The doctor, of course! He was quite taken at how well your poultice and bandaging did to heal what he said were particularly bad bayonet wounds."

"Ah, and is Darcy—Mr Darcy faring well this morning?"

"Like you, he has a bold appetite and seems to have had a restful sleep."

"That is nice to hear, I—well, it is good to hear."

Charlotte studied her closely as she passed the cup of tea across the table. "Do you wish to tell me of the last few days?"

Not lifting her eyes from her plate, Elizabeth shook her head emphatically. "No, I... No, not yet, I mean."

"Forgive me for being forward, but did Mr Darcy behave as a gentleman?"

"Oh yes! He did. I just—" Elizabeth looked up and suddenly felt her lips gently press upon Darcy's as she attempted to quiet him in the shepherds' hut. The memory caused her to drop her gaze from Charlotte's concerned scrutiny. She was painfully aware of the rush of heat that crept up her neck and cheeks.

"He was a perfect gentleman at all times, except perhaps in moments of fever, he may have said a few things that he would not say now. But, other than that, I have nothing to accuse him of."

"Ah. I see."

There was a certain archness in her friend's expression, a slight upwards turn of the corners of her mouth, that increased Elizabeth's blush.

"I certainly hope," Elizabeth declared louder than she intended, "that none of our acquaintances in the militia in Hertfordshire came to any harm during all of this. I hope Mr Wickham is well."

"He hardly deserves your well wishes. But I join you in hoping that none of our acquaintances have been injured."

"What can you mean? Mr Wickham deserves some of our concern, I think."

"He deserves absolutely nothing from polite or even impolite society. He is a scoundrel of the most base kind, I assure you."

"What? Of what are you speaking?"

Charlotte lowered her voice and leant closer. "I have it on very good authority that most of his supposed misfortunes are completely fabricated. You know I do not promote gossip, but this is a fair warning to any ladies who think—" She paused. "—who think well of him. He is not to be trusted."

"Charlotte, you must be more explicit! What am I to think of him after so little information?"

"Mr Wickham told everyone in Meryton that Mr Darcy had refused him the living intended for him. It is not true. He was paid very handsomely by Mr Darcy when Wickham himself stated he had no intention of taking orders. Mr Wickham laughed at the idea of a living in the church. He was paid well over what the living was worth. Everything he has said to the contrary is completely false."

"That is a charge that casts him in a poor light. However, there may be some resentments or slights that we do not know of. Perhaps Wickham still felt slighted somehow."

"No, it is not just the case of the living that was promised to Wickham. In addition to that, there was also a girl of but fifteen years whom Wickham attempted to seduce away from her family for an elopement. A girl of a large fortune. I cannot tell more, but I have it from those personally involved."

She must be referring to Colonel Fitzwilliam! Who else could be so familiar with the particulars? Does Colonel Fitzwilliam have a younger sister?

"If it had not been for Mr Dar—" Charlotte's enigmatic expression shifted Elizabeth in her seat. "—for others interfering in his scheme, the young lady would have been lost in a marriage to a fortune hunter who likely had no sincere regard for her. He gave her up the moment they were exposed."

Elizabeth conjectured that the young lady must have been intimately connected with the Darcys, the Fitzwilliams, or perhaps the de Bourghs. As she bit into her third piece of liberally jammed toast, she reflected on conversations she had had with Wickham. There were certain gaps in his retelling of his interactions with Darcy that she had not noticed at the time. And then there was her own misdirected encouragement and filling in of those gaps. Elizabeth felt some real shame at her own promotion of Wickham's false narrative to the populace in the village of Meryton.

Her sister Jane had been absolutely correct in her refusal to judge Darcy with only one side of the story known.

I had been so eager to listen to a handsome man who preferred my company above all others. Had I really been so blinded by Wickham's simple flattery? I, who value my discernment and judgment so highly?

Elizabeth knew that Darcy's slight to her at the assembly and his 'tolerable' reference about her had fuelled her naivety for Wickham's stories.

The delicious fresh toast stuck in her throat the same way the hard French cheese had just the day before. "Then Mr Wickham is really such a man?" Elizabeth queried softly.

"Yes, and probably much worse. Those are only the instances we know of. I am sure there have been other intrigues that are entirely unknown to us. I hope, my dear friend, that your heart is untouched by this information. I know you enjoyed your conversations with Mr Wickham."

Elizabeth reached a hand across the table to fondly squeeze her friend's forearm, acknowledging the genuine solicitude she heard in Charlotte's voice. "My heart is perfectly well. I appreciate your honesty and your dislike of gossip. It is well to know that such a man lives so close to Longbourn. My sisters are young and not always wise in their choices."

She sat back and looked Charlotte square in the eye with her head held high. "You are correct that I did have a small fondness for Wickham at one time, but it has weakened to almost nothing. I am saddened to hear such horrible things of a man who has been invited into the homes of Meryton and Longbourn and met with hospitality and kindness that he did not deserve." Elizabeth took a breath, then asked, "Should we make this information known to our general acquaintance in Meryton?"

"I have not been authorised to share this with anyone. I am under no promise to keep it secret, but also I have no permission to make it generally known. I leave it to your discretion with whom you choose to share it."

Elizabeth looked up at the ceiling, as if calling upon angels to guide her. "I wonder what Jane would advise? Hmm. I think she would say that perhaps Wickham is attempting to better himself in the eyes of society. This stint in the militia may be his redemption and not to be trifled with by us. No, I may enlighten Jane to his true character, but the information will go no further by my hand. What say you to that?"

"A wise compromise. Besides, with recent events, it is

likely that the militia may be moved out of Meryton to an area of more strategic importance in the very near future."

"And Mr Wickham will be nothing more than a not very fond memory."

"Exactly."

Elizabeth stirred her second cup of tea; the swirl of the vortex within the delicate china walls held her unfocused gaze. "I wish…"

"Yes…?"

"I wish I had not spoken so warmly of Wickham and his misfortunes to Mr Darcy at the ball at Netherfield. It casts me in an exceedingly foolish light to have been so taken in by a scoundrel such as Mr Wickham."

"No, indeed. You would not be the first intelligent woman, nor the last, to be deceived by a handsome, well-spoken man. I believe that Mr Darcy—" Charlotte hesitated. "Well, I suspect you need hardly worry at all about Mr Darcy's poor opinion. In fact, any man of education, sense, and taste would find it quite easy to forgive you of such an understandable mistake."

Elizabeth bit her lip, leaning back from the breakfast with an achingly full stomach, yet feeling somehow unsatisfied. The air between her and Charlotte seemed thick with things left unsaid—the death of Mr Collins, the intimacy she had glimpsed between Colonel Fitzwilliam and Charlotte, Elizabeth's two nights in the woods alone with Mr Darcy—all were subjects that left both ladies unsettled. So, they both silently agreed that the best course of action was another cup of tea, of course.

CHAPTER ELEVEN

Later in the day, Elizabeth ventured downstairs. She moved silently, feeling like a trespasser in the very house in which she had spent so many pleasant days prior to her misadventure. The uncertainty of who knew what of the past several days and how they would judge it, and *her*, prompted Elizabeth to enter each room with an unfamiliar trepidation in her step.

She had always been too confident in herself to waste excessive anxiety on the unknowable opinions of others. But this time, there was propriety and her reputation to consider. After all, the entire country of England had *not* been invaded; only sections in the far east counties of Kent and East Sussex had seen the sky soldiers visit. Would the rest of the country and the rest of society understand the danger that had turned the traditional rule of conduct on its head for several days? She could not be certain, but based upon what she knew of society, she thought not. People would be quick to smirk over any story of her nights alone with Darcy.

Elizabeth crept to the door of the parlour that Charlotte frequented. She silently entered, not wanting to interrupt any conversation with a burst of salutations aimed towards her. No one was within. She took in a slow breath to sigh with relief.

The loud creaking of the chair at the desk next to the door startled her back a step. Darcy was leaning back in the chair, his eyes pressed shut as he placed his left hand tenderly on his right shoulder. The pen he had been evidently holding had dropped from his grasp, and his right hand was flexing and releasing.

Elizabeth's first impulse was to retreat and leave him alone. Then, with a shock, she realised that she wished to see him. That she was actually looking forward to being near him.

I suppose this is natural, being that we have spent so many days exclusively in each other's company. I am quite sure it will pass, now that we have returned to more ordinary circumstances.

Elizabeth cleared her throat. Darcy startled with a wince and made to stand.

"Pray, I did not mean to interrupt you, sir. I just..." Embarrassed, she found she could not tease a complete thought out.

"I am glad to see you in such good health, Miss Bennet." Darcy slowly stood, repressing a mild grunt. "I have been anxious to know how you fared this morning. Please, join me, if you wish," he said with a sweep of his good hand towards the sofa and chair.

Elizabeth, bewildered by this display of courtesy, nodded in agreement and sat. Darcy slowly lowered himself into the chair opposite her. She noticed that he was dressed in highly unusual clothes. Her eyes strayed involuntarily up and down his form with bemused curiosity. He wore only a white shirt, breeches, and boots. His once impeccable appearance was shabby and ill-fitting. Instead of being shocked by the image before her, Elizabeth realised, as she averted her glance, that it was actually quite becoming on him.

As if hearing part of her thoughts, Darcy said, "You must excuse my appearance, Miss Bennet. My wardrobe was at Rosings, and this was cobbled together for me from various sources. Colonel Fitzwilliam is escorting Mrs Collins into Hunsford to select some more appropriate clothing for me. You see, everything I own is either in London or Derbyshire. Except for my horse, of course."

Elizabeth repressed a mischievous grin. "You look perfectly well, sir. Perhaps just a shade less refined than what is usual, but anyone who knows even part of the circumstances of the last two days could not judge you poorly. Why, I know you were hoping to see me again in my muddy gown and breeches, but I have had to don this less flattering gown instead." Smiling, Elizabeth made a gesture to the pale blue dress she wore. "No others were to be found. I am quite distraught."

Her words and smile provoked a warm look of humour from Darcy as the corners of his mouth turned upwards.

"I think that you look very well indeed, Miss Bennet," he muttered as he dropped his gaze from her eyes. "Quite recovered from your adventure, it seems."

Silence filled the room.

Elizabeth glanced back at the desk that Darcy had been seated at. "It appeared that the task of writing was giving you some discomfort."

"Yes, the doctor said that the wound to my shoulder is such that I may be in pain while using my right arm for some time. Perhaps I may always experience some aching of it in foul weather." Darcy paused, clearing his throat. "He also did mention that I can thank your excellent nursing in difficult circumstances for the wounds not taking a turn for the worse."

"Any thanks to me must be directed to our housekeeper at Longbourn, Mrs Hill. She taught me well when I was a child. My enjoyment of rambling walks was pronounced even then, and I had the incurable habit of bringing home every injured animal I came across. I demanded Hill's medical advice and her help in attempting to heal them. She is very wise in many ways. Not to mention her patient indulgence of me."

Darcy stared at her for several moments, and Elizabeth could not discern if it was curiosity or disapproval that his face expressed. She doubted many young ladies of his acquaintance learnt how to heal baby rabbits, foxes, and even the occasional frog.

She shifted uncomfortably and said, "If writing is painful for you, sir, if I may, I would like to offer my services. I can write as you dictate. If the letter is not too personal, that is..."

Darcy sat in silence for another few seconds, examining her. Elizabeth began to feel quite foolish for the offer she had made. Perhaps he saw it as an impertinence on her behalf.

"That is extraordinarily kind of you, Miss Bennet," he murmured softly. "If you have no other plans, I would appreciate your help very much."

Elizabeth, uncertain over such pleasing words from *Mr* Darcy, waited a moment before rising and sitting at the desk.

"I have already completed a letter to my solicitor in London. The matter of Rosings is important to resolve."

"The matter of Rosings?"

"My aunt and cousin both perished. The matter of who inherits Rosings needs to be resolved. It is an unfortunate, but urgent, matter."

"I have not had the opportunity to properly express to you my condolences at the loss of your aunt and cousin."

With a sigh, Darcy rubbed his eyes. "Thank you. I am sorry for the loss of your cousin, as well. Have you written to your family yet?"

"Not yet. I will attend to it as soon as we finish your correspondences. I suppose the matter of who shall inherit Longbourn upon the death of my father is also something that needs to be resolved. I imagine Charlotte has already written to her family and my father has been told by the Lucases."

Suddenly Elizabeth realised that, in all the very heated, loud discussions of the fate of the Longbourn entail that she had overheard between her father and mother, there was never any mention of what would occur should Mr Collins die before Mr Bennet. If her mother had ever thought of it, Elizabeth was sure it would have been thoroughly canvassed with every available audience.

Darcy cleared his throat. "I wish you to know that I also wrote a letter to Mr Bingley. I have begun to attempt to put to rights my wrong interference on that score. When I return to London, I will be able to explain all to him and ask for his forgiveness."

"Well," Elizabeth said as she turned to the desk with a rush of satisfaction. That Darcy had made an attempt to correct the thwarted courtship of Jane and Mr Bingley gave her such happiness that she felt she could write scores of letters for him if need be. "It is little wonder that your shoulder aches terribly, sir. You have already been busy this day while I slept too late and ate too large of a breakfast. I shall attempt to make up for it now by being of some little service."

Elizabeth looked at the paper before her.

"It is to my sister, Georgiana."

She read aloud what he had already written down.

Dear Georgiana,

Please allow this letter to ease your anxiety over my welfare. I was indeed injured, but am recovering well. Richard informed me that he has already related to you the tragic events at Rosings. The loss of Anne and Lady Catherine must be exceedingly shocking to you, and I regret that I am not there to comfort you. I am most anxious to have a letter from you to tell me of your health as I know you tend to worry about me, perhaps more than is needed sometimes.

Elizabeth turned to Darcy and saw that he had risen. He stood with his back to the room as he gazed out over the garden, his form silhouetted by the afternoon sun pouring in.

"I am ready to continue your letter whenever you are, Mr Darcy," she said, the pen in her hand at the ready.

"Ahem, yes."

Elizabeth proceeded to write.

Rest assured, dear sister, that you have no cause to concern yourself over me. I am so grateful that you were safe from this French incursion and hope that another such will never occur.

If you will recall, I have already mentioned an acquaintance I have with a lady by the name of Miss Elizabeth Bennet. If you ever have cause to meet her, know that all those who care for me owe her a great debt of gratitude. I am unable to give particulars, but it is she to whom we all owe appreciation for my return to health. If you are so fortunate as to have the honour of her acquaintance, you will see that she is…

Elizabeth lifted the pen and waited, no little amount of anticipation coursing through her.

"Excuse me, if you could cross that last bit out and begin a separate sentence," Darcy said. She reluctantly struck a line through the last incomplete sentence and continued to write as he spoke.

You may note a change in the style of my penmanship. Miss Elizabeth Bennet has graciously agreed to write what I say to her in order to save me from some discomfort in my arm. So you must add this small kindness to the debt of gratitude the Darcys of Pemberley owe to her.

I know how fond of Aesop you are, although you refuse to ride him for fear of his prickly nature. Let me now inform you that he is well. The French soldiers were actively looking for horses, but he managed to escape their notice and had a little adventure on his own for two days in the woods of Rosings Park. Miss Elizabeth Bennet rode him tolerably

"Oh, um, could you strike through that last word, please? Thank you."

…with calm grace. It is safe to assume that Aesop would be as accommodating with you, Georgiana. He appears quite transformed around Miss Bennet. Indeed, much of his proud nature seems to disappear when she is near to him. He is quite taken with her and would…

Darcy stopped short. Elizabeth turned her head to see that he had not changed position from his steady gaze out of the window. Heat filled her cheeks as she turned to stare back down at those last words, uncertain if they were still on the topic of his horse or not. Unwilling to break the silence, she waited.

In closing, I want to assure you that I will be joining you as soon as possible. I look forward to hearing you at the pianoforte, as I can attest that your skill and natural talent at that instrument have few equals.

Your loving brother, Fitzwilliam Darcy

Elizabeth glanced over the previous lines, trying to make sense of the words that pertained to herself. But Darcy's hand reached out and took the letter from the desk. She looked up into his suddenly flushed face, the cause of which was uncertain to her.

"Yes, that is done. Do you mind one more letter to my steward at Pemberley? It will be to a Mr Taylor and is more to do with matters of business."

"Not at all," replied Elizabeth curtly, eager to clear her head of the last letter. They continued on for half an hour more as she diligently recorded matters for his very grand estate. The tracts of land addressed, the amounts of money needed for various supplies for the upcoming late summer and autumn seasons, even matters of new equipment and repairs to existing ones were addressed. He closed by expressing sincere concern for one of the tenant farmers' families and questioning his steward as to the means to aid them through the loss of their father from illness.

Elizabeth was awed by the endless concerns of what must

be an impressive estate. With some chagrin, she realised that she had never witnessed her father being quite so involved and specific in the matters of the much smaller concerns of Longbourn. It was not in her father's nature. Mr Bennet had been born to the role and exerted the minimal amount of effort needed to fulfil the basics of his duties. The important duty of attempting to sire a son, *that* he had apparently taken quite seriously as the flawed result of five daughters could attest.

If only he had tackled the task of efficient estate management with an equal amount of enthusiasm.

"I thank you, Miss Bennet, for performing this service for me," Darcy said, startling Elizabeth out of her thoughtfulness. "I shall not claim more of your time for my correspondences as I know you have several of your own to execute."

"Indeed, I have, sir. But it was my pleasure to assist you."

An awkward quiet filled the room. Darcy opened his mouth as if to say more, thought better of it, bowed, and left the room. Elizabeth was left alone. With an unsatisfied sigh, she turned to the desk to write her own letters.

CHAPTER TWELVE

Elizabeth had spent the rest of the afternoon at the desk writing the necessary letters. She wrote to her father about the death of Mr Collins. She closed by asking if there was any way she might be of service in the legal matters of it.

Next, she wrote a more candid letter to Jane, telling of what had transpired in the past several days. Elizabeth held much of it back, but shared what she was comfortable putting in a letter. She also advised that new information had come to light that should make all the ladies of Meryton watchful when dealing with Mr Wickham. Again, she gave only general information that would prove the depth of his deceptiveness without any particulars that would cause trouble if the letter was seen by another.

As she sealed the letter to Jane, Elizabeth wondered how much she would tell her sister upon seeing her again. She would fill in more details in regards to Wickham, of course. As for her time in the woods with Darcy, if anyone would be acquainted with all that had happened, it would be Jane. But the thought of telling even her most beloved sister and confidant of those moments made Elizabeth's heart race and her courage fail.

She stood and looked out at the garden. Mr Collins's precious bee hives in which he had taken so much pride were buzzing furiously with all the eager anticipation of a warm spring day. They, at least, were unaware of the many changes that had occurred and were still to come. Elizabeth wished she could be so blissfully unaware of the considerations of reputation and fortune in a time of war.

That evening at dinner, Elizabeth, Charlotte, Colonel Fitzwilliam, and Darcy sat in the snug parsonage dining room. Darcy wore slightly more elegant dress, though given that his clothing was usually impeccably tailored, it was not quite up to the traditional standards of his wardrobe. The conversation was sedate. The considerations and worries of all those present made the food dull and the air thick. The warmth of the afternoon had yet to fully break into a cool evening, making the air of the small parsonage dining room stifling.

As they sat in silent contemplation, Elizabeth, her curiosity of the world always present and eager for knowledge, asked, "Colonel Fitzwilliam, is the military concerned about the possibility of more invasions from the air? If so, should there be more methods employed to defend ourselves?"

"I have spoken with the captain of the militia that has been assigned to Hunsford. They arrived yesterday morning, and I wished to offer my services to him, but it seems that there is little to concern him as the enemy has been thoroughly thwarted. But, you are right to believe that we should prepare ourselves for a further attack. This invasion by air scheme of Napoleon's has been known of for quite some time. There are even the occasional cartoons in the newspapers depicting the French in their balloons. Fortunately, the prevailing winds make such an attack untenable and risky, as we saw for ourselves the other day."

"Most of the balloons that have been found appear to have suffered badly in the strong winds, and not many of the French soldiers survived," Darcy murmured, glancing at Elizabeth.

Before she could determine the meaning behind Darcy's look, Colonel Fitzwilliam continued. "It was disastrous. But we did capture the few survivors. One was wandering around barefoot, muttering incoherently in French about a lady fiend." He chuckled, shaking his head.

Elizabeth's eyes shot back to Darcy, who imperceptibly raised his brows. She pressed her lips together in amusement and refrained from commenting while she tried to think of something suitable to say. She remembered the French soldiers in the balloon they had spied running frantically in the wicker basket, trying to manoeuvre the unwieldy thing in the vicious winds. "It seems our gratitude for the success of the day must rest somewhat in the hands of England herself," she observed. "It appears her winds and tides aid in our protection more than I realised."

"That is a very fair view of things, Miss Bennet. It seems you are correct," Darcy said as he took a last sip of wine from his glass. "I believe I shall retire early, as I am feeling tired. If you will excuse me."

Colonel Fitzwilliam held up his hand to prevent Darcy from rising. "I have some news, if you can spare me a few moments. I expected that I should be called up and assigned a posting very soon, but information has reached me that has given me cause to resign my commission."

Everyone stared at him, waiting for his next statement.

"Due to the total destruction of the Rosings manor house and the deaths of Lady Catherine and Miss Anne, I sent an express to the family solicitor in London. No one knows who is in authority to direct the many servants of Rosings or the business of the estate. Many of the servants are displaced, although most are able to find shelter among friends and family in the neighbourhood. I thought it a matter of some urgency to resolve for the sake of them and the village of Hunsford who depend so greatly upon the residents of Rosings. None of us anticipated or discussed this possibility, a lack of an heir, as we all expected Anne to marry."

Here he paused, and Elizabeth noticed Darcy shifting uncomfortably in his chair. She remembered that Darcy had been expected to marry Miss de Bourgh due to an arrangement dating back to their early childhood. What a ridiculous expectation for parents to put on their child at such an early age. It was little wonder that Darcy had rebelled against it. Elizabeth had noticed little warmth of understanding between Miss de Bourgh and Mr Darcy. Dropping her gaze to her lap, Elizabeth recalled that Darcy was indeed capable of warmth and deep passion, even if his daily appearance gave no indication of that side of him.

"For her to marry and have children. In short, in the absence of both Miss Anne and Lady Catherine, I am to inherit Rosings. The express came from the solicitor this afternoon, and I now have the freedom to help house the displaced servants and organise the affairs of Rosings to help the surrounding community through this time of difficulty."

Everyone looked at him in astonishment.

"You? To inherit Rosings?" Darcy exclaimed.

"Yes, I am the next in line of my father's children to inherit. It was never discussed with me as, given Lady Catherine's unusually robust health and expectation of Anne's marriage, it seemed a highly unlikely event."

Darcy winced as he stood and approached Colonel Fitzwilliam with his hand extended. "Allow me to congratulate you. Although the circumstances are indeed tragic, Rosings could not have a more conscientious or capable owner."

The men shook hands with real warmth and regard for each other. Colonel Fitzwilliam turned to Charlotte.

"As my very first act, let me extend to you, Mrs Collins, the use of Rosings Cottage, but a quarter of a mile from here. For as long as you wish, it is yours. I can say after a good inspection today that it is in excellent repair, in no need of improvements, and is but a room smaller than this parsonage."

Charlotte, mouth open in astonishment, stared in shock at the colonel.

"Your dearly departed husband lost his life in an effort to save my aunt and cousin. We are indebted to you."

"But, sir! I had not—I did not—"

Elizabeth could not suppress her smile at the very unusual sight of her friend at a loss for calm, considered words. She imagined any income that Mr Collins had left her would be modest, but probably adequate for an efficient housekeeper such as Charlotte. Besides, Elizabeth suspected, based on the warmth in Colonel Fitzwilliam's eyes, that

Charlotte would not be long out of her black mourning clothes before she received another proposal of marriage. Rosings Park could do much worse than to have the quiet, steady influence of Charlotte to oversee the rebuilding of the manor house and to see to the happiness and prosperity of its residents. It would be a stark contrast to the iron-fisted Lady Catherine's imperious rule, but Elizabeth thought they would rapidly adjust.

She smiled broadly at Charlotte, whose eyes were becoming watery.

"Yes. Well. I am certain you ladies are ready for some time alone," Darcy said as the evidence of Charlotte's full heart trailed down her cheeks.

The two gentlemen left the small dining room with just as much formal courtesy as they had displayed during the opulent meals at Rosings. Elizabeth shook her head at the distinction, but appreciated the consideration shown to them.

After the gentlemen exited, Charlotte slumped over her plate, her hand resting on her forehead as she shook her head. Elizabeth rose and sat in the chair beside her, placing a reassuring hand on her back.

"Charlotte..." Elizabeth said softly. Her friend did not lift her head from the shielding hand for several minutes. To see her imperturbable friend so distressed caused Elizabeth to furrow her brow in a way she never did with her mother and younger sisters. The throes of an emotional affliction were so common at Longbourn that Elizabeth met it with the same surprise that one might greet an expected sunrise. But in the self-possessed countenance of Charlotte, those tears created anxiety in Elizabeth for the welfare of her oldest friend.

Elizabeth stood and poured another glass of wine. Charlotte took it gratefully, and after several sips, she said, "I knew very well what my husband was, and that he could be the most ridiculous man, but we did have small moments of happiness. I know, in his way, he loved me. And I came to find some comfort in his presence. I suppose I was raised to patiently bear silly men. I know how ridiculous my father can be at times. Perhaps it was something I understood, and became familiar, so I knew it well by the time I married Mr Collins."

The truth of her words struck Elizabeth deeply. She bit her lip, agreeing silently, not wishing to say aloud how much her own thoughts mirrored her friend's. Charlotte paused as she gazed into the swirling currents of red wine circling the glass. A calm spread across her face. "I shall miss him, Elizabeth. But I am not devastated by his death. I am mournful, but not broken-hearted."

Several moments passed. With a laugh, Charlotte exclaimed, "It is so absurd! I married him for a secure future. To be in comfort, never to have the spectre of poverty knocking on my door. And now I wonder what was it all for? What is my future?"

Thinking again of the warmth in Colonel Fitzwilliam's eyes when he gazed at Charlotte, Elizabeth said soothingly, "We cannot know the future. Perhaps there is love waiting for you still."

"At my age? I am eight and twenty, with no fortune and middling looks. It is not a propitious beginning towards a second union. A union either of love or convenience."

"No, but you have qualities that those of refined discernment and intelligence value. Do you think that I would have tolerated a friend for this many years who has no genius? No wit? I think not. I am very insulted that you cannot see the great recommendation that my friendship bestows upon you. Think of *my* feelings, Charlotte."

They both laughed. Elizabeth poured herself another glass of wine and took a long drink.

"So, leave me in suspense no longer," Elizabeth said as she leant in conspiratorially. "Are you planning on returning to your family in Hertfordshire? Or, have you grown so attached to the environs of Hunsford, Rosings and its residents, both old and new, that you have no desire to quit it?"

"I do not know! I do love it here. And I know I could be of real service during this time of uncertainty. I would very much enjoy being of service to Colonel Fitzwilliam in organising his affairs."

Elizabeth repressed a smile at this small confirmation of her suspicions. "Was Mr Collins able to leave you with an income?"

"I believe a small income was left to me, yes."

"Then you could live in a quiet way in Rosings Cottage, if you choose?"

"I think so, yes! I think I could!"

"Then, as you will be in mourning for at least a year and may understandably wish to remain close to where your husband died, I believe the decision to stay or return home is entirely yours to make."

Charlotte looked at Elizabeth with wide-eyed alarm, in the best possible way. "You know, you may be right. I think it will be my decision alone! Can you even imagine!"

With a sigh, Elizabeth took the last sip from her own glass. "No, I cannot imagine at all. The only power women in our position hold is the right to refuse a marriage proposal. And even on that point, we are judged harshly no matter what our answer is, it seems."

Charlotte nodded thoughtfully. "Never accept a proposal based on any sort of obligation, from either party. Promise me, Eliza! Promise!"

"Lower your voice! I promise!"

"I have learnt my lesson. I have no regrets in my marriage to Mr Collins, but I shall model myself after you, dear Eliza. Only the very deepest love shall induce me to marry. Again, that is. My first marriage was made under the obligatory need to fasten myself to a financially secure future. Never again!"

"Hear, hear!" Elizabeth concurred and raised her wine glass.

"Only the very deepest love, the most sincere regard, the most handsome—"

"The most handsome in regimentals, that is, but not for much longer, I hear—"

"Lizzy!" Charlotte burst out with a look of mortification on her face.

Elizabeth shushed her with a giggle. "You will rouse the interest of the servants. I think we may be overindulging. It would not do to appear silly before the housekeeper, would it? I mean, I have my dignity, you know. Not many ladies have the beauty and sense of fashion that is needed to wear breeches under a gown, like me."

"Breeches under your gown!" Charlotte cried with laughter, tears of mirth running down her cheeks.

"Did I look too ridiculous?" Elizabeth exclaimed through her own laughter.

The ladies of the parsonage continued their tête-à-tête for another hour while the servants glanced at each other with perplexity as whispers, giggles, and clinks of glass were heard from behind the closed door of the dining room.

CHAPTER THIRTEEN

Elizabeth woke late again the next morning. Her head weighed heavy with the consequence from consuming more wine than was entirely proper. But since she had been rewarded by hearing a laugh from her friend again, it was well worth some discomfort. She smiled to herself as she strode out past the columns marking the end of the parsonage's drive.

True to her promise she had made to calm a nervous Charlotte, Elizabeth stayed mostly in the lanes and only entered into fields that could be easily observed from the roads.

"There may still be some French soldiers about. How could I ever show my face in Meryton again if I had lost Miss Elizabeth Bennet for a second time in one week?" Charlotte had said that morning as she had watched Elizabeth put on her bonnet.

Elizabeth, not ready for a long, solitary tramp through

unknown forests anyway, had decided to heed her friend's advice and stick to well-travelled roads and open fields.

After she had gone some distance from the parsonage, she heard the sound of hoofbeats approaching from behind her. Feeling no inclination for conversation or company, she stepped off the road and a little way into the adjacent field.

Elizabeth was surprised that, as the sound approached, her heart sped up. Recent mishaps had made her more nervous, but she was determined to reassert the independence of her walks as soon as possible to regain her adventurous spirit.

If I do not have my walks, I shall go mad. One bad experience will not quell the joy and comfort of a thousand prior walks.

Keeping that in mind, Elizabeth took a deep breath and turned her face to the road so that she could see who the rider was.

Darcy, sitting tall atop Aesop, came into view. He saw Elizabeth in the field and directed his horse off the road and towards her. Aesop high-stepped his legs and snorted in greeting. She suspected that the animal enjoyed showing off for her. Once they came before Elizabeth, Darcy carefully dismounted. His clothing was still untailored and cobbled together, but his commanding bearing would leave no one in doubt of his station in life.

"Miss Bennet, I was hoping to see you this morning."

"Mr Darcy. I hope you are feeling well. Should you be riding again, so soon, after only a day of rest?"

"The doctor did want me to wait another day, but I find that so much needs my attention, that I am obliged to return to London. The carriage at Rosings is available, but only one of the horses to pull it has been found since they were turned loose due to the fire."

"And the French, as I recall."

"Yes." He frowned momentarily at the remembrance. "Miss Bennet, I must ask you—"

After one look at Elizabeth, Darcy's gaze wandered the meadow as if searching for either words or enemy soldiers. The idea of both of them seemed to give him smouldering anxiety. Elizabeth looked around as well, uncertain if he was going to continue, but feeling his disquietude. Her focus returned to him when he inhaled deeply.

"Miss Bennet, I must insist you relate to me all that passed between us during those two days when I was alternately intoxicated or feverish. I am tormented by scraps of remembrance that may or may not be true. I am accustomed to a certain amount of-of—"

"Regulation in your behaviour?" Elizabeth ventured, smiling slightly at his inability to define this aspect of his nature.

"Yes," he replied, his spine stiffening. "And not knowing if I behaved in a way that was honourable to you is driving me—I am exceedingly distracted and unable to conduct my business as I ordinarily would."

His last sentiment was murmured out in such a gentle fashion, with his gaze dropped, that a compassionate warmth spread through her chest. Checking her first impulse to make light of the entire situation and dismiss it, she turned from him. For a man like Darcy to make such an impassioned plea for something so simple as the truth moved her. Although it was simple, that did not mean it was easy. With resolution, summoning more of her bravery than it had taken to bash the French soldier on the head, she began a faithful recital of all that had happened during those two days, including the most delicate moments: his exclamations of affection, his pressing of her to him, his illusory proposals of marriage—all that she could recall. Elizabeth was very clear in explaining that when they kissed, it was she who had instigated it through a necessity to quiet him. She was adamant that the presence of the French soldiers in the field below had been a very real threat to their being discovered.

When she finished her honest narrative, several moments passed in silence. Her heart pounded and her hands felt like ice as anxiety coursed through her. Elizabeth could not even begin to guess the thoughts that must be swirling behind that stoic countenance. A man so accustomed to being in authority must be resentful and possibly even enraged. *But I have nothing that I can apologise for. Every action I took was with the intent of keeping him alive.* She tore her focus from his face and looked to the forest's edge that lined the pasture. The birds in the trees called back and forth to each other from opposite sides of the field, perhaps retelling in their own language what had been said. They sounded a little scandalised and shrill.

"Miss Bennet." Elizabeth started and looked back at him. In a low, husky voice, barely above a whisper, his dark eyes locked upon her, Darcy said, "I think that it is clear what must happen next."

Her stomach clenched in alarm when she met his gaze. "I-I...do not know what you—"

"We must be married as soon as possible. Your father must be applied to at once for permission. If he refuses, which is highly doubtful given the circumstances of your family, we shall enlighten him as to a few of the details that you have supplied in order to convince him of the urgency. If he still refuses, as a very last resort, we should immediately go to Scotland for an elopement."

"Mr Darcy, I—"

"An elopement *is* scandalous, but perhaps necessary," he continued, beginning to pace back and forth in front of Elizabeth, unmindful of her presence. "Your family is so low in society that it will likely affect my reputation far more than theirs."

"Mr Darcy!"

"People will, in time, forget the scandal of an elopement and accept you. That is to say, as long as ties with your family—who frequently behave, as I am sure you are well aware, in total want of propriety, excluding you and your elder sister, of course... As long as ties with them are minimised and you are rarely seen in public with them, I can—"

"Mr Darcy!" Elizabeth cried. Startled, he stopped his pacing. The birds in the trees were shocked into silence. Even Aesop lifted his head from the grass, ears perked forward as if to better understand this silly human drama that he once more found himself embroiled in.

Elizabeth slowly blew out a long exhale through puckered lips, her eyes squeezed shut, in an effort to calm the maelstrom of fiery, conflicting emotions in her breast. "Mr Darcy, are you proposing marriage to me?"

"Yes. Of course. I believe I was clear about that." He frowned slightly, as if trying to recall his exact wording. "Very clear, of course."

"Thank you, sir, for the honour of your proposal. I thank you, but I must refuse."

Darcy blinked several times in the manner of someone who had just been confronted by a mythical beast that could not possibly exist in real life. "What?"

"I am very grateful that you feel it is your duty to protect my reputation by marrying me...it speaks of the high degree of honour that you possess. However, you have no obligation to me. Few know of our experience. Even fewer know the full truth of it. You and I, Aesop, and the squirrel in the tree next to the hut are the only ones who are familiar with some of the particulars. So, in that light, I release you from feeling any sense of obligation towards me. Indeed, I could say that I am equally in your debt, for if you had not been with me that day, I would have been alone when confronting the French soldier. I am as indebted to you. Therefore, we are equal in this. You have no obligation to marry me."

After managing to calmly state her response, Elizabeth felt too upset to stand still any longer. She began to walk back towards the lane. Darcy pulled on Aesop who, apparently choosing the most inopportune moment to be difficult, refused to budge. With an angry look at his horse, Darcy dropped the reins as Elizabeth passed by them and followed her. Aesop accompanied them both at a discreet distance.

"Elizabeth! I mean, Miss Bennet, please, if you would give me just a few moments more. Perhaps I expressed myself ill. It was not my intention to insult you."

"Mr Darcy, even if you had behaved in a more gentleman-like manner, I would still refuse. A sense of obligation is no way to begin a marriage." She stopped and turned to him, her eyes filled with fire and tears. "You have made it perfectly clear in the past that you find me barely tolerable. You dislike my family. You are shocked by my position in society and my lack of a dowry. I think even some of my spirited nature is offensive to you. If I need to add to this list, I shall. I have two young sisters, as you know, who will argue for hours about something that took place a day before. Their memories are in conflict with each other. Each remembers things very differently. They will scream about this for hours, till the roof shakes with the dispute! All over a conversation with a single officer and what he said and what was meant by what he said. So, supposing for a moment that we did wed. And in a year's time, you remember differently the events in the shepherds' hut. It matters not who is right and who is wrong. You may eventually believe that I have somehow trapped you into a marriage. You can imagine how the resentments will multiply. What you may begin with the best of intentions will end in disharmony."

"I would never dream of accusing you of entrapment! I have full trust and faith in the account you have given. I believe deeply that you are not attempting to lure me into making a proposal under false information. There are few in this world whose opinion and judgment I trust more than yours."

"Sir, you say that now, but I have been witness for many years to a marriage—" Elizabeth paused, an image rising of her mother and father in one of their quarrels, and took a deep breath. "—to a marriage that I suspect was begun under false information. It is not a scene of happy accord. And those surrounding them suffer as a consequence. To rely on my memories alone is to rely on something as changeable as the clouds in the sky!"

Elizabeth twirled around until she found one cloud far overhead that suited her purpose and pointed at it. "There! In that cloud, some will see a dragon ready to kill. Others will see a puppy asleep at the feet of a beloved owner. Memories are just as fickle, variable, and bewildering. The point being, sir, that I shall not build a marriage upon the back of a cloud that can change in form or interpretation. I have told you what happened during our time together. That is what I experienced. If you ever regain your memories and have an alternate view of things through the lens of fever and Chartreuse, it could be very different, and I shall not be burdened with the guilt of knowing I accepted your proposal under those circumstances. All obligations are dissolved. Have a safe journey to London, Mr Darcy, and accept my best wishes for your health."

Darcy continued to stare at her in silence for several moments, his face clouded with angry disappointment and profound confusion. Clearly, of the many endings he had imagined for their interview, there was one that he could not have ever foreseen.

Elizabeth stalked away and stumbled back onto the road, walking down it at a rapid pace. When she glanced back over her shoulder, she saw Darcy standing, watching her, his horse by his side.

Were there enough tree-lined lanes in all of England, from the Highlands to Cornwall, for a girl to walk off her anger from receiving such a proposal? Elizabeth knew that her legs could propel her to every coast, north to south, east to west, and still be unable to quell the storm of passions that raged in her chest.

She was well past the village of Hunsford, her cheeks still ablaze, when she stopped and looked about her. Nothing was familiar in the least. With an exasperated groan, she turned back to retrace her steps and began reviewing every moment of her acquaintance with Mr Darcy that she could recall. All the moments of cool superiority on his face. His high-handed treatment of Jane and Mr Bingley's courtship. She had to pause and admit that Darcy was making efforts to repair his officiousness in that instance. *But is the attempt to heal the breach too late? Is Jane's heart able to forgive and love again?*

In the case of Wickham, though, Elizabeth had to shine the penetrating light of her discernment upon herself. There, she had been the one to falter. Without knowing the full particulars, she was confident enough in what Charlotte had said and—reflecting on Wickham's behaviour with cold impartiality—to acknowledge that she had been too ready to condemn Darcy in that matter. It was she who had acted foolishly and helped to spread a false tale through the neighbourhood out of spite for Mr Darcy's treatment of her and those closest to her. Some of her anger towards Darcy quickly shifted to shame of herself and her actions.

Regardless of his offensive comments and her completely justified feelings of resentment, Elizabeth knew in her heart that she was correct in refusing a proposal made out of the need to oblige a debt. Such a beginning to a lifetime together was wretched. But then she recalled some of his most fevered moments with her, and doubt began to take hold. It cooled her burning heart. Did he really have genuine feelings for her? Did he mention anything of that in his wandering lecture of a marriage proposal?

Elizabeth hesitated in the middle of the road and looked up at the changeable clouds overhead. *He had said so much, those days we spent together, perhaps he assumed that no more needed to be said? There was indeed so much passion in his words then. Does he truly feel deeply for me? Was that said just now? Today?*

After as much calm deliberation on the subject as she could exert, Elizabeth had to conclude that, no, he had not mentioned love today. Although he had listed many reasons in favour of and against a marriage, love had not been among them. For reasons too complex for her weary mind to fully examine, her heart sank low and fury retreated. Suddenly, Elizabeth wanted nothing more than to have a cup of tea with Charlotte and think of Mr Darcy no longer.

What a week this has been. I truly want nothing more than to return to Hertfordshire and see my family, especially Jane.

The thought of Jane, always able to calm Elizabeth with kind words, filled her with a longing for home that was overwhelming. By the time she made her way back to the parsonage, it was much later than she had realised. An alarmed Charlotte greeted her at the door.

"My dear Eliza! I was quite prepared to ask the militia to begin a search for you. Where were you off to?"

"I travelled far past Hunsford. I turned back at a large expanse of fields."

"Goodness, you must be exhausted! It sounds as though you almost made it to the next village. What possessed you to walk so far?"

"I needed to think. Besides, my mind was a bit muddled from too much wine last night."

Charlotte repressed a smile and looked knowingly at her. "We did drink to excess, perhaps. But, given recent events, I think it is a forgivable misstep. Mr Darcy has taken leave of us and travels as far as London this afternoon. I am sorry you missed seeing him off."

"Yes, I...it could not be helped. I am sure he would not wish to see me anyway."

Elizabeth sensed Charlotte peering at her with genuine curiosity, likely knowing that there were things not being said, but she dropped further enquiry and instead offered her tea.

"I have letters of business to attend to this afternoon,"

Charlotte said as she looped her arm through Elizabeth's, "but may I ask a favour of you?"

"Of course."

"Tomorrow morning, I should like to walk to Rosings Cottage. I have never been inside of it. I am seriously considering staying here for a while. Will you accompany me and give me your opinion?"

"Of course! I would be delighted. I should mention, Charlotte, that I am contemplating an early return to Hertfordshire. I am longing to see my family."

"Oh, yes. That is only natural."

"But I shall stay as long as you need! I would hate to abandon you at this time."

"Do not worry yourself in the least. Colonel Fitzwilliam is being very attentive. My mother is coming to visit and help me. In fact, if you stay several more days, you may perhaps be able to use our carriage to take you to the Gardiners in London or all the way back to Hertfordshire. Do any of your family know what you have been through these last few days?"

Elizabeth thought of all that she had experienced, from the French soldier's attack to Darcy's proposal. She felt as if she were the exact same and a completely different person simultaneously than she had been a week ago.

"Only Jane has any hint of what happened," Elizabeth responded as she dropped her gaze from Charlotte's face, knowing that she had not really shared much with Charlotte herself. "I have instructed her to be silent on the subject and give very little indication of what has occurred. As far as my parents and the Gardiners know, I was simply nearby the alarming events."

"I suppose that as long as you are safe and well, everyone shall be pleased."

They entered the parsonage, and Elizabeth looked forward to the healing powers of a warm cup of tea in good company as she never had before in her life.

CHAPTER FOURTEEN

The next morning, Charlotte and Elizabeth walked to Rosings Cottage. Their path took them by the ruins of the main house. The smouldering had finally been quenched by a light rain during the night, and men were busy searching through the wreckage for anything that might be restored.

As Elizabeth stood there, the memory of Mr Collins reciting the prices of the glazings on the windows and the chimney-piece in the second-best breakfast room with such enthusiasm made her forlorn. Such attention to opulence and grandeur that were now gone forever.

Wealth is indeed a fine thing, but it is nothing without happy memories to associate with the things that fortune can provide. It can all disappear so quickly.

The ladies hurried past that place of sadness to the cottage farther down the way. It was a snug cottage, set back in a grove, quite hidden from the sight of the former manor house. Everything was in such good repair that, if Charlotte decided to make the cottage her home, it would need little attention prior to her moving in.

During the walk back to the parsonage, Elizabeth queried, "And so? Has that visit helped you decide what you are to do next?"

Charlotte turned her eyes towards the sky, contemplative of her future. "I believe that I shall stay here. At least for now. I think if I venture home to Hertfordshire, I shall be welcome, but not wanted. I see many ways here that I could be of assistance. And, I have grown to love Kent very much and should miss it if I were to leave. No, the decision is made. I want to stay. As soon as Colonel Fitzwilliam is able to find a new—" She hesitated. "—a new parson, I shall move into the cottage."

Elizabeth smiled at her friend's bravery. To strike out on this path by herself was quite admirable. They made their way slowly back to the parsonage, then halted in shock at the entrance of the drive. There, in front of the house, was a barouche with four horses before it.

"Were you expecting visitors?" Elizabeth whispered.

"No, indeed. I do not recognise it at all. It is a very fine set of horses and carriage, though."

A coachman in livery approached and bowed. "Miss Elizabeth Bennet?" he asked Charlotte.

"I am Miss Bennet," Elizabeth said uncertainly.

"I beg your pardon, Miss Bennet," he replied with a bow. "I am instructed by Mr Darcy of Pemberley to convey you to wherever you choose to go. His carriage is at your disposal."

"What is this about?"

"Mr Darcy wishes to place his carriage at your disposal for as long as you require, ma'am. He mentioned it likely that

you may wish to travel to London and then on to Hertfordshire at some later date."

"But, I-I..."

"I am also instructed to give you this."

The servant returned to the carriage and brought them a
flat box with a sealed letter on top. He handed it to Elizabeth, who glanced at Charlotte in utter astonishment. Elizabeth quietly passed the box to Charlotte and turned her back
to read the letter. She broke the seal and opened it eagerly.

Miss Elizabeth Bennet,

*Be not alarmed, madam, upon receiving this letter that it contains
any renewal of those proposals that you found so unpleasant yesterday. I believe we will always disagree on the importance of remembrances of the past week. I do appreciate what you told me. In some
ways, it has put my mind more at ease. I know it was not easy for you
to relate such things. Despite our disagreements, I must be allowed to
offer my assistance to you. I know for certain that any rational person
who was familiarised with the events that occurred during the brief
French incursion would indeed concur that I am to a small degree, if
that is how you wish to phrase it, indebted to you. If I may be perfectly
honest, in my opinion, it is a debt so large that time and consideration
can hardly do it justice. There are no other women of my acquaintance,
except perhaps for my sister, who would have done half of what you
did. Indeed, I can only think of two men who would display as much
bravery as you did, those fellows being Colonel Fitzwilliam and Mr
Bingley. I hope that the contents of the box go some small way in
recompense for the destruction of your property. It is no replacement
for what I know was a favoured possession of yours, but I believe it
will be a somewhat adequate substitute. Please do not consider it a
payment of a debt or a gift, rather a replacement of an irretrievably*

damaged, valued possession. The carriage is at your disposal for as long as needed. It is from my London residence and, as I will soon travel to Pemberley to visit my sister, I shall not need it in the near future as I do not plan to return to London until I am fully healed in several weeks. I shall employ a small carriage for that journey, so do not concern yourself over my health. Please do me the honour of accepting this small token of gratitude for your support during a truly difficult time.

In closing, Miss Bennet, let me assure you that you retain my sincerest respect and warmest regards. I do not agree with your reasoning in response to my question, but I truly am in admiration of your opinions as they indicate a mind that thinks deeply on subjects and demands esteem from those fortunate enough to claim you as an acquaintance.

Please do me the honour of conveying my respects to your family, both the Gardiners in London and your family in Hertfordshire. Believe me when I wish you the very best for your future.

Fitzwilliam Darcy

Such a letter. Warmly written, but proper in every sense. No resentment or accusations. A wave of warmth spread through every bit of Elizabeth like sunshine after a cold, drizzly morning. Her hand covered her mouth while she absorbed his words for a second, then a third time. It stayed in place to suppress a gasp of astonishment that threatened to expose her to gentle questions from her friend.

Finally, her eyes lifted and she stared without seeing, trying to reconcile her feelings before speaking. But it was a silly endeavour, for her feelings were too chaotic to be tamed. A small shuffling of gravel by her side brought her attention to the present. Charlotte, still holding the box in her outstretched arms, looked at Elizabeth with amused curiosity. Elizabeth suspected that she was repressing a smile.

"Does the letter contain good news, Elizabeth?"

"Yes, it is from Mr Darcy, confirming what his man has just said."

"How very kind of him! Do I ask too much to see what else he sent?" Charlotte nodded to the large box in her hands.

"Oh, my goodness, thank you. I forgot that you have been patiently holding that for me."

Charlotte addressed the coachman. "Would you like some refreshments after your journey?"

"Thank you, ma'am, but we have already reserved some rooms at the inn in Hunsford and can retire there at any time. If you have need of the carriage, we will be ready at a moment's notice."

Elizabeth, recalling the presence of the four horses and barouche, replied dazedly, "Thank you, I do not have need of it today, but I would like to journey to London in the morning."

"As you wish, ma'am," he said with a small bow. He climbed to the driver's seat and began the slow process of turning the carriage and exiting the parsonage drive.

The ladies entered the house, scattering away two very curious servants, and took the package into the drawing room and set it on the table. After cutting off the string, Charlotte and Elizabeth removed the top. There, nestled in fine paper, was a gown of exquisite make and refined style that matched to the thread the colour of Elizabeth's green gown that had been utterly wrecked during her adventure.

"Oh my, that is very fine indeed," Charlotte murmured.

Elizabeth extended her fingers and the fabric slid along

the tips with the most satisfying delicacy. "It is, but I must send it back. I cannot keep it," she whispered.

"No!"

Elizabeth startled at such a strong reaction from her friend. "But I must! It would be improper to keep it, as you are well aware."

"Do you realise, Elizabeth, how exhausted and in pain Mr Darcy probably was when he reached London after a ride of several hours? And in that discomfort, he canvassed London to find a very fine gown of the exact same colour as your absolute favourite gown that was damaged beyond repair? He was so attentive as to find a beautiful gown that is the very thing that you would have chosen for yourself."

Elizabeth gently touched the fabric again. *Not only that, he chose a gown of simple elegance, one that truly suits me.*

Charlotte continued with her heated defence of the gentleman's gesture, standing with her hands on her hips and chin forward. "Anyone who knows even a slight portion of what occurred, like myself, would not be shocked in any way as to the propriety of it. A young lady of limited means ruins her favourite gown, and it is replaced by the very person who received such a kindness? It would be an insult to return it, rather than a nod to propriety."

Elizabeth stared in astonishment at her opinionated friend. "Calm yourself. I shall not return it. I had not thought of it in that way. But, honestly, what am I to say if anyone questions me about it? This is hardly something that would be within my means."

"Say exactly this, 'It was a gift I received while staying at Rosings. Lady Catherine was so very generous.' Those two things are the truth. There is no falsehood. You were here when you received the gift, were you not? And Lady Catherine, God rest her soul, was generous! Did you not observe the shelves in the closet in your bedroom? That was at her suggestion and done by her carpenter."

Elizabeth marvelled at this new vision of Charlotte. She doubted if even Lydia was capable of inventing a response that served the purpose quite so well without exactly being deceitful. Her eyes dropped back down to the gown in the box. It was the perfect colour, with delicate needlework, and beautiful in every way.

"It should hardly fit me, though," Elizabeth muttered, removing it from the box and holding it up to herself.

"No, it certainly will not fit precisely, but my goodness, Mr Darcy did a remarkably good job at reckoning. It looks as though you could wear it this very evening and it would fit decently."

Elizabeth blushed at the idea of Darcy so closely matching her body size from his memory.

"It is nothing more than what you deserve. I think Mr Darcy has a very high opinion of you now," said Charlotte.

"I am sure you must be mistaken. Do you remember with what severity he treated me when he first arrived in Hertfordshire?"

"That was then. You must have noticed how he has stared at you since his coming into Kent. I have often thought that he may have formed an attachment to you. Did you happen to notice a change recently?"

Elizabeth felt dizzy from the gift and the carriage and the remembrances of his proposal spinning together in her mind. She gently laid the gown down in the box, leaving Charlotte's question hanging in the air. "I am certain Mr Darcy thinks I am beneath his notice. In status, beauty, and wit," she said with a light laugh that she did not believe herself.

She was genuinely confused as to his feelings for her. And she was no longer certain of her own staunchly held views of him. Would he truly propose as a way to prevent her from losing her reputation and in order to pay a debt of honour? Was anything Darcy said of his passionate love for her while he was in such pain and under the influence of spirits actually true? She had thought absolutely not. But now, she was beginning to think that Darcy did mean everything he had said of his admiration and love. And, with a rush of emotion, Elizabeth realised that perhaps she was beginning to feel some tenderness towards him.

Elizabeth took a step back from the gown. It was lovely, deceptively simple, and pure. Exactly what she would have chosen for herself. This was the embodiment of his regard for her. Incontrovertible proof of Darcy's affections. Materialised before her very eyes was a manifestation of how deeply he understood her nature. Her heart raced in answer to this call, its beating filling her ears to the exclusion of every other sound. Suddenly, the longing to see him again ached in her chest, demanding to be satisfied. When she realised she might never see Mr Darcy again, the room began to swim.

Charlotte reached out a steadying hand. "My dear Eliza, are you well?"

"I believe I need to lie down for a while. Perhaps, these last few days, I have walked too far."

CHAPTER FIFTEEN

The ride to London the next day was dreary and punctuated by squalls of blowing rain. Elizabeth's concern for the coachmen was acute. It had appeared to be nothing more than a cloudy sky when she left Hunsford. Had she known, she would have gladly delayed her departure for another day.

She leant forward to look out of the window, keenly aware of the emptiness of the carriage's large interior. In addition to the unusual grandeur to make Elizabeth ill at ease, there was a hint of a familiar yet foreign scent within. Something of horses, sandalwood, and limes.

Darcy. It smells of him. Elizabeth stilled as her body heated with awareness. There was no escape. The blasts of rain outside made the idea of opening a window untenable. What should have been a novel trip in an elegant equipage turned torturous. She squeezed her eyes shut and rubbed her forehead.

Perhaps London will come into view around the next corner, she told herself hopefully, but with little conviction.

At last, Elizabeth arrived at the Gardiners' house in London. The surprise upon everyone's faces at seeing her step out of such a fine carriage was enough to make her laugh aloud. The fresh air combined with the friendly faces of her aunt, uncle, and Jane were enough to dispel the discomfort of the journey.

"Elizabeth! Come in. You look pale from your travels, but otherwise very well indeed," Mr Gardiner exclaimed.

Elizabeth stepped inside, relieved to be somewhere that, excepting for Jane, no one knew of her adventures with Darcy. The strain of having to act as if nothing had happened when indeed a great deal had happened was lifted from her shoulders.

Over a rejuvenating cup of tea, Elizabeth related the awful loss of Rosings and its residents. Her family was shocked at the tale and asked a great deal more questions than she was able to answer. Her uncle had read much of the failed invasion and the absolute wonder of people flying through the sky like birds. The strength of the Royal Navy in repelling the French fleet was acknowledged in grateful terms. Indeed, by the time they closed that chapter of the conversation, Elizabeth had learnt more of the entire episode than she had known so far.

"But Elizabeth, we have rattled on about the news from here. Besides the tragic events at Rosings, did you see anything of the French or their balloons?" Mrs Gardiner queried.

Elizabeth could not prevent her mind from returning to that moment when Aesop had spooked, Darcy crashed into her, and the balloons flew by overhead. She covered her discomfort with a too rapid shake of her head.

"It is very well you were not on one of your long, rambling walks at the time, my dear. Who knows what sort of danger you may have encountered."

As Mrs Gardiner spoke the word 'danger', Elizabeth could feel the muzzle of the gun in her hand as she crashed it down on the French soldier's back to save Darcy from death. Again, she shook her head and looked out of the window nearby. Elizabeth did not wish to open her mouth and disabuse them of their misconception with a lie. For a lie she surely must tell. She trusted her aunt and uncle and Jane implicitly, but was completely uncertain how to speak of what had happened. She had hinted at some of the events in her letter to Jane, but did not feel up to making it common knowledge. And, even though they were generally liberal-minded people who would not judge her too severely on anything she had to relate, the idea of telling them of such highly improper events dried the words upon her tongue before they could take flight.

Fortunately, one of her young cousins, Hugh, chimed in with some nonsensical declarations. "If it had been I who encountered a French soldier, I would have given him a taste of steel he'd not likely forget!" He finished his bold strategies with a demonstration of his skill with an imaginary sword as he bounded around the room.

His mother turned back to her niece with an exasperated sigh. "So, do you plan on taking up the offer of Mr Darcy's carriage and returning to Longbourn straightaway? Or will you stay with us here in London?"

"I believe, if you would not be too offended, Aunt, that I wish to return home tomorrow. It has been a trying time.

And I do not want to importune Mr Darcy's carriage for too long."

"It is excessively generous of him," said Mrs Gardiner. "I am shocked, for what I have heard of his behaviour in Hertfordshire, a kindness such as this seems completely out of character for Mr Darcy."

"No, indeed!" Elizabeth countered vehemently.

Everyone turned towards her, eyebrows raised in surprise at her enthusiastic burst.

"I think, that is, I now *know* that such generosity is not out of character for Mr Darcy. We may have been misled by stories told about by him during his time in Hertfordshire. And his natural reserve does not recommend him well to new acquaintances." Elizabeth could feel the eyes on her burning cheeks, but pressed on anyway. "It is true that he has some qualities such as pride that may not be his most engaging aspects, but there are other features that become apparent on closer knowledge of him. I found his company to be more...tolerable...as time went on." A private smile spread across her face as she raised her teacup for a concealing sip.

The quiet around the table lasted for a full minute as everyone apparently attempted to decipher this unexpected new light shown upon Mr Darcy.

"Of course," Elizabeth said as she stretched out a hand to place on Jane's forearm, "Jane was always in favour of not judging him too quickly."

Her sister nodded gently. "His friendship with Mr Bingley always made me suspect that there is more to him than we saw. In fact, Mr Bingley always seeks out Mr Darcy's opinion on matters of great importance."

Elizabeth looked at Jane in astonishment. She was saying

the name of Mr Bingley readily and without the forlorn look of old. There appeared to be in Jane's eye a little of that old sparkle from the past when she spoke his name.

"I believe that Mr Bingley does indeed rely on Mr Darcy's discernment on matters of importance."

There was an awkward silence around the table.

Jane cleared her throat, then spoke quietly. "Mr Bingley has visited here the last two nights."

"Indeed!" Elizabeth exclaimed with ill-concealed joy.

"In fact, the first time he visited," Mr Gardiner chimed in, "it was at an hour so very late that decent company was hardly out and about. I was preparing to retire for the evening. Fortunately, Mrs Gardiner and Jane were still up."

Elizabeth looked at a blushing Jane and then back to her aunt in bewilderment.

"Is this true? Mr Bingley came here to call so very recently?"

Jane looked up, seemingly more in possession of herself. "Yes, it is true. He did call quite late that first evening. He said he had just discovered that I was in town, that I had been in town for some time."

"Hmm, and this he did not discover sooner from his sisters? Despite you having sent two letters to that effect to Miss Bingley?"

"I do not know... There must have been some confusion. When we called on Miss Bingley, she said both of my letters had gone amiss and were never received by her."

Elizabeth and Mrs Gardiner exchanged a look that left little doubt as to their opinion of Miss Bingley's explanation.

"Is Mr Bingley in good health?" Elizabeth asked innocently with a knowing smile upon her lips. Her heart was so gladdened to see Jane in happy spirits. Obviously, true to his word, Darcy had cleared up any misunderstanding that Mr Bingley was suffering under as to Jane's sentiments towards him. It seemed the young man had hardly waited more than a few minutes before making his way to the Gardiners' house once he had learnt the truth.

"He looked to be in very good health," Jane replied. "He enquired as to how long I would be in town and discussed with me the possibility of returning to his house in Hertfordshire in the near future."

"We shall be happy to receive him at Longbourn, shall we not?" Elizabeth replied. "I know Mama will be in raptures to finally have him over for that dinner she had been planning for him. You know how very much our mother looked forward to his company."

A bashful smile was Jane's acknowledgement. Elizabeth believed Jane's heart was mending, and some of her recently faded glow of contentment was returning to her beloved sister's face. Mr Bingley had been told of Jane's presence in London by Darcy, Elizabeth was sure. Had Darcy also told his friend that he may have been mistaken as to the depth of Jane's regard? Since he had renewed the acquaintance so suddenly and with such vigour, Elizabeth could hardly doubt that Darcy had dropped some hint that perhaps Jane did sincerely favour Mr Bingley's company dearly. It was so pleasant to see Jane return to her happier spirits.

I hope Mr Bingley feels secure enough in their mutual attachment to make her an offer and soon. It cannot happen too soon, for I am certain that his sisters will do what they can to prevent him from making a match with my sister.

Elizabeth reflected that had she not been confined with Darcy while he was injured, perhaps he never would have learnt that his meddling had cost his friend a loving companion for life. Had the circumstances not been so dire, Elizabeth would not have had the opportunity to see her sister so happy.

Thanks to a prior invitation, Mr Bingley called again later and joined them for supper. His joy upon seeing Elizabeth was so obvious, she could not help but forgive him on the spot for his previous inattention to Jane. He was so transparent with his regard for Jane that it bordered on comical. But Elizabeth could not find it in her heart to laugh. Two such kind and generous souls who had been thwarted in their journey deserved nothing less than her full support and solemn respect. He spent much of the meal turned towards Jane and engaging her in conversation.

"And Miss Elizabeth," Mr Bingley remarked as he shifted his attention away from Jane momentarily, "I am so glad to see you well. It seems Darcy is forever in your debt for the service you did for him in such dangerous circumstances. Indeed, he hardly spoke of anything else. According to him, your presence in Kent may have saved his life."

The silver that tinkled down upon porcelain prompted Elizabeth to sit up straight and not dare to lift her eyes from her plate.

What has Darcy told Mr Bingley? Why did we not discuss what we were going to tell our acquaintances?

Elizabeth paused for as long as was acceptable, then responded, "Oh? Is that so?"

"Yes, indeed. You coming along to find him when you did, helping him back to the parsonage, probably saved him from suffering more from his injuries. All I can say is, I too am in your debt, Miss Elizabeth Bennet, for saving my friend. Thank goodness you love your long walks, eh? Why, I remember so clearly your appearing at Netherfield to enquire after your sister. What a shock my sisters had! They could speak of nothing else but how far you had walked through the mud."

Mr Bingley let out a small laugh, which quickly faded when he apparently observed what Elizabeth keenly felt— that everyone seated at the table was staring at her in expectation. She became terribly involved in relocating a piece of potato to various new locations on her plate. When the silence became unbearable, she lifted her gaze to her aunt and uncle and inhaled deeply.

"I believe I neglected to tell you that I did indeed aid Mr Darcy when he was injured by an encounter with a French soldier. He was far from Rosings. I helped him return to the parsonage, which was closer at the time."

The looks of horror on her aunt's face and of astonishment on her uncle's caused Elizabeth to shift uncomfortably in her chair.

"It was nothing, truly. Mr Darcy makes too much of it, I am sure. Anyone would have done the same in my situation."

"The same!" Mr Bingley exclaimed. "You rate yourself too low, Miss Elizabeth. According to Darcy, it was an act of bravery that few would have—"

"Yes! Well," Elizabeth interjected, "it was the least I could do, and Mr Darcy has more than repaid any small kindness of mine by lending me the use of his carriage to take me back to Hertfordshire. No more needs to be said of it, indeed."

Mr Bingley, looking puzzled but clearly admonished enough by Elizabeth's pointed comments, fell silent on the subject and turned back to Jane. Through the rest of the meal, Elizabeth glimpsed furtive looks of concern passing between her aunt and uncle Gardiner. Upon completion of dinner, Elizabeth immediately rose, citing a headache and excusing herself for the rest of the evening. She dashed upstairs to her room, closed the door, and extinguished the candle as soon as she could.

As she lay in bed, her heart ached with the knowledge that Darcy was also in London that evening. Hearing Mr Bingley recount how warmly Darcy had spoken of her had left her in a state of confusion and longing that wearied her. Sleep came upon her at last as she wished the dawn to approach rapidly so that she might return to Hertfordshire in the morning.

CHAPTER SIXTEEN

The next morning found Elizabeth feeling much refreshed and ready to continue her journey. The weather was bright and inviting, a perfect day to take the road that led to home after adventure and danger. Being homesick for Longbourn was so unusual for Elizabeth that she wondered if she would ever be in favour of another trip again.

Jane hugged her close while she waited for her luggage to be loaded onto Darcy's carriage. "I would join you, but my visit here is to last for another week and I—"

Elizabeth smiled and squeezed her sister's hands. To leave now when Mr Bingley was so obviously working up the courage to make her an offer would be a difficult hardship.

"You know that I enjoy my own company far too much to regret a solitary journey!" Elizabeth said laughingly to cheer her sister out of anything like regret. "I shall fend very well in this shabby equipage."

Both sisters looked over at the magnificent carriage that

was far grander than anything they had ever ridden in in their lives.

"Oh, Lizzy, I wish we had had more time to talk! You seem to have been through more in Kent than you have been able to share. But I would never press you into a confidence that you are not prepared to admit. I will be home within a week, and then, if you like, you must tell me of all that occurred."

Elizabeth could only nod and give her sister another hug. She squeezed Jane tight to her, suspecting that this was the last time her sister would be solely her own. An engagement was surely around the corner, perhaps even by the end of that morning. Elizabeth blinked back some tears of joy and sorrow. Pulling away, but again holding her sister's hands, she said, "Please convey to Mr Bingley that I regret not seeing him today but look forward to calling on him at *Netherfield* in the very, very near future."

"Oh, Lizzy," Jane murmured as their aunt and uncle joined them.

"Recover yourself from your travels thoroughly, Elizabeth dear," her uncle stated as she hugged her aunt. "We have plans to tour the Lake District and wish you to accompany us. If you are so inclined, that is. Do you believe that you would be ready for such a trip soon?"

"Truly? Yes, I shall be more than ready, I assure you. Oh, that would be wonderful! I have heard such lovely things about the Lakes that I shall anticipate it every day."

"I am quite anxious to revisit the village that I grew up in as well. It is Lambton in Derbyshire," her aunt said with an inscrutable expression.

"Derbyshire?" Elizabeth repeated as her brows knit together.

"I see your concern," Mrs Gardiner added. "It would be unlikely that we should meet with any of the Darcy family. They move in circles far above my old acquaintances. You need not concern yourself about encountering Mr Darcy. I know how exceedingly unpleasant you would find that."

"Oh, absolutely. Yes, indeed, very unpleasant," Elizabeth agreed vaguely, though feeling quite differently in her heart. But to meet him again, after rejecting him so thoroughly! Her heart fluttered at the very notion. But, as her aunt insinuated, it was unlikely that their paths would cross in Derbyshire, or ever again. Perhaps, eventually, if Mr Bingley and Jane wed, they might encounter each other. But such a thing was so uncertain. Elizabeth knew herself too well not to recognise a pang of regret at that thought.

As she stepped into the carriage and her journey home began, Elizabeth had to confront that her heart was in a tangle of emotions. Regret at perhaps never having the opportunity to see Darcy again. Doubt as to the wisdom of her response to his proposal. Speculation that if he ever did wed, what kind of woman he would marry. Anxiety at a chance meeting in Derbyshire.

With a sigh, she watched the last views of London pass by the carriage window. She would be home in Hertfordshire within a few hours. It was not helping her mind settle to be riding in the carriage of the very man she was endeavouring to forget. The irony of it did force a small smile from her as she leant her head against the window.

No matter the future, Elizabeth felt herself right to have refused a marriage proposal made under the weight of a perceived obligation to preserve her reputation and repay a debt. It mattered not that the invitation had come from one of the richest, most handsome men in England. A man whose company she preferred, despite his faults, to the company of any other.

By the time the carriage reached Longbourn, Elizabeth was decided. As she stepped down, she made her face into an unreadable mask of resolution to absolutely not ruminate upon the handsome features, intelligent conversation, or the deliciously warm body of Mr Fitzwilliam Darcy ever again.

The impressive vehicle with its many horses had caused such a stir among the inhabitants of her home that several of her younger sisters issued forth in haste and wonder. Feeling proud of her strength of character, she greeted her sisters and their many questions with the appearance of calm equanimity.

Life back at Longbourn was exactly as Elizabeth had remembered it. Mr Bennet kept to his library after some preliminary enquiries about her visit. Her two youngest sisters were obsessed with the men of the militia. Mrs Bennet pined over the status of Jane and the absent Mr Bingley. On this point, as well as several others, Elizabeth refrained from providing information that would in any way inflame the expectations of Mrs Bennet in regards to her eldest daughter. If Elizabeth shared the fact with her that Mr Bingley had renewed his attention to Jane at the Gardiners' house in London, she would be forced to share with her every minute detail of his visits dozens of times. That was a trial of Elizabeth's bravery that made her quail far worse than a French military invasion.

No, far better for Jane alone to inform our mother. It is her tale to tell, not mine.

No one was overly concerned about Elizabeth's experiences during her stay at Rosings. It was as if the French soldiers had fallen from the sky somewhere far away in the wilds of the New World as opposed to just a few hours away in Kent. Since they lacked the curiosity to ask any significant questions on the subject, Elizabeth felt absolutely no desire to share any details. Sometimes, being the least-favoured child of her mother was quite satisfying.

The one fresh point that Mrs Bennet could grow quite hysterical over was the state of Longbourn upon the death of her husband. With Mr Collins dead, and Charlotte no longer to succeed her, Mrs Bennet found this subject ample reason for uncorking her salts regularly.

She had cornered Elizabeth on several occasions to cajole her into exerting some influence over Mr Bennet in regards to the future of Longbourn.

"Elizabeth! Has your father said anything about Longbourn? About what is to become of us when he is dead?" Mrs Bennet quizzed her after Mr Bennet had left the breakfast table on the morning after her return.

"I would think you should direct your enquiries about the future of our estate to him directly, ma'am. I can know little of it other than that Charlotte does not expect to inherit now as Mr Collins is dead," Elizabeth replied coolly, reluctant to become stuck in the middle of another of her parents' power struggles.

"But I know how often he consults you, Elizabeth, when it should be me he talks to of such things!" her mother bleated.

Elizabeth knew the truth of what her mother said. No matter how shrill and overwrought Mrs Bennet tended to become on important matters, especially those that dealt with their family's future once Mr Bennet died, she deserved to be consulted and informed of those matters as they unfolded. Her father had left off until the last possible moment to inform Mrs Bennet when Mr Collins, the future heir of Longbourn, was coming to visit. Her mother had been left scrambling for an impressive meal on the morning of his visit. Elizabeth strongly suspected that her father was teasing out the legal details of what was to happen now that Mr Collins was gone. If he was, he was keeping those machinations to himself entirely, causing her mother no end of fidgets and loud speculation.

"You know how Papa likes to conduct his business. He wants things settled and firm before he shares it with us." Elizabeth knew that argument to be a weak one in the face of such legitimate concerns. "I promise you, Mama, when I know of anything definite, I shall pass it on to you. It is only proper that you should know your own future and the future of any of your unwed daughters."

Mrs Bennet looked like she was about to respond with an accusation or a tart scolding, but she stopped with a startled look on her face. "Why, yes! Yes, I'm so glad you see what I am saying. Thank you, child."

Elizabeth looked down to hide a smile. She and her mother rarely ever saw eye to eye on subjects. It amused Elizabeth that one of the rare exceptions was a matter of such importance to all of them.

A few days after her arrival home, her father called her into his library and shut the door.

"Elizabeth, I am glad you came home earlier than expected," Mr Bennet said as he waved her into her usual chair. "Lacking the presence of either you or Jane, I have had no one to consult with on the matter of the Longbourn inheritance. Unfortunately, my dear wife and her attendant nerves would cause this entire matter to become more of a muddle than it already is."

"She seems perfectly content debating the matter fully on the limited information that she has. Although I cannot imagine she would have any legal opinions that would aid you, sir, it might be a kindness to her to keep her abreast of developments so that she is more comfortable about our future."

He merely waved this point away with his hand as one would attempt to rid a picnic of a persistent wasp. "As you know, the estate of Longbourn, upon my death, was to be entailed to Mr Collins. But now, as he has predeceased me, the entail is to go to my next closest living male relative."

"Yes? And that is?" Elizabeth asked anxiously.

Her father stood and poured himself a drink, which he drank from deeply before sitting down again. "That is the thing! None can be found! Your uncle Philips is doing his due diligence to discover another to inherit in the place of Mr Collins, but..." Mr Bennet gave a shrug and rapidly drained his glass most uncharacteristically.

"But, what does that mean, Papa? If none can be found?"

"It means I can write up a will and leave Longbourn to whomever I wish. The entail is broken. My cousin is dead. His son, Mr Collins, is also dead. After a set amount of time to search for an heir, I shall be able to leave Longbourn to one of you."

Elizabeth stared at him, dumbfounded. "Can you mean it? Is this the truth?"

"According to your uncle, it appears that once we have shown that a genuine exhaustive effort was made to discover the next male in line to inherit, we shall be done with the silly thing all together and one of my children can inherit! What do you say to that?"

"I am utterly astonished! But are you absolutely certain?"

"Yes, I am not completely useless, you know. You do not think I would entrust a man such as your uncle Philips, good man that he is, with something as delicate as this without reading through everything for myself as well? No, he is a good country lawyer, but something of this nature needs more than one pair of eyes on it."

"Who?" Elizabeth faltered, uncertain how to phrase her next enquiry with tact.

"To whom shall the grand estate of Longbourn be left? Lizzy, do you really *need* to ask? You, who are by far the most lively and intelligent of all my children?"

Elizabeth twisted her trembling fingers together, unable to comprehend what her father said. Suddenly, her future lay before her, set and unyielding. Her mind filled with long winter nights of listening to her mother complain of every chilly draft, aching joint in her body, and slightly under-cooked piece of potato. Long afternoons of listening to Mary practise at the pianoforte with grim determination. Assemblies where the person of greatest interest and insight would be Sir William Lucas. She could not explain it, but as much as her heart dearly loved Longbourn, the thought of never leaving it made her vision resemble the crumbling walls of a fox den, threatening to collapse in on her at any moment. She struggled to take in a full breath. The room dimmed as the weight of inheriting Longbourn pressed down upon her.

From a distance, she thought she heard someone calling her name. She forced her head to turn, and she saw her father leaning over her, patting her hand, a look of concern in his eye.

"Mary!" Elizabeth blurted out before her mind could even begin to approve of such a declaration.

"Yes? Are you well, Lizzy? What about Mary? Do you wish me to fetch her?"

"I think Mary should inherit Longbourn."

An amused smile crept across Mr Bennet's face as he righted himself. "Now, now, this is a very serious matter. Not the time for one of your little witticisms."

"No! You misunderstand me!" Elizabeth grasped at his sleeve before he moved away. "I am in earnest! For the very reason that you just stated, I would not be the best choice." Uncertain how to—or whether she should—explain Mr Darcy's advice that her active mind needed intellectual stimulation and amusement to stay healthy, she took a breath. "Papa, I am not sure I have the correct disposition to be tied down to the running of Longbourn for the rest of my life. But Mary—"

"Surely you jest? Mary?"

"Mary has the ideal disposition for the day-to-day tasks of estate management. In the areas of organisation and mathematics, she is superior to all of us. Her character and interests make her perfectly suited to a life on a quiet country estate. I think, if given a proper, fair chance—" Mr Bennet winced slightly. "She could be the best of all choices. She certainly has the most patience with Mama. And if she never marries and has children of her own, it could be left to her in a way that Longbourn would pass to the eldest of your grandchildren, could it not?"

Mr Bennet turned from her and looked out of the window onto the garden.

"That is not to say that either Jane or I would not do an admirable job of it, sir, but I think Mary is simply the best suited. It is my honest opinion. Jane should be consulted as well, when she returns home in another week."

Silence pressed upon the room for several minutes together. He seemed to be weighing her words carefully. "You have given me much to consider. You may go." His voice had a hint of disappointment in it, but also indicated that he was serious when he said he would think upon her suggestion.

Elizabeth stood and placed her hand upon his shoulder. She gave him a gentle squeeze before she turned to leave.

True to her word, Elizabeth informed Mrs Bennet that things were still unsettled regarding the future of Longbourn's entail. Without getting into the particulars of the search for another male heir, Elizabeth informed her in the most general terms of all that was being done and that Mr Bennet was acting with the interests of his children at the forefront of his thoughts.

Elizabeth was heartened to see that her advice had had some weight with her father, and he seemed to take a greater interest in Mary's opinions. He even called her into his library several times for talks. Mary, although not the most original or insightful thinker of the Bennet girls, would be an excellent steward of Longbourn, Elizabeth was sure. As Mr Bennet made an effort to draw Mary into intelligent conversation more frequently, she became more comfortable and confident in her discussions with him. By the growing air of appreciation that Elizabeth observed in Mr Bennet's eye, he was beginning to realise that much of what he had previously thought was silliness in Mary was really nervousness about making a misstep or misspeaking in his presence. Elizabeth had the very great satisfaction of hearing Mr Bennet eventually agree with her on some of Mary's finer qualities of steadiness and rationality.

In her quiet moments, Elizabeth often reflected on why she had had such a visceral reaction to her father's recommendation of her taking over Longbourn. It had been an instinctual response to refuse and redirect his attention to her sister Mary. She loved Longbourn. She loved her family. But the idea of staying the rest of her life there when she had seen so little of the world felt wrong, somewhere in her bones. Perhaps too much had happened too quickly and she had neglected to lay down a trail of breadcrumbs so that she could return to the girl she used to be.

I have seen things, experienced things I could never have imagined a few months ago!

Seeing the absolute impossibility of people flying through the air like birds. Fighting and winning perhaps the only battle against the French on English soil. Feeling Darcy under her body as she kissed him into silence. These things had happened and had changed her. There was no going back.

Elizabeth was extremely grateful when Jane returned from London several days later; she was eager to talk these things over with her. But any conversation of meaning had to be delayed for the very best of reasons. Jane was hardly five minutes over the threshold of Longbourn when she announced that Mr Bingley had proposed marriage to her and she had accepted.

A maelstrom of ecstatic joy from Mrs Bennet made any rational attempt at congratulations an impossibility.

Elizabeth hugged her sister tightly. "I knew it, Jane! I knew how much he cared for you. He just needed some time away from his sisters to truly work up the courage to address you. Were Miss Bingley and Mrs Hurst aware of how earnestly he had resumed his attentions to you?"

"Indeed, they were not. Both the sisters had been invited to a country estate of another friend for a few weeks. Mr Bingley had been invited as well and was going to join them, but..." Jane blushed.

"But? You were saying?" Elizabeth prompted.

"But Charles discovered that I was in town the very evening before he was to join them."

Elizabeth imagined that the 'discovery' coincided closely to the time that Mr Darcy had sent his letter. With a glow of satisfaction, she meditated on how rapidly he had set about to right an injustice done by his interference into his friend's affairs. How many men would have so readily admitted that they were in the wrong and taken immediate measures to rectify it? In Elizabeth's experience, there were few she could imagine who would have done so.

"So, he begged off joining them and claimed business that he had to attend to."

"I see that 'business' had a very happy outcome for a most beloved sister of mine," Elizabeth said with another tight hug of Jane.

"Yes," Jane acknowledged quietly. "Charles said... He thought... Apparently, he did not believe that I loved him. He did not wish to propose marriage to a woman who did not feel as deeply as he did towards her. That is why he left Netherfield. He could not bear to be in my company, thinking I was unable to return his affections."

"Please, do not let Lydia overhear you," Elizabeth said with a playful poke at Jane's arm. "She will take it as encouragement to be even *more* outspoken about her feelings towards officers she prefers."

They both laughed as they walked arm in arm to the drawing room. Elizabeth could not help but reflect on the two marriage proposals that she had received and rejected. Both had been from men whom she had in no way encouraged by her behaviour to believe that she cared for them. Indeed, she believed that she had been exceedingly explicit in her dislike of both Mr Collins and Mr Darcy. At the other end of the scale, in her quietly modest way, Jane *had* encouraged Mr Bingley, but it had not been enough to elicit a proposal. Elizabeth shook her head at the futility of it all. So many opportunities for misinterpretation and false starts, it was a wonder that marriages of love occurred at all.

As Elizabeth sat down next to Jane, their mother began an excited recitation of all that needed attending to in preparation for the wedding. Elizabeth's focus began to wander after just a few minutes, back to the two men she had rejected. She had absolutely no regrets in her complete rejection of Mr Collins. His belief that he was in love with her had been so comically deluded that it was difficult to feel any compassion towards the recently deceased man on that point.

However, her rejection of Mr Darcy was so complex and her feelings so altered, Elizabeth had to pick up some needlework to dissimulate her thoughtfulness upon this particular subject. Her indifferent pokes at the fabric, however, allowed her mind to wander.

She had never encouraged or sought Mr Darcy's attention. She tried to reflect on any instance of warmth or emotion from Mr Darcy prior to their adventure in the woods of Rosings, but could not bring a single one to mind, unless...

As she had accused Mr Darcy of judging her sister Jane's

true feelings based on false assumptions, had she done the same with Mr Darcy? Just because he was reserved and cool outwardly did not mean that he could not feel deeply passionate towards a woman he loved.

With an accidental jab of her needle into her finger, Elizabeth realised that she had conducted herself no better than Mr Darcy in making assumptions of the heart of another. His wild proclamations of love in the shepherds' hut could not be taken seriously, could they? And he had made no mention of love during his proposal, only insults towards her family and obligations to shield her reputation from damage.

What am I to believe? She distractedly sucked on her injured finger. Her own feelings towards him had evolved to something quite warm. She could not think of those dark eyes of his—desperate and stormy, as he clutched her tightly to his chest—without feeling keenly the loss of knowing that she would never experience that again.

"I know Kitty will prefer a yellow tone, but Elizabeth must always go her own way in such matters, though I think she will accommodate us in this instance, for to do otherwise would be a grave insult to the entire ceremony! Do you hear, Elizabeth?"

She looked up absently at her mother. "Pardon?"

Mrs Bennet rolled her eyes, and Jane glanced at her in mild concern.

"The colours of the dresses you and your sisters will wear at Jane's wedding! Are you not attending, silly girl? Oh, Kitty! Go ask your father what can be spared for all the girls to have new gowns for Jane's wedding!"

"Lizzy," Jane murmured softly, "you seem distracted. Are you feeling well?"

"Just mournful at the thought of losing the best sister a

girl could hope for. And at the same time, so happy that I would not wish a thing to change! Reconciling the two is not easy at all."

Her sister nodded, clearly not quite fully believing Elizabeth, but already being asked her opinion on a fabric from her mother, she had to turn her attention away.

CHAPTER SEVENTEEN

S everal days after Jane arrived home and before Mr
Bingley returned to Netherfield, Elizabeth lightly
tapped on Jane's bedroom door when she thought
most everyone in the house had retired for the evening.

She pressed the door open quietly and stepped over a
particularly squeaky board on the floor to move as stealthily
as she could. Long experience had taught both of the eldest
sisters that any small indication of a confidential conversation caused their youngest sister Lydia's ears to perk up and
nose to twitch much like a hound on the trail of a fox. For
days afterwards, Lydia would prance and preen while dropping hints as to what she may have overheard in an effort to
worm even more confessions from her sisters. It was one of
her least endearing qualities.

Jane set aside her book. Elizabeth sat on the edge of the
bed and twirled several tassels of the coverlet into a braid as
her worried eyes wandered the room.

"Lizzy, what has been bothering you? There has been a

restlessness about you ever since I arrived home." Jane placed a hand on Elizabeth's arm and asked earnestly, "Are you that upset about my marriage to Charles?"

Shocked, Elizabeth looked her sister solemnly in the eye. "No! No, Jane. No one could be happier for you than I am. Well, perhaps Mama may be happier. But for other reasons, I am sure. To see you engaged and made so happy by a man whom you truly love and who truly loves you is the most wonderful thing in the world."

"Then what is it?" Jane paused and chewed her lip reflectively. "Did something happen during your stay in Kent? Did something upsetting occur at Rosings?"

Elizabeth could only nod and turn her head. The tears that threatened to cascade down her cheeks were held back by fierce blinking.

"Oh, Lizzy."

That was all it took for her to collapse in Jane's arms and stifle her sobs against her sister's shoulder. When she gathered herself together sufficiently, Elizabeth retold everything that had occurred from the time of crashing into Mr Darcy at the base of Tall Oak Hill to the awkward proposal in the field before he departed and the receipt of the gown that she had not dared take out of the box since arriving home. The only thing Elizabeth left out was Mr Darcy's confession of his role in concealing Jane's presence in London and casting doubt into the mind of Bingley.

The two girls sat in silence for some time after Elizabeth had stopped speaking. The tale was so wild from beginning to end, involving so many trials of the heart and the body, that once told in its entirety, she could hardly believe the only ill effect of it were a few tears. But she knew she was bold, clever, and healthy. Had it been any of her other sisters, she was not certain the outcome would have been so relatively happy.

"I should not have bothered you with this tonight, Jane. Mr Bingley is expected tomorrow, and I know you will want your rest."

"Lizzy, stay! Please. Till your mind is quieted. It is just...it is quite a lot to take in!"

Elizabeth nodded silently in agreement.

"So, you do not believe Mr Darcy truly loves you?" Jane queried, skipping over any concerns for the improprieties and making her main concern Elizabeth's heart.

"I do not know! He made no mention of it during his proposal, although he made plenty of mention of warm feelings earlier when deluded by drink or pain or fever. But were those moments sincere?"

"You were very correct in questioning the properness of entertaining a proposal made in that way. Though, if Mr Darcy has no real affection for you, it speaks very highly of his honour to wish to preserve your reputation by offering you his hand."

"I have no doubt that Mr Darcy is one of the most honourable men I have ever encountered."

Jane raised her eyebrows. "But his treatment of poor Mr Wickham, Lizzy. How do we reconcile that?"

Elizabeth rolled her eyes with a sigh and began a retelling of the few bits of information that Charlotte had passed on to her about Mr Wickham. It was very vague, but coming from Charlotte gave it an import that impressed both girls with its veracity.

"Oh my," gasped Jane. "I always thought there must be more to the story of Mr Darcy's treatment of Mr Wickham than what was widely known."

"And you were correct, as usual."

Jane shook her head at the compliment and pressed on. "But if Mr Darcy does truly love you, and never showed it before the proposal, it makes his case a sad one indeed, does it not? Why, Charles himself said that he hesitated to make me an offer because my countenance in public was always so serene. In some ways, Mr Darcy may be suffering due to the very same reasons that I have suffered. Like myself, he may not be adept at sharing his feelings in public places."

Elizabeth squeezed her eyes shut at this painful validation of her suspicion. "To think I spoke so warmly of Mr Wickham and so ill of Mr Darcy," she groaned. "I have never felt so misguided by my wit in all my life. To have made so many public proclamations against a man who behaved so honourably, towards both myself and Mr Wickham. I am ashamed."

"You are too hard on yourself. You did save his life. I think that makes up for many missteps, do you not?" Jane gave Elizabeth an earnest look. "Besides, if you felt no affection for him, you were right to refuse him. And, even if you do feel affection for him, his proposal was such that it would have been inappropriate to accept. As you said, a marriage should not be made in an effort to repay a service or even to protect a reputation. Either way, you were correct, I think."

There was a pause of several seconds. Jane cleared her throat and ventured timidly, "You do not have any affection for him, do you, Lizzy?"

"I do not know anymore!" Tears began to meet again in her eyes.

Jane leant in and gave her hug. "You will know. You are so clever, you will discover the truth. And if he truly does love you and you him, he will make an offer of marriage that is respectful and pleasing."

"What if we never see each other again?"

Jane gave a small shrug. "He may come to our wedding, but I do not know for certain."

In the end, comfort for one she loved was all she could give. She merely held her sister's hand as they both gazed at the rising moon, full and brilliant through the window.

True to expectations, Mr Bingley arrived in Hertfordshire the next day to re-open Netherfield. His reception at Longbourn was loud and exciting. There could be no doubt to anyone within a mile of Longbourn as to Mrs Bennet's feelings on the subject. Jane was, of course, very happy in a much more quiet and dignified way to see her betrothed.

The weeks flew by uninterrupted while the happy couple exchanged visits. Calls were made all around Meryton. Preparations were made at Netherfield for the arrival of a mistress. Clothes and menus were organised for the wedding day breakfast.

Mr Bingley's sisters were noticeably absent through all of this, but if anyone was in mourning over their loss, they made no comment. Elizabeth perceived that even the eternally magnanimous Jane had her suspicions as to whether Mr Bingley's sisters truly wished them well. Mr Bingley did not mention them as often in conversation; it appeared to Elizabeth that he knew of their involvement in attempting to hide Jane's presence in London from him. To have managed to incur the disfavour of two such kind individuals as Mr

Bingley and Jane Bennet was a feat Elizabeth imagined few could boast of.

Mr Bingley frequently mentioned his friend Darcy in glowing terms, and Elizabeth hoped that all had been forgiven in that particular case. There was no hint of him knowing anything more of the events at Rosings than what he had already shared. It seemed Mr Darcy had confided in no one, not even his closest friend, as to what really occurred. For that, Elizabeth was grateful. Only Jane knew of what had truly happened, and Elizabeth knew her secrets were safe.

The only thing that marred those lovely weeks was the continued presence of the militia in Meryton. Due to the busy schedule of wedding preparations, Elizabeth saw less of the officers, and therefore less of Mr Wickham, for which she was secretly very grateful.

Although she had told Jane what little she knew of Mr Wickham's true character, Elizabeth was hesitant to share it with her family and the neighbourhood, for the sentiment in favour of him was so strong. And since she could provide few specifics as to the nature of his misdeeds or to whom they were directed, she was only very vague in expressing an occasional doubt as to how implicitly he should be trusted or believed.

One morning at breakfast, when Lydia heard her speak of Mr Wickham in terms that were not glowing, she rolled her eyes with a snort. "Lizzy! Your vanity is injured that poor Wickham pursued Mary King! You are no longer his favourite and wish to degrade him in the eyes of others. I think it's very unkind of you."

"I can give no proof to you, but I think all ladies should use caution with Mr Wickham."

"No, you are just jealous and it isn't fair," Lydia scolded her. "You will no longer have to worry about him flirting with others more than you, for the militia is to depart very soon."

Elizabeth was well aware, and quite relieved, that the militia was for Brighton. She took a sip of her tea and replied, "I think it a good thing that then we can focus more on the wedding and less on the redcoats."

Lydia smirked slyly. Elizabeth attempted to ignore her as they finished their meal, but then Lydia looked at Mrs Bennet and began to giggle uncontrollably.

"I shall *not* be saying goodbye to the militia anytime soon," her sister cried. "I have had a letter from Mrs Forster to be her particular friend and join her in Brighton. All of you can stay here and plan Jane's wedding as you wish, for I am to be with the wife of Colonel Forster and shall be the belle of the ball! Many balls, I should imagine."

"Mama!" exclaimed Kitty. "Is this true? It isn't fair!"

"Yes, yes. It is all true, your father and I have consented. It will be a terrible shame not to have Lydia at the wedding, but imagine the fun she will have in Brighton!"

"And at relatively little expense to her family," Mr Bennet added.

"But," Elizabeth stuttered out, "is it wise to allow Lydia to be there unsupervised? She is but fifteen years old!"

Lydia stared daggers at her sister from across the table. "Lizzy, don't try to ruin this for me! You had a fun adventure in Kent. I want some adventures of my own! Besides, I shall be with Harriet. What can possibly go wrong?"

"Papa, do you approve of this?"

Mr Bennet lowered a book that he had brought to the table. "What? Oh, Brighton, yes, I approve. I should think you and Jane would be delighted, for there will be one less sister to contend with during all your wedding business."

"But the wedding is not until autumn! It is but May, there will be plenty of time for us to organise everything. Do you think this is wise?"

"Worry not, Lizzy. All will be well." Her father rose to leave.

Elizabeth left soon after him, only to be confronted by Lydia as she put on her bonnet for a walk.

"Lizzy!" she hissed. "Do not try to persuade Papa from allowing me to go to Brighton, or I shall never forgive you!"

"Lydia," Elizabeth said in her most conciliatory manner, "I only raise legitimate concerns because I care about you. You are too young to be travelling to such a place unguarded, and I wish our mother and father could be made to understand that. I say these things because I worry about you."

"Ha! I should behave better than you out in the world. It is a laugh that you lecture me when you behaved as you did."

Elizabeth froze. "What do you mean?"

"As if you don't know." Lydia peeked at Elizabeth from the corners of her eyes.

"I have no idea what you are talking about, you silly, foolish girl." Elizabeth turned her back on her sister and tied on her bonnet. Her cheeks burnt with uncertainty of what Lydia knew. Had the girl eavesdropped on her private conversation with Jane when she told of her time with Mr Darcy? It had occurred before.

Elizabeth stalked out of the house and broke into a run down the lane to feel the sensation of the wind on her face. If she walked far enough, fast enough, she almost felt that she could outdistance the oppressiveness of her family embarrassments. To think she had been so eager to return here from Kent, only to be just as eager to leave. Once Jane was gone, how could she bear to remain at Longbourn? The idea of living out the rest of her days there in such company brought her little joy.

Elizabeth alternated between walking and running as far as she could before she collapsed upon a hill breathing hard. Her bonnet was untied and tossed to the ground beside her so that she could allow the sun to bathe her face in warmth. She sat up and looked out at the countryside. She now had little doubt that her minx of a youngest sister had indeed heard *something* of her conversation with Jane that night. How much she was able to glean was unknown. Asking her would only reinforce the fact that Elizabeth was concealing something and give Lydia greater reason to drop spiteful hints about it before her parents and others. Lydia was a master of faulty logic and bold accusations, but she was also inordinately adept at extracting secrets from someone before they realised they had let anything slip. In a family of five sisters, nothing caused more grief than allowing Lydia to discover secrets to hold over them.

Are all families as trying as mine?

She remembered poor Mr Bingley and his waspish sisters. Say what one would of the Bennets, none of them had ever actively worked against the true happiness of another. Of course, Lydia would disagree with her on this point, after Elizabeth had raised objections about her visit to Brighton. But those were legitimate concerns that called into question Lydia's ability to make rational decisions whenever a man in a red coat was about.

The best I can do is attempt to advise her to be on her guard for men with intentions that are not entirely honourable. Perhaps I should name Wickham directly.

Elizabeth plucked at several strands of grass and a few flowers and began a braid, hoping the activity would organise her thoughts on how to broach that tricky subject with Lydia. After a few minor adjustments, it was a rather pretty crown. A crown suitable for a fairy princess. She tied the crown of braided grass and flowers around her head.

"Of all I survey, I am mistress!" she declared with a giggle, sweeping her hand at the miles of rolling landscape below. She had once done this very thing frequently when she was upset—run as far as she could, make a crown of flowers or grass, and proclaim all she saw as her queendom. It was a silly ritual that had cheered her since childhood.

An image of Mr Darcy flashed before her, asleep on the floor of their hut, his shirt open and the light covering of dark hair on his chest rising and falling with each breath. The thought made her heart race as she stood. Frowning, she tore the crown from her head as she reluctantly turned her steps towards home.

Elizabeth paused on the footbridge over the stream and stared at the swirling water below. She held out the grass crown and let it drop from her hand into the water. It flowed down a few feet, caught on a root, broke free, caught on another root, struggled, broke free again, then sailed quickly downstream and out of sight. For reasons unknown, this made her heart swell with happiness. She returned home in a better mood than when she left it and began to think of preparations for her northern tour.

CHAPTER EIGHTEEN

In July, Elizabeth departed Longbourn with the Gardiners. With an eager heart, she saw her beloved home disappear in the back window of the carriage. If she had to listen to one more conversation about fabrics, dishes, or the flowers easily procured in autumn, she thought her tattered sanity would be all she could offer as her wedding gift to Jane.

With a large exhale, she turned and smiled at her aunt and uncle. "I cannot tell you how excited I am about this trip. Mama's enthusiasm for Jane's wedding is almost more than I can bear at times." They both smiled at her, understanding in their faces.

Mr Gardiner's brow furrowed. "I do have some bad news, Elizabeth. There was confusion with a shipment from overseas, so I shall not be able to be away from my business for as long as I hoped. I am afraid that we shall have to cut our time short and limit ourselves to going only as far north as the county of Derbyshire."

"Oh! Well," Elizabeth replied with shock that melted into ill-concealed disappointment, "you have always said that Derbyshire is the most beautiful of all the counties, have you not, Aunt?"

"Yes, it is my belief that nowhere else in England has anything to compare to Derbyshire. I hope you are not too disappointed."

Elizabeth, pondering the location of Pemberley in Derbyshire, shook her head to reply as cheerfully as she could, "I am not at all disappointed! I trust you implicitly. You both are far more travelled than I am, so your judgment that Derbyshire is the fairest of them all is enough to assure me that our trip will be wonderful."

Mrs Gardiner gave her a sympathetic smile, clearly not entirely convinced, but ready to be placated that Elizabeth would still enjoy the trip. "Lambton, the village where I was raised, is but a few miles from Pemberley—the very estate where Mr Wickham and Mr Darcy grew up. I know the association with Mr Darcy is unpleasant, but the connexion to Mr Wickham is not so bad."

"A few miles? So close?" Elizabeth asked, her mouth turning down.

"I would not worry about it too much, dear. The family is frequently in London. And when they are at the estate, they visit Lambton but rarely."

Elizabeth nodded and gazed out the window. Falling away were the sights she knew so well that she could walk the lanes blindfolded. Each turn of the carriage brought a vista that was entirely new to her eyes. The few places she had travelled to, such as London and Kent, were south of Hertfordshire. Anticipating a new adventure before her, she was assailed with a flutter of excitement. Perhaps if she were to examine those butterflies beating their wings in her belly and chest, she suspected she would discern that some were the result of knowing that she would be so close to the home of Mr Darcy.

After a few weeks seeing sights in the farthest north of Derbyshire, settling into the inn at Lambton was very pleasant. Elizabeth enjoyed meeting old friends of Mrs Gardiner; imagining her as a girl before becoming the busy wife of a prosperous tradesman and the mother of a young family was quite diverting. It seemed to Elizabeth that a bit of a girlish twinkle returned to Mrs Gardiner's eye when she was recounting some funny tale of a scrape they had got through or a boy that they all had admired. Elizabeth wondered whether one day she and Jane would be laughing over the events of the past year. Perhaps then Jane would be able to smile at the misunderstandings that had delayed her happy ending.

One morning, over breakfast, Mrs Gardiner said, "I have learnt from the serving girl that the Darcy family is currently away from Pemberley. I have always had a very great curiosity to see inside the place. I grew up hearing much of it, but have never been to it. What would you say to a trip there this morning and we could apply to see within? I understand it is open to the public for a tour."

"Ah, my dear, what a capital idea for an outing! We have no other engagements for the day," Mr Gardiner added.

Elizabeth had remained silent through this exchange, her appetite suddenly vanished. The thought of visiting Pemberley made her head swim for a moment. She glanced up and saw that her relations were watching her expectantly.

"Is it certain that the family are not presently at home?" Elizabeth asked, trying to sound nonchalant. "It could be embarrassing if they were. Even if they are not presently at home, it seems awkward without a proper invitation."

"We visited other fine houses in the north of Derbyshire and there was no awkwardness in those instances," Mr Gardiner reminded her.

"I would not care about it if it were merely another fine house, Lizzy. But the grounds are delightful. They have some of the finest woods in the country."

Elizabeth knew that there was nothing that could tempt her more surely than a statement such as that. She nodded her assent and Mr Gardiner called to have their carriage prepared.

'Another fine house' was not really a fair category to put Pemberley in. To Elizabeth, it fulfilled all the qualities of the other fine houses they had seen. But then it exceeded those inferior structures with an added refinement that the other massive stone buildings did not possess. It seemed to be more of a kindly, beloved regent as opposed to a tyrant imposing its will on the environs. Pemberley melted into the landscape in a way that made it difficult to say where the building began and where nature ended.

It is exactly what an estate house of taste should be. Precisely what I would have built for myself.

She half expected that the interior would be mouldy and dark for such an older building. But no! Upon applying to the housekeeper, Elizabeth saw that the interior carried on the pattern of real elegance without pretension that the exterior implied.

As they paused in the particularly bright and cheerful music room, she stood at a tall window that looked out over the lake. Somewhat mournfully, she muttered, "Of all this, I might have been mistress..." Smiling ruefully, she turned to join the others. It was difficult to walk those halls with equanimity, feeling that her heart might have been so happy there in so many ways. Something like regret of her fastidious sense of honour gnawed at her.

When the tour was at an end, Elizabeth was grateful to be out of doors again. The sense of Mr Darcy in every room was so overpowering, it was reminiscent of her journey in his carriage. Mrs Reynolds, the housekeeper, had been so effusive in her praise of her master that it was difficult for Elizabeth to rid herself of him in her thoughts. When Elizabeth enquired as to the favoured walks on the grounds, the housekeeper had been kind enough to recommend several that they might find enjoyable. She particularly recommended a fine avenue of old trees that lined a lane seldom used since an improved drive had been built. Elizabeth's interest was piqued, and she hurried to consult her aunt and uncle after thanking Mrs Reynolds.

"I think, my dear, that I must beg off," replied Mrs Gardiner. "I am feeling like resting upon this bench for a bit before we travel back. But, by all means, you should enjoy your walk, Lizzy."

"Yes, Elizabeth, have one of your rambles!" Mr Gardiner assured her. "I wish to walk for just a pace beside this stream that feeds this pond. It looks quite promising for trout fishing. Not that I will get the chance of it, but I do enjoy admiring such a well-kept stream as this."

Elizabeth looked at the stream. Indeed, it had not been overly manicured by too many opinions over too many generations. Nothing had imposed upon the natural beauty of the waterway. It took a special kind of tasteful restraint to allow nature to sing her own praises rather than man forcing it into an artificial beauty. Just enough of the plants natural to England had been allowed to flourish without choking the practical use of the stream as a fishing spot.

Mr Gardiner waved her off, assuring his niece that he would stay within sight of his wife while Elizabeth had her walk. Elizabeth's smile was hidden by her bonnet as she hurried towards the entrance to the shaded lane. A towering medley of sweet chestnuts and oaks shaded the path so that it had a perpetual feel of twilight. She could not help but think that if the fairy folk still wandered in England, this might be one of the spots they frequented.

Pemberley is finer than I imagined. I am glad we stopped here, though it would not have been at all possible had Mr Darcy been present. How awkward that would have been for the both of us.

Even as she thought it, Elizabeth shook her head. After her treatment of him, there was no possible way Mr Darcy could imagine her to be mercenary. She was now certain that at some point in the future they might meet, since her sister was about to be connected to his closest friend. Her heart raced at the thought.

I wish we had understood each other better. But it matters not, as we shall rarely, perhaps never, meet again.

Elizabeth's chest ached, causing her to gasp in surprise. She gazed up at the branches overhead, then spun in a circle half a dozen times, with her arms outstretched, to cast off the gloominess. She stopped, stumbled to the side slightly from the dizziness, and turned to retrace her steps back to her relations.

Before her mind could register it, her ears and spirit heard hooves approaching her from behind. Flustered, she instinctively retreated to stand off to the side of the lane, framed between two tree trunks. The rider, likely—she hoped —the steward or a tradesman, approached, but she knew herself to be fairly well hidden. She hugged one of the trees and peeked around it.

It was Mr Darcy, staring straight ahead, riding towards Pemberley!

She pulled back and bit her lip, not knowing where to look or how to act. Never had her face burnt so much in her life as sheer panic set in.

I shall let him pass, then run back to my aunt and uncle and insist we leave immediately. I shall claim a headache and exhaustion. Yes. That will do. We will leave at once before he has an opportunity to realise we are here!

As the horse neared, Elizabeth held her breath, one hand on the tree. But Aesop, being the social fellow that he was, knew immediately that she was there. The horse pulled up out of his canter to a trot, then a walk, then a full stop. The gentleman nudged him forward, but the horse was having none of it. Mr Darcy pulled his stallion round to circle and move on when he glanced up and saw Elizabeth standing there. The thunderstruck look of astonishment on his face would have been comical if she had not been so desperately uneasy.

Aesop walked forward on his own and tossed his head, demanding some affection from her. Elizabeth stared at Mr Darcy; he stared back at her. Neither spoke. Both were likely shocked into senselessness, especially at the improbability of the moment.

Finally, Mr Darcy, still ashen but clearly recalling that he was on his property, slid from the saddle. He walked slowly towards Elizabeth. Aesop wandered off to select from the sparse grass along the lane.

"Miss Bennet."

"Mr Darcy."

"What an unexpected surprise."

"Yes," she said, her face burning hotter.

"But a pleasant one," he said quickly. "Did I say pleasant? I meant to say pleasant."

"No, sir. You did not say pleasant before. You have said it now, though." She looked away from his unexpected awkwardness.

"Well, I meant to say it—" He glanced down the lane towards Pemberley. "What an unexpected, pleasant surprise. Seeing you here, that is."

Elizabeth nodded, feeling for the first time in her life that her arsenal of clever words had been misplaced.

"Is your family well?"

"Yes."

"And all your sisters?"

"Yes."

"Ah, I see." Mr Darcy nodded and appeared not to know where to set his eyes.

Elizabeth took pity on his discomfort and finally managed to speak more than one word. "I am visiting Lambton with my aunt and uncle Gardiner. My aunt grew up in Lambton."

"Did she?"

"Yes."

There was a pause as both took the opportunity to look anywhere but at each other.

"And you are staying at...?"

"The inn."

"At Lambton?"

"Yes."

"Of course. I see."

"We would not have presumed to impose upon you, sir, but we understood the family was away. We would never have asked to see the house and grounds otherwise. My aunt was particularly keen as she had never seen the house before. And she grew up so near."

"I am very glad you have come and seen Pemberley for yourself. Do you—do you approve of it?"

Elizabeth finally smiled. Mr Darcy noticeably relaxed.

"Who would not approve, sir? It is the most beautiful house and grounds."

"Yes, but I seem to think that you are not easily over-whelmed by opulence alone," he said, smiling back at her. "To earn your good opinion, something more must be added. Therefore, your good opinion is more worth the earning."

Elizabeth, not used to such words of warmth and approval from him, looked away, confused.

"Will you permit me to walk with you back to your party?"

She glanced back and found him still smiling. She nodded.

"Let me just retrieve my horse." Mr Darcy dashed back and grabbed Aesop's reins. The horse was surprisingly obliging, perhaps feeling tired from long travel.

Elizabeth gave the stallion an affectionate pat. "Did you ride Aesop from London?"

"Yes, but we made the journey leisurely, over five days. It is nothing to him, of course." Mr Darcy nodded at Aesop. "Georgiana is a few hours behind me, in the carriage. I had some business with my steward, so came ahead."

"Ah, I see."

Mr Darcy's eyes lit up with inspiration. "Would you— May I introduce my sister to you?"

"Of course! I would be delighted to meet her."

They walked in silence for a few moments before Elizabeth asked, with genuine concern, "Your injuries, Mr Darcy, have they healed?"

He dropped his gaze, appearing to flush. She bit her lip and chided herself for asking such an improper question, but having been through so much to preserve his life, she felt she was entitled to know.

"I am mostly recovered, thank you for asking. I still experience some discomfort when writing many letters. It is such a simple activity, but my shoulder will start to ache from it after a while."

"Consider me at your disposal, sir, if you have need of a scribe. I would be happy to assist you while I am in the neighbourhood." Elizabeth spoke with a tease in her tone, but the sincerity of her offer was clear.

Mr Darcy scrutinised her face until Elizabeth looked down self-consciously. "That is very kind of you, Miss Bennet. Your offer is appreciated."

Another silence descended as they walked, though to Elizabeth's mind they were not walking as quickly as they could be. It seemed to her that Mr Darcy was as anxious to extend their time together as she was. Pemberley's lake was coming into sight, and Elizabeth could still see her aunt sitting on the bench.

"And you, Miss Bennet? Are you fully recovered from—" He raised a hand as if to conjure the word he sought.

"Our adventure?" she asked with a nervous laugh. "I believe so. It was a trying time, but...I would not change a thing about what happened to us."

Her words seemed to strike Mr Darcy forcibly. He paused and turned towards her. He gazed at her intently, gathering his thoughts behind those dark eyes. Elizabeth held her breath.

"Miss Bennet, the last time we saw each other, just beyond Hunsford, was...I wish to say how sorry I am that I—"

"Elizabeth! There you are! Mrs Gardiner was becoming concerned!"

She tore her gaze from Mr Darcy and saw her uncle coming up over the hill towards them.

"They must be quite worried about me. I believe I was gone for longer than they anticipated."

"Of course." Darcy frowned at the approaching man, unhappiness at his speech being interrupted clearly written across his face. "Will you do me the honour of introducing us?"

Once a visibly concerned Mr Gardiner had joined them, introductions were made. Elizabeth felt a surge of pride in her well-spoken, intelligent relation who gave no cause for shame. The men spoke for several minutes about various innocuous topics before settling on the joys of fishing.

They walked back to join Mrs Gardiner, and more introductions were made. Elizabeth stayed mostly quiet as she marvelled at Mr Darcy's ease at conversing with her relations. Her aunt thanked him for the use of his carriage to convey Elizabeth home after the trials of her stay in Kent, and Mr Gardiner enquired as to his health. To all these polite enquiries, Elizabeth saw Mr Darcy display calm, confident composure with no hint of dismay at the degradation of being in the society of her relations in trade. Indeed, it was more than Elizabeth could reconcile, and she was glad when Mrs Gardiner hinted that her energy for visiting was at an end after the long morning of walking through the house and gardens.

"May I speak for my sister and invite you all to dinner tomorrow evening?" Mr Darcy asked.

The invitation was accepted readily by Mrs Gardiner whose expression revealed she was concluding rapidly that things were very different between Elizabeth and Mr Darcy than she had previously been told.

Mr Darcy cleared his throat. "I failed to mention earlier that there will be additional members of the party. Although Mr Bingley is much involved in matters at Netherfield, my sister is accompanied by Miss Bingley and the Hursts."

Elizabeth could not help but sag slightly under this new piece of unwelcome intelligence. But her heart was already so full of other, more positive emotions that even the prospect of Mr Bingley's sisters could not lessen her joy at the idea of the dinner engagement tomorrow.

"I would have thought," Elizabeth ventured, unable to resist, "that Miss Bingley would have been very busy helping her brother in preparations for his impending marriage to my sister."

Mr Darcy could not hide a wry smile as he responded drily, "Yes, I was also imagining that her next trip would be into Hertfordshire, but it seems that she wishes to anticipate that joy for as long as possible."

The look that passed between herself and Mr Darcy left

Elizabeth wanting to laugh, but since the Gardiners were standing there, she simply dropped her gaze as they arrived at their carriage. Mr Darcy handed her into it, allowing her hand to linger in his for longer than was necessary.

Elizabeth rode in thoughtful silence. Mr and Mrs Gardiner expressed their appreciation of Pemberley, the grounds, and the master, but neither asked Elizabeth her opinion of any of the subjects. Tomorrow loomed large in her mind—being a guest at Pemberley, meeting Miss Darcy, renewing the acquaintance of Mr Bingley's sisters. Even the tranquil landscape of Pemberley and Derbyshire could not calm her thoughts.

Before she went to bed that evening, Elizabeth took a moment to open her trunk and pulled out the wrapped, paper bundle on the bottom. By candlelight, she gently untied it to reveal the gown of green that had been given to her by Mr Darcy. She laid it out upon the wooden chair near the fireplace and stood back to gaze upon it. It was so beautiful to her. She had never been overly attached to her clothes, but this gown was so special. So perfect.

Elizabeth then turned her head to gaze in the mirror and imagined with some twists and turns how she would arrange her hair. Her hands snaked up through the fountain of black curls, pushing them one way, then another. She sighed and allowed her locks to tumble as she realised that, although the gown was exceptionally fine, her hair would have to be a simple affair. Her lack of a skilled maid to assist her made that a fact to be faced.

She looked back at the gown and then her reflection. *Why am I so nervous over this meeting tomorrow? Is it the Bingley sisters? The finery of Pemberley? Meeting Georgiana Darcy, whom Wickham said was so proud and unpleasant?*

Her mind danced around the immovable truth with the finest skill of a highly trained ballet master. She allowed herself to examine every other possibility with her sharp mind, slicing away the detritus until she could eliminate it as a cause of her discomfort. The true cause of her anxiety was too big, too brilliant for her to look at directly. So, she kept her nervous body and mind busy with other, less plausible reasons.

Elizabeth moved to put the paper wrapping back in the trunk. As she slid it off the table, something hard hit the floor. She bent to pick up the flask from the French soldier's pack. Elizabeth smiled down at it; the metal flask, round with its cork top, brought memories flooding back.

She had grabbed it from the depths of the pack before Charlotte's housekeeper had whisked it away. Tucked up under the gown seemed like the safest place, for no one had seen the gown or the flask but Elizabeth when she returned home. She had been quite insistent in keeping those two things private. It had been her hand alone that had made the small alterations to the gown in the privacy of her bedroom at night. It was fortunate that the rest of the household had been so involved in the approaching nuptials of Jane or preparing Lydia for Brighton, otherwise news of the secret gown might have got out.

Elizabeth ran a finger over the smooth metal of the flask and turned it over in her hand. She uncorked it and smelled the opening. Although empty, the lingering scent of Chartreuse remained. It was still quite a strong odour. After she recorked it and began to place it back in the trunk, she hesitated. Mr Darcy had given her the gift of the gown, even though he knew she would not approve.

I shall return the favour.

With a mischievous smile, Elizabeth wrapped the flask in the paper that had held her dress. Once she wore the gown tomorrow, there would be no need to conceal it any longer. Her relations and Mr Darcy's friends and relations would have seen it.

While she tied the flask up in the paper with some simple brown string, she recalled the exact wording that Charlotte had advised her to use if any were so curiously uncouth as to ask her how she had acquired the gown.

It was a gift I received while at Rosings. Lady Catherine was so very generous.

Elizabeth smiled. She was not usually given to even harmless subterfuge, but she knew that if anyone possessed the slick gall to press her on the subject, it would be Caroline Bingley. If Miss Bingley asked further questions, Elizabeth would hold a handkerchief to her nose and become temporarily overcome by the fond memory of Lady Catherine de Bourgh.

I despise a lie, but it is no lie that I tell. Both sentences are the truth. Besides, if anyone deserves a taste of her own medicine, it is Caroline Bingley. Jane's two letters both gone missing in the mail, hmmph. I cannot believe she told that fib straight to Jane's face.

Elizabeth at last felt more equal to anything the next day would bring. With a slightly calmer heart and mind, she prepared for bed and extinguished the candle. She still refused to look squarely at the truth of her feelings and slipped into the blissful slumber of denial.

CHAPTER NINETEEN

The next day, Elizabeth entered the sitting room to meet with Mr and Mrs Gardiner before the carriage arrived to take them to Pemberley. The light pelisse she had on did nothing to conceal the gown beneath it. Her aunt noticed almost immediately. Then her uncle, apparently noting the pause in the flurry of leaving, turned to glance at her as well.

"That is a very pretty gown, Elizabeth. The colour suits you." He continued pulling on his gloves.

"Lizzy," said her observant aunt.

"Yes?" she responded with wide, innocent doe eyes.

"Is that a new gown?"

"Oh, you mean this?"

"Yes, I mean that," Mrs Gardiner responded, looking at Elizabeth from the side of her eyes.

"This? Oh, yes. It was a gift I received while staying near Rosings. Lady Catherine de Bourgh was so very generous."

Mrs Gardiner looked askance at Elizabeth and opened her

mouth to make further enquiries. To Elizabeth's relief, the door opened and the carriage was announced. The three of them went to meet it and travel to Pemberley.

When the three guests entered Pemberley's music room, Mr Darcy rose to greet them. He stopped, frozen in place. His eyes were locked on Elizabeth; she felt his gaze travel down to what she wore.

After a brief, awkward pause, he continued his intrepid voyage forward across the room while the eyes of his sister and other guests watched with keen interest. Except for Mr Hurst, of course, who only ever keenly observed the decanter of any room with the most loving reverence.

Greetings and introductions were made all around the room. Elizabeth had the great satisfaction of seeing another of Mr Wickham's declarations dissolve in its veracity. Miss Darcy was nothing more or less than a lovely, shy, sweet, somewhat awkwardly tall young woman. Elizabeth had no doubt that time and confidence would nudge her into the beauty that she was destined to become.

She sat with the girl on a sofa and entered into conversation very naturally. Other than needing a little more encouragement than usual to speak her mind, everything Miss Darcy said was careful, correct, and intelligent. After several minutes, Miss Darcy noticed the paper-wrapped package that lay in Elizabeth's lap.

"May I take that for you, Miss Bennet? I can place it aside."

"You may indeed take it for me. But if you would not mind acting as a courier, you can deliver it to your brother.

Tell him it is from me. It is an item of his that he left in Kent quite by accident. I am returning it to its proper owner."

"How very kind of you. I shall. At once."

Elizabeth moved to restrain her; she had meant for her to deliver it later, in a more private setting. But Miss Darcy, evidently eager to please, got up and walked to her brother who was conversing with the Gardiners.

Elizabeth saw Miss Darcy speak to her brother in quiet tones and hand the little package to him. Mr Darcy looked over at Elizabeth quizzically and then unwrapped the package. When he saw what was within, his countenance went through a rapid change. First a frown, then his face and eyes lit from a fire within, then to a small upturn of the corners of his mouth, as if he subdued a smile.

He glanced up at Elizabeth, both of them struggling to smooth a smile from their faces. Suddenly, Mr Darcy's expression became much graver when he looked with powerful emotion across the room at her. The fervent ardour of his gaze swept over her, causing all else in the room to fade from her vision until she felt that they two were alone in the world. Her heart soared until a movement caused her to drop her gaze in a confused wave of embarrassment.

Miss Bingley had risen and undoubtedly taken it upon herself to see what this highly improper delivery of a package from an unmarried woman to an unmarried man could possibly be about. Her face had nothing of humour in it as she said, "What is it that is so amusing, Mr Darcy? May I see? I was unaware that we were expected to bring *gifts.*"

The last word was dripping with so much venom that Miss Bingley could have been speaking of snakes. She stared down at the little metal flask and curled her lip in disapproval. "If we were supposed to bring gifts, as indiscreet as that would be, I imagine mine would have been much finer," Miss Bingley said with a studied tinkle of laughter.

Mr Darcy stood, obviously offended by the multiple implied slights to Elizabeth's honour. "It is not a gift at all. I found this while walking in the woods around Rosings. It was misplaced during my injuries and the fire. Obviously, Miss Bennet found it and very kindly returned it. Sometimes, Miss Bingley, in order to be kind, to do the correct thing, the rules of propriety may be bent a little. It speaks of a greatness of spirit, not an inadequate understanding of what is right and wrong."

Mr Darcy looked at Elizabeth intently.

"But," Miss Bingley countered, unwilling to leave the field of battle so early in the evening, "if all you required was a flask, I am sure I could have directed you to the very best shops in London. A much finer replacement could have been easily acquired. *I* could have been of great assistance to you in that. Indeed, this thing looks hardly fit to be used by your stableboy!"

Miss Bingley laughed at the ridiculousness of the little metal thing that Mr Darcy cradled in his hand. She glanced around the room to see if anyone else found humour in the situation. Other than an uncertain titter from Mrs Hurst, everyone else in the room was silent.

"It is not the monetary value of the thing that interests me in the least, Miss Bingley," Mr Darcy responded. "It has very fond memories attached to it. And therefore, despite its ragged condition, it will always be a most beloved possession. Indeed, I consider it priceless."

He crossed the room to Elizabeth and bowed formally. "I thank you, Miss Bennet, for the return of my flask. I am in your debt," he said quietly.

Elizabeth could not resist rolling her eyes slightly, as no one else in the room could see her with Mr Darcy standing before her. "Let us not talk of debts, sir. There are no debts between friends, I think. Do you not agree?"

Before she could think better of it, with a blush, she held out her hand. Mr Darcy took it and they shook on the resolution. Elizabeth's breath hitched when she looked up into his eyes. There was a burning intensity there that startled her.

She withdrew her hand hastily, before anyone could see. Mr Darcy dropped his gaze down for the briefest of seconds to indicate the green gown that she wore.

"You look very fine this evening, Miss Bennet. Summer travelling has given you a glow of health. That and your sense of fashion are very becoming."

Elizabeth looked to the side, uncertain how to answer.

At that moment, Miss Darcy joined them, looking eagerly from one to the other. "Miss Bennet, would you do us the honour of playing some music for us? My brother said you have a delightful style that is pleasant to hear."

Elizabeth could not help but look at Mr Darcy quizzically. She repressed a smile and said, "I shall, thank you, Miss Darcy. You do me a very great honour, and I will attempt to live up to your brother's estimation of my abilities."

She played as well as her limited instruction and sporadic practising allowed her. Everyone seemed quite pleased with her playing that had sparkle and wit to recommend it. Except, of course, for Miss Bingley and Mrs Hurst, who did the bare minimum of applause.

Next, Elizabeth insisted that Miss Darcy perform. The young woman was hesitant at first, but after some encouragement, she sat and began a sonata. Elizabeth moved towards Mr Darcy, determined to sit beside him. Miss Bingley was ready to intercept.

"Miss Bennet. I do not believe I have ever seen you in that particular gown. It is somewhat out of character from your usual wardrobe."

Elizabeth seethed at the woman's thinly veiled insults. Having so many sisters, she was accustomed to holding her own in conversation against slights and jealousies. But even Elizabeth was beginning to lose her patience for such a tactic. She inhaled to cool her rising temper.

"It was a gift I received while I was at Rosings. Lady Catherine was so very generous."

Miss Bingley stood, silenced for a moment while she processed this unusual bit of intelligence.

"But, who exactly did you—" she began.

Elizabeth withdrew her handkerchief, pressed it to her nose, and blinked rapidly. "Excuse me." She retreated to the window and looked out over the lake, hoping Miss Bingley would not follow. But the lady, perhaps chastened by Elizabeth's performance, did not press her further.

As she pulled away in the carriage with her aunt and uncle later that evening, Elizabeth looked back at Pemberley. It was a completely different creature at night with the bright, rising moon silhouetting it from behind. The building, which blended so well into the surrounding landscape in the day, took on the appearance of a hulking, protective dragon at night. Several torches on either side of the doorway illuminated the figure of Mr Darcy. He stood there as they drove away. Only the rising of a small hill cutting off her view of him caused her to turn back around. Her aunt looked at her meaningfully, but said nothing. Elizabeth felt a real pain in her chest at the separation as she gazed at the dark woods on either side of the carriage. Her brow furrowed at the thought of leaving Derbyshire soon. She regretted that she would not be spending more time with the Darcys—especially Mr Darcy.

That evening, Elizabeth tossed and turned in her bed, trying desperately to find some comfort. But repose was elusive. The events of the evening had her mind spinning. Just when she would settle into a light doze, an image of Caroline Bingley looking down her nose at Elizabeth's gown arose. With raised eyebrows, Miss Bingley would turn to Mrs Hurst and whisper sharply. That would cause Elizabeth to jump suddenly and awaken fully. Then the warm remembrance of Mr Darcy, looking up at her with the metal flask in his hand, would flood through her. She would begin to doze again, feeling warm and unusually happy, only to have the image of Caroline Bingley reappear. It was very late by the time sleep finally overtook Elizabeth for good.

CHAPTER TWENTY

The next morning, as Elizabeth and the Gardiners were just about to set off on a walk, the post arrived with three letters for Elizabeth. Her aunt and uncle decided to continue with their outing to leave her time to read her correspondences in private.

The first letter of the three was from Jane. Elizabeth saw it had been misdirected due to Jane's writing being hurried. Without pausing to inspect the other two letters, Elizabeth sat and opened it. Jane, usually a very faithful letter writer, had been remiss in her duties of late. This caused Elizabeth a little concern for her dear sister, and the letter would soothe away any anxieties, she was sure.

My dear Elizabeth,

Time is not a luxury that I am in possession of these days, so I apologise for not writing sooner. Mama is so very demanding over every detail of the wedding that she is constantly calling out my name to attend her. This would not be so difficult a thing to bear, but the addition of our cousins to the house has made things more chaotic than it would usually be. Fortunately, the children have their highly competent nurse to attend to them. Also, Kitty has been so very obliging in helping to keep an eye on the dears and inventing new diversions for them. I am quite exhausted by the time night falls. But please, Lizzy, do not take this as any sort of reprimand for your travels. I am so very happy for you. These little trifles are of the happiest sort. Preparing for my marriage and looking after our cousins are activities that leave me in a very glad state of weariness every night.

I have enjoyed your letters very much and am so glad to hear of the county of Derbyshire. Will you stop in at Pemberley? Charles tells me how very beautiful it is and well worth seeing. But perhaps you will feel it is not an entirely comfortable outing. If Mr Darcy is not there, you could visit with no feeling of apprehension. I know you are not always at ease in the company of Mr Darcy.

Elizabeth glanced heavenward with a laugh. If only Jane knew.

Mr Bingley informs me that Mr Darcy plans to be at the wedding, so it may be well that you see him prior to that event. I really do believe that, in many ways, his nature may have been misunderstood by us.

Dear Lizzy, my eyelids droop as I write this. The only quiet time for me is just before bed, and I think that it is becoming too late for me to make proper sense of anything that I have to tell.

Be assured that we are all well and I look forward to a snug tête-à-tête with you upon your return.

Your loving sister,

Jane

Elizabeth folded the letter with a smile. Jane was bearing

the ecstasies of their mother better than she would be able. Perhaps the Gardiner children were providing a nice diversion for both Jane and Mrs Bennet.

Elizabeth picked up the next letter, seeing that it was from Charlotte and had originated in Kent. She read through it fairly rapidly. It contained no bad news, only a thoroughly well-ordered account of her friend's move to Rosings Cottage and all that it entailed. Indeed Charlotte was proving to be quite useful in helping Colonel Fitzwilliam to organise the rebuilding of Rosings. It seemed he was growing dependent on Charlotte's taste and judgment for the renovation of such a grand estate and had rented a small house nearby in order to devote his time and energy fully to the project.

At the close of the letter, Elizabeth had the very great satisfaction of imagining that more than just Charlotte's taste and sense brought the colonel to Rosings Cottage for frequent consultations. Elizabeth hoped she could visit Kent again to attend a wedding in the not-too-distant future.

Finally, Elizabeth picked up the third letter. The handwriting was entirely unfamiliar; although it was postmarked from Brighton, the handwriting did not belong to Lydia. Elizabeth assumed it must be from Colonel Forster's wife. Curiosity was swept aside by concern for Lydia. If something untoward had occurred, she would have received news of that sort from her family in Hertfordshire, would she not? Her confidence in Lydia's good sense was so low that it was with a skip of her heart that she tore open the last letter.

Miss Elizabeth Bennet,

I hope this letter finds you well. I am writing to you to convey that I have come into some information about your recent past that I am sure you would wish not to be known to the general public. It was related to me by the most reliable of possible sources. But you may rely on my honour, my dear lady, that I have made very clear to the source that it must never go any farther. However, I must point out to your generous nature that the trials and difficulties of keeping such information quiet can be very costly to my finances. I feel compelled to relate to you that it will become increasingly more difficult for me to remain abreast of the burden of work that silence on this subject will require.

The one sure way to ensure that nothing of this terrible incident is known is to provide me with the means to sustain the silence that I am ensuring. The means, being financial in nature, would amount to about 10,000 pounds. With your connexions in trade and knowing how particularly intimately you are acquainted with certain people in Derbyshire, I am sure this sum is but a trifle to your generous heart. Indeed, it is almost insulting to ask for so little, I blush at it. But as you know, my misfortunes at the hands of those same acquaintances have been grave indeed, so I must be reduced to the service of which I speak. I am happy to keep your past well concealed. It would be my pleasure to aid you. You may think of me as your knight in shining armour, prepared to defend your reputation from the slightest hint of ignominy.

I shall be in Derbyshire on July 20. There is a spot known as Clements Knoll just outside of Lambton. If you would do me the honour of waiting upon me there at 11 o'clock in the morning with the requested just compensation, I shall be very grateful.

Your faithful servant,

George Wickham

Elizabeth was dumbfounded. She read through the letter again to make absolutely certain she understood the veiled threats being made to her. Every word on the paper was dripping in such false propriety and backhanded compliments that she could barely comprehend them. It was impossible.

But no, it was entirely possible. Her wretched little sister, Lydia, had indeed been eavesdropping outside the door the evening she spoke to Jane of her adventures in Kent. In some moment of weakness gained by flattery and flirting, Wickham had cajoled the information out of Lydia. *Goodness only knows how much more acquainted those two have become during their time in Brighton. Stupid girl! To risk so much to gain the favour of such a man!* Her entire family would now suffer from Lydia's lack of foresight and Elizabeth's actions in Kent. Would this end Jane's future with Mr Bingley? He had been swayed by his sisters in the past. Would he allow himself to be guided by them again in the face of such a scandal?

Ten thousand pounds! It was such an enormous sum, there was no way in heaven or on earth that her family could even begin to assemble it! Even with some help from Mr Gardiner, it would be an impossibility. And what assurances could possibly be valid from such a man as Wickham that he would not attempt to blackmail them again in the future? He would surely run through the money and come back again and again till her entire family was destitute.

What had begun as a day to anticipate, full of walks and conversation and perhaps a call from the party at Pemberley, had devolved into a grim nightmare of a future that was impossibly dim. Elizabeth looked at the three letters on the table before her. Each so different. To imagine that one slip of paper, nothing in itself, held the power to utterly wreck the happiness of so many for years to come—it was more than Elizabeth could bear. She placed her face in her hands and let tears of frustration slip through her fingers.

A knock at the door caused her to jump up and face the

fireplace to hide her streaks of tears. The maid announced Mr Darcy. He entered and the maid left.

"Good morning, Miss Bennet. It seems you are alone this morning. Your aunt and uncle are well, I hope?"

She could not turn. Speech failed her. Mr Darcy shifted uncomfortably behind her.

"If I am intruding on your privacy, please forgive me."

Elizabeth was frozen in place under the weight of that letter. If she moved, she would collapse. If she opened her mouth, she would sob. There was nothing to do but focus on the clay vase upon the mantel and hope that Mr Darcy would leave.

Instead, Elizabeth felt his hand on her shoulder a moment later. She tensed but said nothing, even as he moved forward and could see her face. The tears still hung off the edge of her chin, suspended witnesses to the depths of her sorrows.

"Good God! Miss Bennet! Elizabeth, is something the matter? Are you unwell? Shall I call the maid or a doctor?"

Elizabeth just shook her head. Through her teary eyes, she saw Mr Darcy glanced behind them at the letters that were scattered upon the table.

"Was there some disturbing news in one of these letters?"

Elizabeth could only nod. With that meagre acknowledgement, her resolution failed her. She turned to Mr Darcy and fell into his embrace. Sobs wrung out of her as she rested her head upon his shoulder. He held her firmly, and finally Elizabeth allowed herself to be guided to a chair.

Mr Darcy knelt before her and held her hand. "May I look at the letter?"

Elizabeth just nodded again, still not trusting herself to

speak after so recently regaining a small portion of her self-control.

Mr Darcy turned from her and scanned through the first two very rapidly. The last, the most dreadful one, stayed in his hand for several minutes. The look of deep resentment that spread across his face as he read and re-read that missive was profound. A storm formed in his eyes that would have given pause to the bravest of men.

He roughly ran his hand through his carefully combed locks of black hair, a fierce frown making him look severe. Elizabeth sat in the chair, feeling suddenly chilled and weak. Mr Darcy opened his mouth to say something, but then shut it again quickly. Another moment of silence passed.

"You have long been desiring my absence," he said suddenly. "I have some urgent business that I need to attend to. Goodbye, Miss Bennet. Please convey my regards to Mr and Mrs Gardiner."

Elizabeth hardly heard as a fresh wave of tears washed her face. What gentleman would possibly condescend to open himself up further to dealings with a man like George Wickham? And to involve themselves in a family such as hers that would happily spread such secrets open to the world? *Secrets that could damage his reputation as well as mine. He must want to distance himself from anyone with the last name of Bennet.* She was disappointed in Mr Darcy's silence. But what had she expected? A third marriage proposal from a man such as he? That would be an impossibility.

Perhaps Lydia is not the only stupid sister in my family.

Elizabeth sank farther into the chair by the fireplace and hung her head in her hands. With a fresh wave of shock running through her, Elizabeth looked up at the letters on the table. *Did he read through Jane's letter before Wickham's? Did*

Mr Darcy see Jane's mention of my feelings towards himself? He must believe her to still dislike him, though that was not in her heart at all anymore.

With a new worry to pile on the mountain that pressed down on her, Elizabeth could stand it no longer. She took up all three letters, rose up, and ran into her bedchamber. The door was shut to the world, and Elizabeth was alone, free to read through the letters and let regret dwell upon her miseries.

When her relations returned from their walk, Elizabeth could only say that she was feeling unwell and wished to be alone. They had heard from the parlour maid that Mr Darcy had paid her a visit and were concerned that she was ailing. Through the closed door, Elizabeth insisted that the visit from Mr Darcy was perfectly ordinary and that a sudden, intense headache made her unequal to any company.

"Truly, I assure you, it is nothing but a headache that will pass by tomorrow. My recovery will be more rapid in silence."

Reluctantly, her aunt and uncle consented. Elizabeth spent the rest of the day in isolation, trying to conceive of what she should do next. To bring the Gardiners into the knowledge of the letter from Wickham would require her to explain some of what she had kept hidden from them that had happened in Kent. The thought of more and more people knowing what had occurred, especially when they had not been there to see the French soldiers on English soil with their own eyes, or to see the blood pouring from Mr Darcy's wounds, made Elizabeth ache with embarrassment at their likely reactions and comments.

I wish I had the power to run away to a new life. To escape this tangle! Mr Darcy will surely want nothing to do with me now. I can only pray Jane will escape this entire faire fiasco *unscathed. I hope my actions in Kent will not ruin her happy marriage.*

It was a dismal thing indeed to spend the rest of the day meditating that her actions, no matter how justified and brave, would be looked at as scandalous by many in society. Elizabeth tried to recall one moment that she would have chosen differently. If she could go back in time and alter one of her actions, would she? She examined each decision carefully, turning it over in her mind and scrutinising it as though it were a multifaceted gem and she was trying to discover a flaw. Each time, with each moment, the answer was always no. There was nothing she would have changed. She could look back with pride on how she conducted herself at each moment of consequence. *If I had done anything different, Mr Darcy may not be alive today.* That thought made her very sad indeed.

It was a restless night of semi-sleep that awaited Elizabeth. Somewhere, in the absolute darkness of the middle of the night, she decided that she would go and meet Mr Wickham. She would explain she had nothing to give him. Perhaps she could speak to the good in his nature. Perhaps he could be brought to feel some semblance of compassion. Jane said that there was a chance he was attempting to do good in his life now. Elizabeth doubted that gravely, but she had to hope. It was all that she had left.

CHAPTER TWENTY-ONE

The next day passed with little of note happening. Elizabeth was pale and distracted, and her aunt and uncle became progressively more worried about her health. Elizabeth continually wondered whether to take them into her confidence or not. Mr Gardiner was doing well in his business, but the amount of money that Wickham desired for his silence was no small sum. It could be the Gardiners' undoing. To ask him to make such a sacrifice for a niece he was fond of was something that Elizabeth could not even begin to entertain. She had spent enough evenings in her father's library, helping him to arrange the books and finances, something neither of them were especially adept at, to know that there was no possibility of the Bennets paying out such a sum.

Elizabeth suspected the Gardiners were eager to ask her questions; she had overheard them wondering why they had heard nothing from Pemberley since their dinner two nights earlier. If they privately discussed what was clearly a complicated history between herself and Mr Darcy, they made no sign of it to her.

She hoped, rather desperately, to hear something from Mr Darcy. But as the day led into night with no indication from him as to what his thoughts were, Elizabeth became increasingly morose that tomorrow was to be borne by her alone. She was determined to meet with Wickham and attempt to reason him into doing the honourable thing by her. Through words, pleading, and recollections of their pleasant conversations, there was a chance that the man could be made to understand how much pain he was causing. It was her only chance. Elizabeth knew her powers of persuasion were formidable, but would they be effective upon one such as Wickham with such low morals?

I can only hope my appeal to his good nature that must be buried deep in his soul will carry the day. If that does not succeed, I will be forced to confide absolutely everything to my family and pray that something can be arranged with this scoundrel of a man.

The next morning, Elizabeth again begged off accompanying her aunt and uncle to their social engagements.

"Lizzy, I believe we should cut our trip short." Mrs Gardiner pressed her hand to Elizabeth's forehead to check for a fever. "What could I say to your mother if you became gravely ill during our trip and I did nothing to return you home early? My conscience will not allow me to continue in this way."

Her uncle agreed quickly. "We shall prepare to return you to Hertfordshire unless you begin to feel better. You have looked awfully peaked this last day or so. Are you certain that your digestion gives you no discomfort?"

"I shall be fine, I am sure. I need only to have another day of rest. Please, do not allow my silly headache to delay you on your morning calls. I would not wish to be the cause of cutting this trip short. Especially on your account, Aunt! I have seen how very much returning to your home village has meant to you."

Elizabeth knew her aunt was unconvinced, and it vexed her exceedingly to withhold the truth from them. But until she could have a word with Wickham, so that she could be certain she had no recourse but to negotiate with him and to help him recall his better self, she would not include others in her troubles. If she could look into the man's eyes and truly see that there was no hope of an honourable solution with him, then she would surrender herself to the guidance of her family.

Once the Gardiners were well out of sight of the inn, Elizabeth sat down to write them a note explaining whom she was to meet and where. She had little fear of Wickham attempting to take advantage of her. If he was indeed as mercenary as he seemed, to press himself on Elizabeth might jeopardise any chance of gaining money from her. Highly improper as it might be for her to meet alone with such a man, she was desperate to try to change his mind.

I am so compromised already, what can this do to add to the list of my indiscretions?

She left the note sealed on the table with their names on it. Elizabeth returned to her room to gather her meagre funds and was preparing to leave for Clements Knoll when the parlour maid entered and announced the arrival of Miss Georgiana Darcy. Elizabeth glanced out of the window and saw that one of the Darcy carriages was indeed stopped before the inn. Miss Darcy entered, looking pale and concerned.

"Miss Darcy. I was just about to step out for a walk. Are you well?"

"I am well, but my brother—I know not—"

Mr Darcy? Despite her need to leave, a new concern rose up in her. She offered the young woman a seat. "Would you care for a cup of tea? Or a glass of wine?"

Miss Darcy demurred and wrung her hands together. "I am concerned over my brother. Has he been to see you today?"

Elizabeth bit her lip and looked down at her hands, feeling a flare of melancholy that Mr Darcy had not shown the least interest in how she was to handle this wretched situation. He was the one person who could have condoled with her. Company in this misery would have eased her heart a little, at least.

"No, Mr Darcy has not been here to call upon us today or yesterday. Were you expecting him to call here? Were you to meet him here?"

"No! He left earlier this morning, with the steward of our estate, Mr Taylor. I do not know where he went, but, by accident, I heard them discussing a man. George Wickham."

Miss Darcy had whispered the name out as one speaks of a ghost that terrifies children and makes closets into haunted horrors. Elizabeth's brows contracted as she reached a hand out to touch the girl lightly on the arm.

"I know they are not on friendly terms, but surely you do not fear Mr Wickham harming you or your brother, do you?"

"I do not fear him, Miss Bennet, but…" she said, not terribly convincingly. She paused and looked about the room, battling within herself over something. "I do fear what Fitzwilliam may do to him. You see, last summer, I was led to believe—but no, I also have some claim in this. I decided that I was in love with Wickham and was convinced to elope with him. My brother found it out at the last moment when I was at Ramsgate. I was saved from what would have been an unhappy marriage."

Elizabeth had suspected that the young woman saved from Wickham had been somehow intimately connected to Mr Darcy, but she had not suspected it to be his sister! With a deepening concern, Elizabeth thought back to Miss King in Hertfordshire whom Wickham had pursued. It seemed to her that Mr Wickham took great interest in very young, very vulnerable, very wealthy young women. A flash of concern for Lydia crossed her mind. Perhaps wealth was not always a prerequisite for Wickham.

Then it struck her. Mr Darcy had read the letter from Wickham to herself. She had foolishly thought that he had fled to save himself from the taint of her sullied reputation. It had all been such a brutal shock that she had not thought clearly at the time. And, of course, Mr Darcy's typically stoic response left her in doubt as to his true feelings. How could she believe that he would be capable of abandoning her at that moment? Suddenly, it all became clear.

"Miss Darcy, you have no reason to be ashamed. You were acting in good faith and under the belief that he loved you. Anyone who is acquainted with your disposition would understand. Wickham is a despicable blackguard, but hand-some and persuasive. It is no wonder that he excels in deceiving young women."

"But why was Fitzwilliam discussing him with our stew-ard? And when I asked him where he was going this morning, he would not tell me! I am sorry to bring this to you, Miss Bennet, but I am frightened. He seemed so angry, so determined. I have rarely seen him like that."

Elizabeth, aware of the passing time, did not want to be late in meeting with Mr Wickham. But she also did not wish to abandon Miss Darcy at a time when the girl was so fragile.

Miss Darcy twisted her handkerchief in her fingers, looking ill at ease.

"Is there something else that troubles you?"

The girl looked around hesitantly, as if searching for the courage to do some monumental thing. Elizabeth remained silent as she watched her worriedly.

"I must confess, Miss Bennet, that my brother asked me to call upon you this morning. Not that I would not have gladly done so anyway. I quite enjoyed our talk the other evening."

Elizabeth smiled; Miss Darcy managed a weak one in return. "I too enjoyed our time together. Your brother was perhaps trying to keep both you and I out of harm's way." Her smile disappeared as she sat back, worried. "But now I am concerned as to what your brother may do to Mr Wickham. Or what Wickham may do to him."

"What can you mean?" Miss Darcy appeared nearly hysterical. "Is Wickham here? In Lambton?"

"I do not know where Wickham is, but he is staying nearby."

"Oh, I fear for my brother!"

At that moment, Elizabeth heard the laughter of her aunt and uncle upon the stairs, returning from their morning calls. They must have been brief in them so that they could return to check on her welfare.

"Miss Darcy, promise me you will stay here until either I or your brother returns."

"What do you propose to do?"

"Do not worry about me. I must hear you promise, though, that you will stay here with my aunt and uncle."

"Yes, I promise."

Elizabeth grabbed the letter on the table and gave it to Georgiana. "If neither your brother nor I are back within the hour, give this to my aunt and uncle. But, truly, all shall be well," she added, attempting to convey a resolution and confidence that she did not feel.

She gave the girl a quick hug, grabbed her shawl and bonnet, and ran through the door of the sitting room and past Mr and Mrs Gardiner as they ascended the stairs.

"Lizzy! What in Heaven's name?"

"Pardon me, please! Miss Darcy is upstairs and needs attending to. I must run. I recalled a previous engagement, so please keep her here until either I or Mr Darcy returns!"

Elizabeth bounded out the front door of the inn and took off down the street at a rapid pace towards Clements Knoll. She had gleaned the directions the night before from the chambermaid, assuring the girl that she and the Gardiners were avid walkers.

She went down the farm lane, across the field, and into the forest of silver birch that followed the hill upwards through some rocks and boulders. The forest turned into thick, expansive oaks that created a shady, welcome canopy, but by this time, even the hale Elizabeth was panting hard. She broke through the grove into a long, grass-covered hill. Here was the knoll she sought, but where was Wickham?

Off to her left, a horse she recognised was tied to a tree with another, unfamiliar horse. That one horse she knew well enough. Aesop. The other must belong to the steward, Mr Taylor.

She ran through the tall grass feeling that her plunging heart would burst with exertion and panic. To move more quickly, she hitched the hem of her dress up to her knees. Her bonnet had already ripped off her head from her dash and trailed down her back. Locks of her hair were flying loose as she determinedly forged ahead with gasping breaths.

Under the shade of several trees at the top of the knoll, she could see the men standing in a small circle. Even from this distance, Elizabeth could recognise Mr Darcy and Mr Wickham and feel the anger and hostility that emanated between them.

"Wait!" she cried. "Please!"

All four men turned and looked at her. She could see a flat wooden box between them, being held by one of the other men. A box that she was certain contained a set of duelling pistols. She still had time to stop them.

"Darcy!"

He stepped towards her, and without a care of what the others thought, she threw her arms around his neck and hugged him so tightly that he almost tumbled backwards. Darcy returned her embrace and buried his nose in her tangle of curls. He inhaled deeply.

"Elizabeth," he whispered into her ear.

"You cannot duel Wickham! Please."

"Georgiana was supposed to occupy you for a while," he murmured.

"If you thought I would not see through that, you have much to learn about me!"

He smiled down at her, a look of relief and happiness spread across his face, before reaching a hand to brush her riotous curls off her cheek and forehead. "I look forward to that more than you can possibly know. But I must do this."

With a pained look, Darcy pulled away and held her at arm's length. "You should not be here. It is not safe. I do not want you anywhere near Wickham."

"I am not leaving, and you will not force me to abandon you at this moment. I think I have more than proved that, in a pinch, I can take care of myself. If you insist on seeing this through, I will be with you."

Elizabeth took both his hands in hers and brought them to her lips. Darcy took a deep breath, then pulled back his hands and turned to Wickham.

Wickham wore a cruel smile. "Miss Bennet, I am sorry that we could not arrange matters privately. I am shocked that you chose to involve this man after you knew of his particular mistreatment of me."

"Indeed, sir, I completely agree with you. He did not treat you correctly. He showed mercy and compassion when you deserved no such consideration. I know how well you were compensated. I know how you choose to treat those who have extended to you kindness and favour. I know how you squandered it. I am sorry that it cannot be me to face you on the field of honour, sir."

Such a hard speech led Wickham to blink and shift his gaze down in what Elizabeth hoped was shame. But in another instant, he had tossed his head up and the rakish smile had returned. Both Wickham and Darcy turned to the open box with the pistols.

"Since the pistols are mine," Darcy said, "you may have the first choice. They have been loaded."

Wickham's eyes shifted from one pistol to the other and back. Elizabeth could only imagine that he guessed at duplicity and deceit in everything, since that was how he himself would behave. Real nervousness was now showing in Wickham's face. He blinked rapidly and grabbed the pistol nearest to Darcy out of the box. Darcy's face was unreadable with no indication of either relief or fear.

"Wait, I shall take the other!" Wickham exclaimed, replacing his first for the one he had left behind. He again raised his eyes to stare at Darcy before something of childish frustration erupted into Wickham's countenance.

Darcy removed the remaining pistol, and the two men stood back-to-back. They walked away from each other, pacing out to ten. Elizabeth felt faint with fear, but she stood tall and emotionless. If Darcy could face this horrible man with such equanimity, she would do nothing to cause him anxiety. No hysterics or worry could be detected on her mask of calm.

At the pace of nine, however, Wickham spun and raised his gun to Darcy's retreating back.

"Darcy!" Elizabeth screamed.

Darcy spun, eyes wide, and began to aim his pistol, but too late.

Click!

There was no explosion from Wickham's gun. A misfire. The disbelief on his face quickly dissolved into sheer panic. He looked up to see he was in the sights of Darcy's aim. Wickham collapsed to his knees and proceeded to beg for mercy. Using every word and tactic he could devise, Wickham clasped his hands together before his chest in a torrent of pleas to recall how they grew up together, how he would be a better person, how magnanimous Darcy was. It was when Wickham dared to bring up the spectre of the late Mr Darcy that Darcy lost all patience.

"Do not dare to bring the memory of *my father* into your pathetic ramblings," he growled.

For a moment, Elizabeth could see a grave conflict battling in Darcy's soul. She squeezed her eyes shut and silently pleaded with him to show mercy, however unearned, to Wickham—truly a sorry excuse for a man.

A shot exploded. Elizabeth's eyes flew open. Darcy was holding the smoking gun with its barrel pointed towards the ground. His second, Mr Taylor, declared, "Deloping, an intentional miss by Mr Darcy. He extends you forgiveness, Wickham. Although you hardly deserve it. A thoroughly cowardly show of it, man. You would have been tried and hanged for murder if you had shot him in the back at nine paces."

Elizabeth looked wide-eyed at Darcy, who turned to look her in the eye. Although shaking, she felt frozen to the ground from the sheer terror of the past few minutes. Darcy turned back to Wickham.

"There now, old man. I have something terribly compromising to tell of you. Who could live down trying to shoot a fellow in the back at nine paces during a duel? I will have no compunction about letting everyone you ever encounter know of your behaviour here today. After that, what are the chances anyone will believe a slander you spread of me or anyone else?"

Even Wickham's second, another younger officer from his militia, looked upon Wickham with thinly veiled disgust. It seemed that Darcy might not even have to spread the story himself. Mr Taylor walked over to Wickham, still on the ground from his pleading for his life, and took the duelling pistol to put back in the wooden case.

Wickham was helped to his feet by his fellow officer. For a moment, Elizabeth feared that he would attack Darcy again, for he raged and grabbed about his person as if for a weapon. His second gripped his arm and whispered angrily into Wickham's face. No doubt the prospect of being a party to the murder of one of the richest men in England gave even that young officer pause. Wickham slumped, and they walked away in the direction opposite of Lambton.

"Mr Taylor, thank you for being my second here today." Darcy extended his hand and the two men shook. "I shall escort Miss Bennet back to Lambton. Will you please take Aesop with you back to Pemberley?"

"Of course, sir." He gave Elizabeth a slight bow and walked back towards where their horses were tied.

"Miss Bennet." Darcy held out his arm to her.

With a grateful smile, Elizabeth wove her hand through his arm, and they began to travel down the hill and back towards Lambton.

CHAPTER TWENTY-TWO

"Were you truly going to meet Wickham here by yourself?" Darcy asked as they entered the oak woods.

Now that she was not in a mad rush of panicked running, Elizabeth looked around at the beautiful grove. "You met him with your own plan of combat," she responded. "I was prepared to meet him with mine as well."

"And your weapon of choice? I see that you carry neither pistols nor sword. How did you think you were going to best Wickham?"

Elizabeth could not be sure, but she thought that she detected a mild lilt of teasing in Darcy's voice that she had never heard before. She looked up at his face, but his gaze was forward and his mood hard to read.

"How can you be certain, sir, that I have not stashed ten thousand pounds in the lining of my bonnet?"

With a smile, Darcy glanced at the bonnet dangling down Elizabeth's back, forgotten during her travels. "I believe that you are capable of anything, Miss Bennet. Nothing would surprise me."

"I think I know you well enough, Mr Darcy, to take that as a compliment. Am I correct?"

"Take it in any manner you see fit. It is the truth."

Elizabeth laughed aloud at this bold assessment of her character. Darcy looked down at her with a smile of admiration.

"I do not think I ever understood your clever wit, Mr Darcy, until very recently. It is so subtle that it has a way of sneaking past." She pressed his arm to ensure he understood her praises. "As to your query, I planned on appealing to that morsel of goodness that must lurk deep in Mr Wickham somewhere. I had no physical weapon, but I was planning on using the weapon of my mind to rationalise him into realising his better nature."

Darcy let out a snort of disbelief. "Although I hold your intelligence in the highest possible regard, I think that would be past even *your* prodigious abilities, Miss Bennet. It certainly has been past my abilities for these last ten years."

"Well, we shall never know since you dashed my chance away from me. Besides, it was my only choice."

"Not your only choice." Darcy stopped and turned to face her. Elizabeth had not even noticed that they now stood among the silver birches. The dappled sunlight that reached through the slim canopy of leaves danced on Darcy's face as he looked into her eyes.

"You could have asked me. I would have done anything for you. Anything."

"But so much money? And to such a man who has hurt you so many times already?"

"Remember, Miss Bennet, there are no debts between friends. You made me shake hands on it."

Elizabeth blushed and dropped her gaze down. Darcy was standing so near, her heart felt ready to beat out of her chest from his closeness. She turned and, as they continued their walk back, the silence between them was electric. The copse of trees ahead was thinning, and they were nearing the winding farm road that led back towards Lambton. Time was slipping away, and these precious moments alone with Darcy were coming to an end. She inhaled deeply and summoned every ounce of her courage.

He has already seen me behave so improperly, so frequently, what can one more instance matter? I must settle this, once and for all.

Elizabeth placed herself directly in front of Darcy. He stopped, startled. His open countenance gazed at her in puzzled wonder.

"Mr Darcy, I realise how completely ridiculous this sounds. I wish you to know that, if you wanted to, if you were still interested—" Elizabeth squeezed her eyes shut, too embarrassed to see his face as she spoke. "—if you wanted to propose to me, again, things may be different."

She kept her eyes shut, almost in physical pain at the ludicrous statement she had just made. The only thing she could hear was the dry rustling of the leaves around them. Finally, she cracked her eyes open. As soon as she did, Darcy gripped both of her hands in his and pulled her against his chest.

"Elizabeth, will you marry me?"

Elizabeth had pressed her lips so rapidly to his that the last word was possibly left unsaid. In her enthusiasm to give him an unequivocally positive response, she leant so firmly against Darcy that the two floundered till his back was against the trunk of one of the slim, stately birches. His hands circled her waist, holding her close. There they stayed for several more minutes, silently working out the details of just who was the happiest about their freshly minted understanding.

Darcy was the one who finally, very reluctantly, pulled his lips away. In a voice a bit thicker than usual, he said, "We should be getting back to Lambton, before my sister and your aunt and uncle send out a search party."

After clearing his throat and straightening his cravat, he reached around Elizabeth and set her bonnet atop her head. He untied the ribbon and retied it very carefully for her as she stared happily at him, her heart warm with this small gesture of concern. When he finished, he tenderly took her face in both his hands and kissed her again.

They walked back towards Lambton in the complete happiness that only two souls so well suited—who have finally understood each other, through so many obstacles, dangers, and misunderstandings—could ever experience.

CHAPTER TWENTY-THREE

I n Lambton, a clearly very worried Mr Gardiner was exiting the front door of the inn, pulling his gloves on. He met Darcy and Elizabeth at the front stoop, visibly relieved beyond measure to see his beloved niece back safely from her unknown adventure. All three returned upstairs.

Georgiana flew to Darcy, expressing enormous gratitude that her brother was safe. Both Elizabeth and Darcy quickly averted the volley of queries with brief, vague answers, once they had the opportunity to speak. Darcy recommended to Georgiana that they should return home and invited the entire party to dinner that evening at Pemberley.

Mr and Mrs Gardiner looked to one another, obviously uncomfortable with not knowing all that had occurred that morning between Elizabeth and Darcy. But when they looked at Elizabeth and surely saw the glow she felt beaming from her face and the slight nod of her head, they agreed to the dinner engagement.

After the Darcys had left, Mrs Gardiner stood before Elizabeth, taking one of her hands, and scrutinised her. "You know that I have full faith in you and your judgment, but I must insist upon a measure of your confidence. I am very uneasy from how ill you were these last few days and now a disappearance this morning with no word as to where you were going? What has happened?"

"Aunt, a girl needs a little privacy to accept a proposal of marriage, do you not think?"

"Lizzy!"

After several hugs and a request for a pot of tea, Elizabeth sat with the Gardiners and explained some of what had happened to her in the last several months. Most of what had happened would only ever be known by herself and Darcy. All of what had happened would only ever be truly known to Elizabeth herself. While telling of the recent encounter with Mr Wickham, she was abused by several admonishments from both of them for not telling them all that was occurring.

"Yes, you are absolutely correct. But how was I to tell you of why I received this letter from Mr Wickham without relating everything else that had occurred in Kent? I beg your pardon for not being more candid, but you see what awful mischief has arisen from relating all to Jane, being overheard by Lydia, then blackmailed by Wickham. No, it was my decision that the fewer who knew of all of our adventures together in the woods of Rosings, the better. Perhaps I should have decided differently, but it is done. Now all that is left is for me to beg for your forgiveness."

After a few more half-hearted sermons on the importance of honesty and transparency with those who bore responsibility for her well-being, all was forgiven in a shower of hugs. Elizabeth, feeling more than a little worn out by the morning's adventures, insisted on retiring to her room for a few moments to freshen up, rest, and write a letter to Jane with the good news of her acceptance of Mr Darcy's proposal.

That evening at Pemberley, Miss Darcy greeted Elizabeth with a warm embrace. She must have been told the news of their engagement, for she positively glowed every time she looked at either her brother or Elizabeth. Obviously, Miss Bingley and Mrs Hurst were still unaware of any developments as there was no change in the level of their cold acknowledgements of Elizabeth. She could only wonder at their future behaviour towards herself and Jane.

Indeed, I must begin to look upon them as sisters, I suppose. Well, I shall survive. I have ample experience with sisters who embarrass or endeavour to make me look bad. It is no great trial.

She glanced over at Darcy, who was speaking with Mr Gardiner. Darcy met her gaze, and his eyes lit up with love. She smiled back at him with so much affection that the corners of his mouth upturned ever so slightly.

No, I shall be able to tolerate two more silly sisters very well indeed. For I also gain another sister, almost equal to Jane, in the bargain.

Elizabeth glanced fondly at Georgiana, who spoke quietly with Mrs Gardiner, delighted by the obvious regard between the two ladies.

After dinner, the ladies retired to the music room. Elizabeth was sure that Darcy would address her uncle to receive at least a nominal approval of their engagement before he could formally ask Mr Bennet. It would be no great feat to find a moment of quiet with Mr Gardiner as Mr Hurst was already showing signs of red cheeks and empty cups.

When the gentlemen joined the ladies, Darcy came straight to her and sat.

"Did you speak with my uncle?"

He nodded. "In the stead of your father, he has wished us joy and blessed our engagement. I shall return to Hertfordshire and stay at Netherfield," he murmured quietly. "I seek your father's permission then. Your uncle seemed to think that, other than you being your father's favourite child whom he has no wish to part with, there should be no objections."

"He will not stand in our way, not once I speak to him about you." Elizabeth looked down with some discomfort. "I am afraid he may still be under the impression that I do not hold you in high esteem."

"Indeed?" Darcy said with a touch of that old haughtiness returning to his countenance. "And why is that?"

Elizabeth's face burned with mortification even as she lifted her chin defiantly. "I had a bad opinion of you based upon our first encounter. At the Meryton assembly. My pride had great difficulty recovering."

"What occurred to wound your pride?"

"I accidentally overheard you tell Mr Bingley, after he was encouraging you to dance with me, that I was tolerable, but not handsome enough to tempt you. And that you had no wish to dance with ladies slighted by other men."

Elizabeth regretted having told him as much as his eyes clouded and his mouth frowned. Darcy seemed not to quite know how to respond to the consequences of his pride laid upon his doorstep. That his flippant disregard for the feelings of others had nearly cost him the woman who captured his heart was almost enough to quell the happiness of the evening. Seeing this change in his expression, she decided to call upon her most abundant resource, her humour.

"So, there, Mr Darcy! You see now where my repulsion of the word 'tolerable' originates! If you had not been so handsome, intelligent, and distinguished that first night we met, I am sure my dignity would not have been half so offended."

She gave him the slightest nudge with her elbow and the warmest of all possible smiles. His face brightened slightly.

"Can you ever forgive my stupidity?" he asked, blunt and raw from regret.

Elizabeth ached with wanting to reach out and clasp his hand and kiss away the regret from his face. But the ever-watchful eyes of Miss Bingley were upon them. She had no doubt already witnessed several warm looks and the little bump of encouragement that Elizabeth had risked.

"There is nothing to forgive. I have not always spoken and acted in a way that I can look back on with satisfaction. And you were only being honest, I think. That is an admirable quality, is it not?"

"But such a disregard for the feelings of others is nothing for which I want to be known," responded Darcy.

"A new resolution, then, similar to the one we agreed about in regards to debts. From this moment forward, we shall forgive each other for past actions and words. No more need ever be said of it. With one stipulation. That you, Mr Darcy, refrain from the use of the word 'tolerable' as much as you are able to in the future. I have a distinct dislike for it."

Again, she held out her hand for a shake. Darcy, smiling at this, took it up immediately and squeezed it as they shook upon it. Embarrassed, Elizabeth withdrew her hand quickly.

Miss Bingley, perhaps seeing and sensing that things were rapidly slipping beyond her grasp, rose from where she sat and approached them.

"Miss Eliza, how has your family been coping with the

tragic loss of the militia that was stationed at Meryton? I hear some are quite heartbroken over the loss of Mr Wickham's company." Miss Bingley tilted her head to one side, in a mockery of mournfulness.

Silence fell on the room. Miss Bingley looked around at her sister, apparently to gain some support at this unexpected reaction. Georgiana stared at her hands in her lap, seemingly too overcome to look up.

"Indeed, you are mistaken," Elizabeth replied, sitting up straight. "It has been no loss for my family. And, after the scare we had in Kent, I do not regret extending hospitality to those men who may very well lay down their lives for the safety of England. It is our duty, I should think. Would you agree, Miss Bingley?"

The lady clearly was not expecting the conversation to turn into a referendum on the strength of her patriotism. Her eyes narrowed as she was obviously working out how to best respond to this unusual assault on her character. It was almost enough to make Elizabeth feel sorry for her while she watched Miss Bingley trying to reclaim what she could of the exchange. If only the lady knew what pain she caused Miss Darcy with the reference to Mr Wickham. But any time Mr Darcy was in the room, the consideration of the feelings of others was none of Miss Bingley's concern.

"I have nothing but the highest regard for those men who, if they must choose a profession, choose the militia. I am sure I meant no slight to them."

"Indeed, I am sure you did not," Elizabeth assured her. "You are well known for your thoughtfulness towards others."

Miss Bingley cast a glance at Darcy, apparently hoping

that some sign from him would help her to gather her resources for another attack.

Poor Miss Bingley. She looks to the absolute last person in the room who would have anything unpleasant to say of me.

"And Mr Darcy," Miss Bingley pressed on, in complete ignorance of the impossibility she was facing in her attempts to prod Darcy into disparaging Elizabeth, "you will have to return to Hertfordshire in the near future for the marriage of my brother. I am sorry that you will have to return to a part of the country that afforded you so little pleasure in the past. I remember comments you made on the sharp contrast between the city and the country."

Elizabeth felt Darcy stiffen at this reference to past rudeness that he may have shared with Miss Bingley. His face had returned to that impassive, unreadable mask that he usually reserved for those he found the most distasteful.

"I did not always look upon Hertfordshire in the most pleasing light. You are correct there."

Miss Bingley glowed with a burst of superiority. Undoubtedly, she felt she had provoked the Darcy of old whom she delighted in.

"But," he continued, "I learnt something in Hertfordshire that has encouraged me to think more deeply on matters." Darcy turned his head to gaze at Elizabeth and said, "Kindness, friendship, honour, intelligence, and beauty can be discovered in the places one thinks they are the least likely to be found." Elizabeth felt the loss of his riveted attention when he turned back to address Miss Bingley once more. "I am very glad to be returning to Hertfordshire. In fact, I shall be travelling there earlier than expected. Once Mrs Annesley, Georgiana's companion, returns from her visit to her parents in another week, I plan on joining

Bingley at Netherfield. I am looking forward to it exceedingly."

Elizabeth smiled warmly at Darcy, delighted to know this piece of information, for she was to leave Derbyshire with the Gardiners within a few days. The possibility of a long separation from him had been the one dark cloud in her thoughts.

Clearly incredulous at the dawning understanding that perhaps Mr Darcy had formed some sort of serious attachment to Miss Elizabeth Bennet, Miss Bingley turned to sit beside her sister. Elizabeth managed not to laugh as she overheard several whispers behind fans while the ladies held a war council about a battle that was already lost.

By the time the evening concluded, Miss Bingley had already retired to tend to a headache. Aside from Mrs Hurst, who was still watching Elizabeth and Darcy with acuity so that she could likely relate every detail to her sister in the morning, and Mr Hurst, who was asleep on one of the sofas, everyone was sorry to see the evening end. Many warm handshakes and proposals for meeting the next day occurred as Elizabeth and the Gardiners were settled into their carriage.

"Well, Elizabeth," Mr Gardiner said as they rode back to the inn, "for what my seal of approval is worth, it has been stamped upon your union most happily. I think that you and Mr Darcy are very well suited to each other and will make a successful marriage. I am quite glad you held out for a marriage of love rather than convenience. I cannot speak for all married couples, but love is the most important pillar to build upon."

He turned to look at his wife sitting beside him, who smiled approvingly back at his statement.

"Yes, Lizzy," Mrs Gardiner added. "Any doubt I had in regards to your feelings or Mr Darcy's has been quite vanquished. Some small-minded people, I daresay there were one or two of them present this very evening, will no doubt spread about that it is a marriage of convenience on your part. Indeed, I myself thought it quite odd that your feelings about Mr Darcy underwent such a rapid change. But I am well convinced of your deep regard for him. And of his regard for you."

Elizabeth dropped her gaze. "After how willing I was to proclaim my dislike of Mr Darcy to any who would listen, it will be an odd thing for people to accept that I truly do love him."

"If people see you staring at Mr Darcy with half the warmth you displayed tonight, there will be no doubt in anyone's mind as to why you have accepted him. Your mother made it very well known that you had already turned down a proposal from Mr Collins on the basis that you had no real regard for him, although it would have secured your finances. They surely cannot now assume that you made a marriage for the sake of money."

Elizabeth beamed her bright smile through the dim light of the carriage. "There is no need for me to marry at all, if Mary is to inherit Longbourn and Jane to marry a very generous man of means. I can honestly say that I accepted Mr Darcy from a sense of love and nothing else."

As she turned her head to look out at the moonlit woods on either side of the carriage, she added, "Of course, it definitely did not *hurt* Mr Darcy's suit that he is master of Pemberley."

She looked slyly at the Gardiners and then broke out into a teasing laugh.

CHAPTER TWENTY-FOUR

The month of August flew by in a whirlwind of preparations and social calls. Now that Elizabeth was back home at Longbourn and Darcy was stationed nearby at Netherfield, they saw each other nearly every day. Her parents never received a full account of all that had occurred in Kent when Elizabeth and Mr Darcy were thrown together by such unusual circumstances. The very thought of relating the full story to her parents mortified her in a way that had not been a consideration with the Gardiners. Somehow, the image of her scandalised mother winking at her and congratulating her on an excellent scheme at catching a rich husband intensely embarrassed Elizabeth. And the thought of her father looking at her over his glasses, not quite believing the severity of the circumstances because in his opinion all women were prone to exaggeration, made her feel frustrated at the very thought of a detailed retelling. So, all they ever knew was that circumstances had thrown them together in Kent, but not to what extent or level of intimacy.

Mrs Bennet was happily overcome by her wealth of good fortune. Two daughters, one marriage ceremony, so many gowns to have made, friends to relate every detail to, smelling salts to be whiffed. She was clearly in heaven. And she was overjoyed that she still had three daughters to marry off, for an experience this exquisite must be repeated many more times. Though, in candid moments, Mrs Bennet declared that the marriage of her younger three daughters could not be nearly so glorious. Such eligible, wealthy bachelors as Mr Bingley and Mr Darcy did not come into this part of the country that often. Or did they?

Mr Bennet was indeed stunned and slightly dismayed at Elizabeth's engagement and tried his best to convince her that she could be in possession of that blissful state of unwed, solitary existence that he himself envied.

"Elizabeth!" Mr Bennet implored after he had given his approval to Mr Darcy. "You have no need to wed! Jane would be happy to accommodate you and will be able to easily afford it. And Longbourn will stay in the family after I am gone from this world, ensuring that you will have a home here if you choose! You know, you were very correct in your opinion that Mary would make an excellent estate manager. This summer, I have taught her all I know, and she has made several improvements of efficiency on the farms that have saved us money. I wish I had started teaching her years ago! We could be much more comfortable with our finances."

Elizabeth smiled. "I saw Mary reading a very thick book on modern soil improvement techniques just the other day. I think Longbourn will do well under her guidance, and that will free you to pursue your reading in more depth."

"And allow time to journey to all the fine houses I shall have to visit to make sure my daughters are being properly treated by their husbands," he added with a smile. "You have not told me *why* you are marrying such a proud, disagreeable man, when you have no need. Mr Darcy is so very rich, to be sure, but will he make you happy? Why did you accept him?"

In all seriousness, Elizabeth looked her father in the eyes. "Because I love him. Mr Darcy is generous, brave, forgiving, and funny, if you listen carefully enough. We have the most interesting discussions. And he listens to what I have to say, he does not dismiss my opinions as many other men do without a thought as to their being correct or incorrect. I am so happy with him, sir, as I have never been in my life."

Mr Bennet shuffled some papers on his desk, cleared his throat, and wiped at his eye. "Then he truly deserves you. And I give you my blessing with all my heart, Lizzy."

Elizabeth was surprised at how well Darcy tolerated the loud civilities of Mrs Bennet. It seemed that nothing could sway him from his happy state with his betrothed. He bore all that the Bennet household had to throw at him with quiet politeness, apparently counting the seconds until he could respectfully ask Elizabeth to go for a solitary walk.

The one person whom Darcy made a real effort to get to know was Mrs Hill. He paid several visits to the kitchen to enquire after her health and bring her a token of his esteem. Everyone else in the Bennet household viewed this unusual friendship with utter astonishment and could not guess as to the meaning of it. It was eventually accepted as an eccentricity of the very wealthy, and none dared to question him about it.

Once, before they were to go on a walk, Elizabeth had been delayed by her mother on some point of flowers or music. When she extricated herself from her mother, Elizabeth heard a laugh coming from the kitchen. She entered and saw that Darcy had stationed himself on a stool at one end of the kitchen table while Hill had her forearms covered in flour from the dough she was kneading. They both quieted upon Elizabeth's appearance. Darcy took his leave of Hill and offered his arm to Elizabeth. They exited the house together and made their way to the overgrown part of the park that had several spots that could not be seen from the house.

"What do you and Hill find so amusing?" Elizabeth queried.

"She was telling me of the time when she came into the kitchen and found you sitting in a puddle of cake batter, licking it out of your hair. Apparently," he continued, beginning to laugh, "your love of cake caused you to tip a bowl of batter over your head in an effort to sneak a taste."

Elizabeth looked at his smiling face, astonished. "I was three or four years old! How dare you laugh at such a silly story about me!"

"Three or four? Why, Hill said that this occurred just last week!"

She could not help but slap Darcy's arm while he continued to chuckle. She was always delighted when his humour showed through, even though that meant he occasionally teased her.

"And how are you two bachelors getting on at Netherfield? I hope there are not too many late nights playing billiards."

"When we cannot be here at Longbourn or you and Jane cannot come to Netherfield, we manage to get by. Bingley and I are both very eager to enter into the married state. It is but another week and we shall be man and wife, Elizabeth."

The thought made him smile, and he pulled Elizabeth behind their favourite tree in the corner of the little walled-off garden. His back against the bark, Darcy embraced her and pressed his lips to hers. There they stayed for quite a while until they heard her mother calling them for tea.

Elizabeth pulled away and looked up into Darcy's eyes. "I have always wondered one thing. Why were you at Tall Oak Hill that day when the wind blew the soldiers in from France?"

Darcy frowned a little. "I may have heard you mention the night before that you intended a long walk there. I was worried that you would be unattended and thought to make sure you were safe."

"I knew it!" Elizabeth laughed. "You did follow me there. I have always suspected. Is that the *only* reason you followed me there that day? To ensure my safety?"

"Yes...I mean, no. When we were in the field where we paused on our way back to Rosings, I was going to propose to you. I had even begun in some earnestness when the balloons appeared in the sky and the chance slipped away."

Elizabeth stared at Darcy, startled. There was no teasing in her voice when she asked, "You were going to propose? At that moment?"

He squeezed her tight to him again, obviously uncomfortable in the remembrance. "I had it very clearly memorised what I was going to say. I was starting to recite my proposal when the balloons appeared."

"Did you make any mention of love in that first proposal that was interrupted?"

Clearing his throat, Darcy drew his brows together pensively, clearly attempting to remember the particulars of his speech. "Well, I think, yes, I think I made mention of how much I loved you during that speech that I never got to complete. I do not recall it entirely, but I must have intended to say that I loved you."

"Because, when you proposed in the field near Hunsford, you neglected to mention love. You only spoke of saving reputations and my embarrassing family."

"Yes, well, obviously I had forgotten some of my original proposal at that point and was muddling through the best I could."

Incredulous and trying desperately to suppress a smile, Elizabeth said, "You mean to tell me *that* was part of your original proposal?"

"Modified, to be sure, but yes."

"So, just to be clear, you attempted to propose once after Tall Oak Hill. Then you *did* propose while feverish in the shepherds' hut, mentioning love several times, which I dismissed as rantings of false delusions. You proposed again outside Hunsford in a modified version of your original proposal. And then for a final time when I asked you to propose to me?"

"When you put it that way, I sound a bit ridiculous," Darcy murmured, frowning.

Elizabeth bit her lip, her heart full to bursting at Darcy looking so sheepish. She placed her hands on the sides of his face and raised his dropped gaze to meet her sincere one.

"Thank goodness you are such a stubborn, persistent man whom I love with all my heart." She kissed him tenderly, several times.

They were in a good way of forgetting all about a thing called tea when they heard Mrs Bennet call for them again, with more shrillness than before. They reluctantly parted and began to walk back.

Darcy took Elizabeth's hand in his and brought it to his lips. "Shall I propose one more time, just to be absolutely sure?"

"No! I do not think I could survive a fifth proposal."

Laughing, Darcy said, "They were truly that bad, were they not?"

"Let us say the last one, the simplest one, achieved the best results. And I was finally wise enough to say yes."

Darcy brought her hand to his mouth once more and grazed his lips along the back.

They continued their reluctant tread back to the house, both of them jealously protective of any moments they had alone together. Elizabeth reflected on all the walks that had led to her present state of happiness and could not resist laughing aloud.

Darcy turned to look at her and joined her in her laughter, although he had no idea what was the source of her mirth. He was developing the highly unusual habit of laughing whenever Elizabeth laughed, before even knowing what it was that made her so merry. But of all the questionable habits one could develop from being in love, this was surely the most desirable.

"What is it, my dear?"

"My habit of walking! Do you realise that if I was not such a dedicated perambulationist—"

"Is that truly a word?" Darcy asked sceptically.

"Of course it is! If I had not been such a dedicated stroller of the world, we may never have had so many adventures together! I may never have found you on top of Clements Knoll and forced you at gunpoint to propose marriage to me."

Darcy laughed heartily. "I do not recall events happening

in quite that way, but you are correct, I think we owe a great deal to your slightly scandalous habit of walking so long and far."

"Scandalous, who said that?" Elizabeth turned and looked up at him with a shade of mild offence in her arched brow.

"I do not recall exactly, but I do remember hearing it mentioned that Miss Elizabeth Bennet was an excellent walker."

"Is that so? Hmm... 'Mrs Elizabeth Darcy is an excellent walker.'" Elizabeth smiled as she looped her arm through Darcy's and hugged him close to her side. "I like the sound of that."

The End

ACKNOWLEDGMENTS

Thanks to Quills & Quartos for their wonderful support. Thanks to Katie Jackson for another stellar job of editing for a flibbertigibbet like me. It is a better story because of her attention and suggestions. Thanks to James Ferrell and Sally Zeigler for being patient, kind beta readers—and a special thanks to James Ferrell for being a patient, kind father! Thank you to all the wonderful JAFF readers out there and the lovely, passionate JAFF community. And of course, thank you, Jane.

ABOUT THE AUTHOR

Lyndsay Constable is a Taurus Sun/Scorpio Rising who runs a small vegetable farm in Virginia with her husband. She has loved Jane Austen since her teens and often ponders 'what would Jane do?' If she is ever stuck for an idea, you can find her in the fields picking kale or digging up sweet potatoes or watering the greenhouse–or a myriad of other activities that keep the farm running and help her organize her muddled thoughts. She is an excellent walker.

- facebook.com/lyndsay.constable
- amazon.com/Lyndsay-Constable/e/B0B98XNZXF
- bookbub.com/authors/lyndsay-constable

ALSO BY LYNDSAY CONSTABLE

Never Inconstant

Unjust I may have been, weak and resentful I have been, but never inconstant.

MISS ANNE ELLIOT COULD NOT HAVE FORESEEN the happiness she would find as the wife of Captain Frederick Wentworth but neither could she have envisioned the life he led when they were separated for eight heartbreaking years. Now years into her married life, Anne Wentworth finds a cache of letters written, but never sent, to her by the then-heartbroken Navy captain.

AMID PERIL ON THE SEA, Captain Wentworth faced heart-wrenching loneliness throughout their years apart. Anne reads the letters to gain a deeper appreciation of the constant and ardent love her husband possessed and still possesses for her, and learns far more about the true character of her old, persuasive friend Lady Russell.

This sequel to Jane Austen's *Persuasion* journeys into the years after Frederick Wentworth made his second and final proposal to his beloved Anne Elliot.

Made in the USA
Monee, IL
01 February 2023

26898538R00152